SIEGE OF VRAKS

More tales of the Astra Militarum from Black Library

KRIEG
A novel by Steve Lyons

DEAD MEN WALKING
A novel by Steve Lyons

MINKA LESK: THE LAST WHITESHIELD
An omnibus edition of the novels *Cadia Stands, Cadian Honour, Traitor Rock* and several short stories
by Justin D Hill

SHADOW OF THE EIGHTH
A novel by Justin D Hill

THE FALL OF CADIA
A novel by Robert Rath

CREED: ASHES OF CADIA
A novel by Jude Reid

DEATHWORLDER
A novel by Victoria Hayward

LONGSHOT
A novel by Rob Young

KASRKIN
A novel by Edoardo Albert

OUTGUNNED
A novel by Denny Flowers

CATACHAN DEVIL
A novel by Justin Woolley

STEEL TREAD
A novel by Andy Clark

VOLPONE GLORY
A novel by Nick Kyme

WITCHBRINGER
A novel by Steven B Fischer

VAINGLORIOUS
A novel by Sandy Mitchell

SIEGE OF VRAKS

STEVE LYONS

BLACK LIBRARY

A BLACK LIBRARY PUBLICATION

First published in 2024.
This edition published in Great Britain in 2025 by
Black Library, Games Workshop Ltd., Willow Road,
Nottingham, NG7 2WS, UK.

Represented by: Games Workshop Limited – Irish branch,
Unit 3, Lower Liffey Street, Dublin 1,
D01 K199, Ireland.

10 9 8 7 6 5 4 3 2 1

Produced by Games Workshop in Nottingham.
Cover illustration by Igor Kieryluk.

A CIP record for this book is available from the British Library.

ISBN 13: 978-1-80407-694-1

Printed and bound in the UK.

For Marty.

For more than a hundred centuries the Emperor has sat immobile on the Golden Throne of Earth. He is the Master of Mankind. By the might of his inexhaustible armies a million worlds stand against the dark.

Yet, he is a rotting carcass, the Carrion Lord of the Imperium held in life by marvels from the Dark Age of Technology and the thousand souls sacrificed each day so his may continue to burn.

To be a man in such times is to be one amongst untold billions. It is to live in the cruelest and most bloody regime imaginable. It is to suffer an eternity of carnage and slaughter. It is to have cries of anguish and sorrow drowned by the thirsting laughter of dark gods.

This is a dark and terrible era where you will find little comfort or hope. Forget the power of technology and science. Forget the promise of progress and advancement. Forget any notion of common humanity or compassion.

There is no peace amongst the stars, for in the grim darkness of the far future, there is only war.

PROLOGUE

THE SPARK

810.M41

The assassin held his breath.

He had his target in his sights. One shot, that was all it would take. The most important shot of the assassin's career.

The Cardinal-Astral had emerged from his palace, as always surrounded by his fawning retinue. His white silk robes, festooned with jewelled rosaries, marked him out from the flock. A tall, brimless white toque hat lent him the illusion of above-average stature. He was an old man – by conventional standards, if not by those of his exalted office. Dry skin stretched across his cheekbones; white eyes lurked in the foxholes of their sockets.

The most holy man in the Scarus Sector...

The assassin didn't think about that now. He didn't doubt.

His masters believed his target deserved to die – or at least that his death would serve some higher purpose – and so, although not privy to their reasons, he believed it too. The learned minds of the Ordo Hereticus were far wiser than the dull-witted labourers of this grey armoury world, so besotted had the latter become with their shiny new demagogue.

Getting into the citadel had been the easy part. The assassin had posed as one of the thousands of worshippers welcomed daily through the St Leonis Gate. He had lain for three days, face down on a ledge jutting from the towering main spire of the basilica. His stealth suit rendered him all but invisible to sensors. He drank in nutrients through a feeding tube and kept his trained muscles rigid.

To his right, the ground dropped steeply away into the Citadel Ravine. Splayed out before him was the palace's outer courtyard, steaming in the mid-morning sun after a recent downpour. His target was moving across this, a clear shot blocked by other heads and marble pillars. He would be out of range in only seconds.

The assassin's finger tightened on his trigger. *One shot...*

Seconds later, he was running.

His cumbersome equipment, including his rifle, lay abandoned on the ledge, with a melta charge timed to destroy all evidence of his identity. He had squeezed back into the spire through a narrow window and pelted down an equally narrow spiral staircase. In the archway at its foot, he collided with a wide-eyed acolyte, who froze in his path. Whipping out a pair of pistols, the assassin blew a hole in the young man's chest.

Sirens wailed out from the Cardinal's Palace. The courtyard was filling up rapidly with uniformed disciples, already converging upon the assassin's tower as if they had known all along where he would be.

Just as his target, too, had come prepared...

The assassin had taken his shot, and could at least take pride in its precision. His bullet had punched through an inconvenient pillar on its way to Cardinal-Astral Xaphan's head. It should have been a good, clean kill. Instead, a violent flash of golden energy had revealed that Xaphan was protected.

The assassin had loosed off two more shots in haste. A second hit might well have overwhelmed whatever obscure piece of archeotech had created a refractor field around his target. Too late. Xaphan was already lost, behind a crush of devotees eager to take the bullets for him. Two had their wishes granted, staining mosaic flooring with their blood.

He had failed in his mission and was unlikely to get another chance. The assassin had no higher purpose at this moment than to save himself.

His escape route through the courtyard was definitely blocked. He ducked through the nearest doorway back into the basilica, then raced along a high-vaulted passageway, firing over his shoulder to discourage pursuers. Strangled yelps informed him that some of his blind shots had struck true, but still the echoing clatter of booted footsteps slowly gained on him. A bullet whistled past his ear.

He heard more cries and footsteps, closing in ahead of him.

The assassin was cornered, at last, in the building's ancient vaults.

Though three more guards fell to his blazing pistols, never was his fate in question. The assassin died in darkness, in a hail of small-weapons fire, choking on grenade smoke, amid the disapproving ghosts of long-departed pilgrims.

By day's end, his corpse would be paraded through the citadel's streets. The spectacle would be vid-linked across the planet, sparking furious riots. Strident preachers would call the assassin a tool of traitors in the highest Imperial offices. They would say that the golden light of the Emperor Himself had foiled their plans, but would warn that more attacks were sure to follow, and that one man alone could defend this world against them. The people would listen, and believe; and thus their hearts and minds were captured.

Just as their messiah, the Cardinal-Astral, had intended all along; just as his sage advisors had foretold.

One shot – that was all it would have taken. One shot to end a single life, and in so doing save many millions more. The most important shot of the assassin's own life. His dying thought – his final, numbing realisation – was that he had been lured into a trap.

One shot could have ended a bloody war before it had even begun.

It had ignited one instead.

ACT ONE

OPENING SHOTS

812-815.M41

Vraks would not be brought to heel without a long and bloody fight.

Its major assets, its citadel and star port, were heavily defended. They possessed sufficient firepower to blast a fleet of cruisers out of orbit. Blockades would take too long to have an effect. That left only one option.

An army would be landed on the planet's surface. They would win back Vraks' barren ground inch by hard-fought inch.

The Astra Militarum turned to the Krieg, of course. Soldiers bred upon that world – my world – are siege specialists, uniquely equipped for the grind of long wars of attrition. We were chosen for that reason and, I believe, one other.

There were an estimated eight million people on Vraks. It had to be assumed that most were under its new ruler's thrall. Our tacticians calculated that each of their lives would cost only two of our own. We were glad to make that sacrifice.

By the time I came to Vraks, I had already lived a longer life than I ever imagined. Like most of my comrades-in-arms, I had gone there to die.

Instead, Vraks was where I was reborn.

– Extracted from the account of Veteran Colonel Tyborc,
261st Krieg Siege Regiment, seconded into the
service of Inquisitor Lord Oddo, c. 845.M41

I

A black train snaked its way across the rocky plain.

A mighty engine bellowed with the strain of pulling its heavy carriages. Its steel wheels shrieked and threw off sparks as they resisted old, worn brakes. They were wrestled to a juddering halt, at last, the engine's black nose nuzzling the buffer where its track abruptly ended.

For a minute, it sat groaning with relief, marinating in steam, sweating pungent oil. Then the doors of its carriages flew open. Grey figures were disgorged by the thousand. They guarded their identities beneath greatcoats, plasteel helmets, and rebreather masks with round, blank eyepieces. It was almost impossible to tell one from another, as they set about the barren ground with picks and shovels.

These were the soldiers of the fabled Death Korps of Krieg. They had come to save this world by re-establishing the Emperor's control over it. Right now, that meant establishing a foothold here, at the end of the line.

* * *

Confessor Ignea Tenaxus stepped down from her carriage.

She strode through the busy Korpsmen, who parted before her, maintaining a deferential bubble of space around her. She planted her oak staff in the ground, disturbing ancient layers of volcanic dust. Her nose wrinkled at the sulphur smell, but she was used to it by now. She straightened her back and allowed her chest to swell as her eyes drank in the sight before her.

The Citadel of Vraks. Constructed upon the remains of a long-extinct volcano, it loomed above the surrounding flat expanses. Its tallest structure, its sensorium tower, drew the confessor's admiring gaze. She thought about its faithful choir of astropaths, torn apart by a fearful mob even as they sent a distress message out into the warp. It was elsewhere, however, that her true interest lay.

The Basilica of St Leonis the Blind. Just a glimpse of its ornate spires sent a thrill of devotion through her unworthy body. The blessed Leonis' shrine was one of the holiest sites in the sector. Its likely desecration by the apostate cardinal and his band of brainwashed traitors was almost more than Tenaxus could bear.

It pained her to be standing here, so close and yet so very far away.

Too much time had already passed since the first drop-ships had put down on the planet's far side, out of reach of the citadel's laser defences. For almost a year, Krieg Korpsmen, supported by a sizeable penal labour force, had dug trenches, erected standard-pattern Munitorum facilities, laid railroad tracks, and unloaded vast quantities of weapons and provisions from supply shuttles. Almost a year, during which the apostate cardinal had stayed safe behind his walls and poisoned who-knew-how-many minds with his blasphemous teachings.

Now, at last the Krieg were ready to wage war upon their enemies.

Black carriages stretched out for over a mile behind her. Grey figures poured unabated from them, spreading out across the Van Meersland Wastes. Their orders were to establish a forward depot here, from which they could dig towards the first of the enemy's defence lines, thirty miles ahead of them.

Imperial tactician savants had calculated that it would take twelve years to win this war. Twelve years before Xaphan would be punished for his sins. Twelve years before Tenaxus could set foot inside the holy shrine again and assess the damage to it.

Around her, the Krieg were working tirelessly, painstakingly, as they always did. They gave Tenaxus faith that they would meet the expectations placed upon them. She prayed to the Emperor to grant her but a fraction of their patience.

At 166813.M41, the first shot of the war was officially fired.

Dawn's light found the forward trenches packed with rows of grey soldiers standing stiffly to attention. For the first time in months, the clatter of their activity had ceased. Vraks had no native fauna and the air was still that day, so not a breath of sound disturbed the utmost silence.

Then a vox-console crackled into life. Its terse message rippled through the earthworks, passed down from officer to officer. Lieutenant Marot heard it from his company captain, who in turn had received her orders from Colonel Thyran.

'Open fire!'

Marot's barked command echoed out along the trench to each side of him. A moment later, though, all voices but the ones in his earpiece were drowned out as Vraks' silence was irrevocably shattered. A thousand gun crews, including the four under his command, jerked into practised action. Their Earthshaker cannons and bombards were already aimed and loaded, and now their pent-up fury was unleashed.

Their targets were the enemy's bunkers and pillboxes, connected by low reinforced ferrocrete walls – but vox-reports from spotters with magnoculars confirmed that their explosive shells were falling short. They pulverised rocks and punched new craters into the ground, as if punishing the very planet for the actions of its people. This was only as expected.

The enemy, so quiet these past months, was soon returning fire. The vast stores of Vraks were theirs to plunder, so of course they had no shortage of weapons of their own, forged for the Emperor, now turned upon His followers instead. Few of their shells would make it to the Krieg trenches either, but there was always the small chance of a lucky shot.

Even over the guns' incessant roar, Marot heard a fearsome blast and felt the ground tremble. One of his crews was showered with grey dust and red-hot shrapnel, which clattered off their helmets. A Korpsman stumbled, the heavy shell that he and a comrade were hefting almost slipping through their fingers. Marot admonished the Korpsman and bawled at the rest of his gunners too – to work harder, faster, more efficiently: 'Just one more shot can make a difference, take a life that tips a balance.'

Few of his words would reach their ears, but in truth it didn't matter. They knew the words by now, and knew their duty. The soldiers of Krieg knew what the Emperor required of them.

The artillery duel continued throughout the morning.

It was briefly interrupted, in the early afternoon, by one of Vraks' frequent lightning storms. The crashing of thunder in the heavens almost matched that of the now-stilled cannons. The Krieg took shelter in their dugouts as rivers of grey slime lapped against the wooden slats of duckboards.

With the storm's abrupt cessation, the air felt thick and warm and newly sulphurous – not that the Krieg could feel or smell it through their layers of filtration and protection. They returned to their stations and resumed their pitiless bombardment. Its effect, if any, at this distance was impossible to know, but the enemy's guns seemed muted. Imperial commissars maintained that the traitors were losing their nerve, lacking the fortitude that faith in a just cause granted.

They said rather less about the shell that struck the 413th Battery, destroying an Earthshaker and cremating its eight-strong crew. Lieutenant Marot heard the news over the command vox-channel but kept it to himself. His Korpsmen were used to living under death's long shadow. He had already lived too long himself, to which the stripes on his shoulders testified.

Regardless of the ever-present threat, life in the trenches settled into a repetitive routine. Marot bunked in a hollow cut into the side of a claustrophobic dugout, which he shared with four other junior officers. Each moonless night, the thunder of the Krieg guns lulled him into a dreamless slumber. On the twelfth night, the less familiar sound of raised voices jerked him out of it.

Intruders had broken through a tunnel wall and been challenged by a sentry. By the time Marot and three score of Korpsmen crowded onto the scene, the matter had already been settled.

The bombardment had served its primary purpose. It had provided cover for the members of the 158th Regiment to slip out into no-man's-land and start to dig. They had begun with foxholes, six feet deep, then worked for three days underground, connecting those foxholes with tunnels, creating a network – which they had extended back towards the Krieg's existing trenches.

'We had to take a detour to avoid a large granite deposit,' a sergeant explained. He looked like a statue, his uniform caked with grey dirt apart from the finger-shaped smears across his gas mask's lenses. 'It threw us several degrees off. Still, our squad is the first to make it back – is that confirmed?'

The question was directed at a Korpsman behind him, who had been murmuring into a concealed comm-bead. 'It is, sergeant,' he reported with something like pride in his tone.

'The going is heavy down there?' Marot asked.

'No, sir,' the sergeant replied. 'Mostly, it is as we have seen everywhere else – light, porous rock like pumice, barely a challenge.'

'That is good to know,' said Marot.

'It should certainly speed up operations,' the sergeant agreed.

'That was not my meaning.' Marot turned on his heel and marched back towards his dugout, continuing over his shoulder, 'If I am to lie forever in this planet's dirt, it is good to know that it will be nice and soft and comfortable.'

Those words came back to haunt him the very next day.

He was summoned away from the front lines to a meeting at the landing site. The seventeen company commanders of the 143rd Siege Regiment crowded into a briefing room to await their commander's arrival. Marot was there on his captain's behalf, as she was nursing a shrapnel wound. He felt an unfamiliar tingle in the pit of his stomach, which might have been anticipation.

His regiment had been the first to arrive on Vraks. They had worked long, punishing shifts to secure the landing site, and hadn't stopped working in the year since then. Marot knew that every mine laid, every crate unloaded, every entrenching tool thrust into the dirt, was a vital step towards their goal. Even so, he had caught himself wondering when he might see combat again, when his turn might come to be sent out to expend his life in the Emperor's service.

That moment was suddenly here.

The arrival of a noisy locomotive rattled the room's shuttered windows. Hardly a minute later, Colonel Thyran and his entourage strode in. Though the air was breathable and he was far from the fighting, Thyran wore the standard-issue gas mask. Unlike the officers of other worlds, he displayed none of his many honours. His eagle-crested helmet, red sash, and rank insignia sufficed for battlefield identification.

Thyran's polished breastplate and riding boots were legacies of his previous service in a Death Rider company. His greatcoat, at the insistence of the Departmento Munitorum, was tailored from fine mukaali hide.

At the colonel's shoulder was Commissar-General Maugh. He too was masked, although as far as Marot knew he was an off-worlder, as most commissars were. Having outsiders maintain morale within each unit was another departmento requirement. Most Krieg took little notice of them, considering them to have a negligible effect upon combat performance.

Colonel Thyran brought news of the latest battle plan. His aides transferred schematics to a holo-projector, and the assembled officers pored over its tabletop display. The Citadel of Vraks was shown, almost surrounded by its three dense defence lines. The only break in these was to the south-east, where the land was pitted with deep canyons and gorges – impassable.

The units of the 88th Krieg Siege Army appeared too, as black skull icons. Four of its line korps formed a near-solid mass to the citadel's west. First Line Korps was pushing north and eastwards, probing for a weakness along the northern walls, but so far had found none.

Colonel Thyran drew his sabre, brandishing it like a pointer. He circled it over the icons of the 12th Line Korps, of which his regiment was part. They were stationed towards the southern end of the western walls. The colonel's aides obligingly zoomed the holo-map in to this area, labelled *Sector 46-39* by scrolling glyphs.

'According to intelligence,' said the colonel, 'this is the weakest point in the citadel's defences. The guns of 21st Bombardment Korps have been moved up to concentrate their fire upon this sector.' A few of his captains nodded. He continued, 'Once they have softened up the traitors, we shall make our first infantry assault upon them. The 150th Regiment will take point, but I have secured for us the honour of supporting their left flank.'

More details followed. The Krieg would advance in three waves over two days, between them comprising some half a million foot-soldiers. Once, and only if, they gained purchase in the traitors' first defence line, then the 61st Tank Regiment would roll forwards to blast through it.

Marot could only imagine such a glorious scene. He knew he wouldn't likely live to see it. His regiment's role, as part of the first wave, was to seek out the enemy's weak spots by deadly trial and error. Their casualty rate was projected to be seventy-eight per cent. They were to make their move in five days' time.

Thyran paused after making that announcement.

'Ideally,' he resumed, 'we might have given the bombardment a few more days or weeks to have an effect. You should know that this option was considered. It was felt, however – by the 88th Army's command staff, and Lord Zuehlke in particular – that time was of the essence.'

The commissar-general spoke up. 'The Krieg have undertaken to retake Vraks in twelve years. We need to make a bold push and secure an early victory, in order to fulfil that promise.'

'Understood, sir,' one of the captains said, and Marot joined in the murmurs of agreement.

'Most of us will not see our ultimate victory,' said Colonel Thyran. 'In no way does that diminish our part in its achievement. Any Korpsman who dies well enough tomorrow can be sure the sacrifice will make a difference.'

Marot felt pride in his heart as, in a deathly tone, Maugh added, 'That life will be counted.'

At 212813.M41, the first Korpsmen went over the top.

The 143rd Siege Regiment moved on the second whistle. The first squads of Marot's platoon clambered up the scaling ladders. He fixed his bayonet and waited as the crush of warm, musty grey bodies thinned out. His heart pounded in his ears.

These first few minutes would be crucial. The enemy knew this attack was coming. They had to know, for why else would the Krieg guns have fallen silent?

The traitors' guns had been muted for several days; spotters were confident that many had been shattered by the shells of Imperial bombards. More than a few gunners had also died in flames, while others must have had their morale sorely tested. The rest, the ones still unbroken, would be scrambling back to their weapons emplacements, clearing rubble from them. How swiftly could they act?

The answer to that question came sooner than Marot had expected. From somewhere south of his position – from where the 150th Siege Regiment had been first out of the trenches – he heard a heavy bolter's steady crump.

His turn on the ladder came at last. He heaved himself over the parapet, gloved hands sinking into earth still mushy from the latest storm. Marot weaved through coils of razor wire, along a path cleared under the previous night's cover. He kept his head down, eyes on the boots of the soldier ahead of him. He could see little further as the smoke of no-man's-land drew curtains around him.

More bolters spluttered into life behind those curtains. It sounded as though some were directly ahead of him. He began to hear breathless casualty reports through his earpiece. Bright flashes pierced the fog, and suddenly he stumbled over a Korpsman's body. 'Keep moving,' he instructed his platoon by vox.

'Turn back now and we only give the traitors a clear shot at our backs,' the voice of one of his sergeants agreed with him.

The bolters' chatter merged and swelled into a persistent rumble. Suddenly, the Korpsman in front of Marot reeled backwards and collided with him. Soft ground gave way beneath his heel and the pair of them slid into a fresh shell crater. Marot struggled to disentangle himself from his comrade, who flopped onto his back with a groan. A spreading patch of blood darkened his coat; his laboured breaths rattled around his re-breather tube. It was just a shrapnel wound; prompt medical attention could save him, but the colonel's orders had been clear.

'Delta Squad, sir. We've lost our sergeant. Two of us left, both wounded.'

'Bodies piling up in front of us, sir. Unclear if any made it through.'

'Keep moving,' Marot growled into his comm-bead.

A storm of bullets raged above his head. As soon as it let up, he planted his knee in the sucking dirt. To the dying soldier beside him, he muttered, 'Your life counted.' Then he levered himself back to his feet.

More Korpsmen lay dead and mortally wounded all around him, but thousands more surged forwards to replace them. Marot reinserted himself into their flow, letting himself be swept along by it. A fresh salvo of bullets cut down figures to the left and right of him.

The calm, authoritative voice of Colonel Thyran cut across all regimental vox-channels. *'The traitors are better prepared than we expected,'* he admitted, *'but we have numbers, faith, and grim determination on our side. They can't gun us all down before we overrun them.'*

Almost as if the enemy mocked his words, the shattering blasts of cannons added to the tempest. A shell hit close by to the north, sending tremors through the ground and a wave of gritty heat over Marot. *Keep moving…*

As if he could have turned back had he wanted to. As if lying face down in the dirt would have saved him from the next Earthshaker shell…

The next voice in his ear was that of his captain, who had taken to the battlefield despite her fresh stitches. *'Forward! Forward! The worth of our sacrifices today will be measured in ground soaked in enemy blood!'*

A fierce burst of static followed, and then a long, ominous silence.

Then another voice, which Marot didn't know: *'I regret to report…'* The speaker broke off, coughing. *'Fifteenth Company…'* His company. *'First Platoon was just scaling the ladders. We lost two squads, and the captain… She had just raised her head above the parapet when…'*

The words dissolved into coughing again. Another voice, more self-possessed, cut in: *'Direct hit on the forward trenches. Extensive casualties. Fifteenth Company captain, 143rd Regiment, confirmed to have perished.'*

Marot didn't know how he had survived. He never knew. Why him? Why him again, when so many better soldiers, his captain included, had fallen?

The attack had been called off at nightfall. The second infantry wave had doggedly followed the first across the battlefield and shared their grisly fate. There had been a few glimmers of hope. As predicted, some Krieg, through force of numbers, had made it through the gauntlet. They discovered that the enemy had not been idle all this time, and that their walls were deeper and stronger than ever.

The newly settled silence rang in the lieutenant's ears. His memories of the past eight hours were jumbled and frenetic, driving out all memories before them. He remembered shredding his gloves on razor wire coils. He remembered yelling out a warning as he realised that he was in the middle of a minefield.

He remembered hauling himself out of the dirt, once, twice, three times and maybe more. His left shoulder ached and was sticky to the touch. He remembered stifling a scream with gritted teeth as he dug a bullet from it with his knife. He had no memory of being shot. His head swam. He was concussed.

He still had his duty to perform.

Marot couldn't make vox-contact with any other company officers. He was likely the last of them. It was up to him to gather the survivors and lead them out of there. No-man's-land was strewn with bodies, piled three or four high in some places. Some clung to life yet, and a fraction of these could walk or crawl.

His ragtag force of the walking wounded grew, salvaging as many guns as they could carry. For what felt like hours, they stalked that fog-shrouded graveyard like grey ghosts. Marot feared they were travelling in circles, but then the lights of illum flares fired from the Krieg trenches, more commonly used for sighting targets, marked a path for them to follow.

More grey-coated corpses lined their route, their faces covered, eyepieces staring blankly. Some were soldiers he had worked, eaten, slept and fought alongside, even shared brief moments of grim introspection with. Unless he read the numbers of their dog tags, Marot couldn't know for sure. Even had he taken off their masks, he may not have known their faces, and that was for the best.

The third wave of the Krieg assault was launched at dawn.

Marot was surprised to hear it, given the failure of the earlier waves to make a breakthrough. The sound of whistles briefly disturbed his exhausted sleep – though, as far as his trench was from those of the other companies, he thought he may only have dreamt them.

He woke in the afternoon to unsurprising news. The third wave had been repulsed. The overall cost of the assault was still being tabulated, but it was certainly horrific. *Half a million foot-soldiers...* It wasn't the number of Krieg lives lost that rankled him, but the feeling that they may have died for nothing.

A quartermaster had bound Marot's arm in a sling.

He had declined to join the sad procession of the wounded, back to the depot and from there to a medicae hut at the landing site by locomotive. The rank-and-file Korpsmen needed leaders among them to look to, and there were so few left. 'I can still give orders one-handed,' Marot had grumbled, 'and operate a weapon if it comes to it.'

That night, he dialled up the stimulant content in his water supply and manned his old captain's command post. His decision was proved justified when a sentry reported movement in no-man's-land. Lieutenant Marot hopped up onto a fire-step and pressed magnoculars to his gas mask's lenses. Through the lingering smoke haze, he made out distant silhouettes. 'Could they be ours?'

'Unclear, sir,' said the sentry, 'but they aren't responding to vox-hails.'

'Sound the alarm,' said Marot.

The figures grew swiftly in number, until they were everywhere he looked. Too many to be routed Krieg Korpsmen from the third wave coming home. Too many and too purposeful in their advance. These were soldiers who were not defeated but triumphant. A grumble of engines reached his ears in confirmation. Around him, roused Korpsmen were taking positions on the steps to the shrill beat of the alarm bell.

'Enemy infantry incoming,' Marot barked at them, 'some in armoured personnel carriers. Pick a target. Fire at will.' He relayed the same information over the command vox-channel and requested artillery support.

The cracks and whines of lasguns and heavy stubbers filled the trench. 'The traitors have made a tactical error,' the lieutenant asserted. 'They believe us broken. They think we are cowering back here, those few of us remaining, licking our wounds. They should have stayed behind their walls.'

New, familiar shapes came looming from the fog: repurposed Imperial Chimeras with hull-mounted heavy bolters and multi-laser turrets. Squadron after squadron ground the bones of the dead beneath their tracks. Small weapons fire could do no more than chip their armour. Tank traps awaited any vehicle venturing too close, along with krak grenade launchers, but Marot knew it wouldn't be enough.

He yelled into his comm-bead, 'We need those cannons. We can't hold the line here without them.' He received confirmation that his request had been relayed, but there was no response as yet. A faulty vox-relay might have been to blame; such equipment was temperamental even under better circumstances. Either that or his superiors just had nothing to say to him at present.

Marot drew his laspistol: a light weapon designed for one-handed firing, which was just as well in his present circumstances. The trade-off for this was a limited range. While his comrades sprayed no-man's-land with withering fire, he bided his time. He waited and watched for those enemies who made it close enough, targeting each of them individually.

For a time, it felt to Marot as though the Emperor was with him.

The traitors were being dealt a bitter taste of their own medicine. Whether they ploughed forwards or turned back, as some cravenly did, they were scythed down with pitiless efficiency. Then a Chimera ground to a halt, its tracks tangled up in wire, and disgorged twelve more figures. With his best shot yet, he punched a hole through the head of the first, but the others surged forwards; meanwhile, another Chimera was pulling up behind them, then another and another behind that.

The Krieg's guns – at least their medium artillery, their mortars and quad launchers – had woken at last. The thunder of their discharges rolled forwards over Marot's head. Their shells' explosive detonations, however, seemed a long distance away – and immediately, he knew what that meant.

'It seems the enemy is attacking on multiple fronts,' he reported. 'Our heavy guns are defending more vital sectors. Our duty is clear. We must hold these traitors at bay for as long as we can. Kill as many as we can. This, just this, is the reason our comrades died – to lure them out to us. Each and every enemy that falls will weigh against their noble sacrifices, as well as our own to come.'

Confessor Tenaxus had never met Lieutenant Marot.

She would remember his name, all the same. She heard so few Krieg names. They used them rarely, especially between themselves. Krieg officers referred to the Korpsmen under their command by their assigned numbers, always numbers.

Tenaxus had been in the war room: a large, prefabricated structure bustling with ordinates, vox-operators, technicians, high-ranking officers and their command staffs, far behind the lines. The atmosphere had been highly charged but focused as urgent calls for assistance had crashed in, one upon another. Decisions had been made efficiently and tersely, providing much-needed support to one company here, condemning another to its fate with the stroke of a stylus there.

She may have heard Marot's first request for artillery support;

she couldn't recall. She had certainly come to recognise his voice, its tone more urgent with each contact, albeit never tipping into panic.

There had been a tragic inevitability to his last-but-one report: a breathless snippet, set to a soundtrack of chainsword roars and screams, in which he revealed that traitors had breached the Krieg lines, invading their trenches. Tenaxus had observed an intense conversation between Colonel Thyran – the commander of Marot's 143rd Regiment – and his counterpart in command of the 150th, which had ended with a grim nod of acceptance from the former.

'Too many… We will fight to our last breaths, but depleted as we are… I have lost my arm… bleeding out. Too late for us, but… colonel, turn the Earthshakers upon our own positions. Wipe out the traitors before they can spread further… and Emperor, forgive us our failure…'

The voice had faded – for the last time, the confessor had imagined, but the vox-channel had remained open, nightmare sounds intruding upon the room's detachment, and the voice had returned a moment later as barely a whisper, with the words that would stay with her: *'This is Lieutenant Marot… signing off…'*

Colonel Thyran had muttered something into his comm-bead that she hadn't caught. She wondered if his words had ever reached their intended recipient. He had spoken to his fellow officers again, in a tone that brooked no argument. Then, with General Durjan's consent, the artillery commanders had issued fresh orders.

The fighting was all over now, or at least at a pause. Three days of violent clamour had subsided into sullen near-silence. The Krieg's ill-starred offensive had seen them losing rather than gaining ground, and Tenaxus had scrolled through impossibly long lists of fatalities on a data-slate.

Many Krieg had been slain by their own guns, as Marot had suggested. They lay buried in the flattened rubble of the forward trenches – but thousands of the apostate cardinal's traitors lay with them. Word came down from Lord Commander Zuehlke on Thracian Primaris; he was satisfied with the progress made.

Tenaxus stepped from a black train carriage once again. She was returning to the front lines to preach to the soldiers stationed there, to lift their spirits and to weed out any doubters concealed among them. A decorated commissar had assured her that there was no necessity. The Krieg, he had said, were a dedicated breed, and even such a massacre as they had suffered here would not deter them in the slightest from their duty. She had prepared her sermons, anyway.

She would tell them of Leonis, martyr of the Scarus Sector, who had had his eyes gouged out for spreading the Emperor's holy word two thousand years ago. She thought she might tell them about a hero of their own too: Lieutenant Marot, who had fought so courageously and given up his life without a qualm for that same higher purpose. She would make him an example to which all could aspire.

The trenches were still a highly dangerous place to be. The guns of each side continued to harass each other intermittently, so death could strike anywhere with little warning. Though it was the middle of the day, a pall of gun smoke now blocked out the heat and light of the Vraksian sun. The planet's scarred surface seemed bleaker and greyer than ever.

A pungent smell reached the confessor's nostrils, carried westward on a reedy breeze. The bodies abandoned by necessity in no-man's-land – hundreds of thousands of them, friend and foe – were beginning to rot. She donned the gas mask given to her by Commissar Oblonsk and was grateful for his foresight.

She could no longer see the great citadel through the suffocating gloom. Strain her eyes as she might, she couldn't even make out the outline of it. Saint Leonis felt further away from her than ever, now that even the uplifting sight of his spires had been denied to her.

God-Emperor willing, if she did her duty, one day she might see them again.

II

The captain's goal was in his sights.

He could almost see his enemies' eyes through their firing slits, behind their muzzle flashes. They'd been caught off-guard this time, but now were mounting a sturdy defence of their positions. Bolter shells burst above the captain's head. He was crouched in a razor wire tangle; between this and the camouflage of his brown and grey uniform, he didn't think he had been spotted.

With a hefty pair of cutters, he sliced through the wire as quickly but methodically as possible. He had practised this countless times in training, back on Krieg. The final strand parted and the captain rolled into the ditch beyond it, a stray barb tearing at his greatcoat, finding no purchase there. The enemy had dug this tank trap for their own protection, but now it protected him. He kept his head down as the rest of his command squad tumbled after him. He returned his cutters to his satchel and drew his laspistol.

No one else had made it this far before.

His comrades had given him every advantage. Over months,

they had furtively extended their trench network to within a few hundred yards of the enemy's first wall, just south of its north-western corner. The 19th Bombard Korps had subjected the sector to sustained shelling and had taken out the traitors' largest weapon therein: an Earthshaker. Quad launchers had covered the advance of the captain and his company.

He had been the first out of the trenches and so was first to make it here. Already, though, his other squads were tearing through the wire, sliding down the slopes to join him. Many, as expected, had been lost in no-man's-land – he didn't know how many yet – but enough had made it across to start filling up the ditch.

Now came the most dangerous part. As the captain gave the order to advance, he felt the weight of all his fallen predecessors on his shoulders.

His Death Korpsmen tackled the climb, knowing just what awaited them above but unafraid of it. A series of sudden, sharp explosions tore through the first two squads, telling him that the slope itself had been mined.

The captain had to make a swift decision. To turn back would be suicide, of course; but then nor could they linger in the ditch. The traitors knew where they were by now. It would only take them minutes to recalibrate their cannons...

'Follow me!' he bellowed. 'Up and over.'

He was one of the lucky ones, again.

The captain hit no mines on his scramble to the top of the glacis. He heard and felt a flurry of detonations on his heels but didn't see the carnage wrought by them, although he could well picture it.

He had to keep focusing ahead. He was inside an enemy stronghold. His sudden appearance, however, had startled its defenders, common labourers cajoled or press-ganged into service. They were swiftly abandoning their posts in the face of their first real challenge. A row of rockcrete pillboxes stood before the captain, but only one remained active.

Once more, he charged into a welter of weapons fire, yelling to his command squad to form up on him. A Korpsman at his shoulder was struck square in the chest; the bolt burst inside his shattered ribcage, leaving little behind. Something hit the captain's left leg and lodged in the muscle; only later would he have time to examine it and find a fragment of his comrade's bone.

Though the traitors had lost most of their gunners, reinforcements were swiftly arriving. Renegade militiamen swarmed up from underground shelters. These were former members of Vraks' garrison auxilia, as evidenced by their soiled uniform fatigues. They wore gas masks as did the Krieg, connected to air tanks on their shoulders. On the front lines, there was little choice: the decay of unburied bodies had laced the air with virulent infections.

Many would have been veterans of the Emperor's armies, but now they held the citadel for the apostate cardinal instead.

The captain, his eyes fixed on the pillbox, was intercepted mere yards from it. He tried to bull his way through, firing wildly. One traitor gave way initially, only to leap on him from behind with a lunatic screech. His weapon was a long blade strapped to his forearm, hammered out of scrap but sharp enough against the captain's throat. He dropped to one knee and, before his attacker could consolidate his hold, he flipped him over his right shoulder. The traitor landed hard on his back, the wind knocked out of him. The captain punched a las-beam through his head.

More Krieg climbed up from the tank trap and closed with the traitors, tearing through barricades of chem drums and sandbags to reach them. Pain lanced through the captain's leg as he straightened up. The bone shrapnel worked its way deeper with his every movement. He braced himself against the back of his veteran watchmaster, his longest-serving ally. With his pistol's bayonet, he slashed at any traitor daring to approach him. Those that learned to keep their distance, he picked off with carefully placed shots.

Not one was a match for a trained Death Korpsman, in his judgement. They fought with their makeshift blades and cheap autoguns, in scraps of armour defiled with blasphemous symbols. The real fruit of Xaphan's captured armouries, he guessed, was reserved for his more valued servants.

The melee now raged, thick and brutal, all around him, but the captain saw an opening and took it. He ducked between two traitors, one of whom shot at him but only hit the other in the shoulder. He primed a frag grenade and dropped it through a pillbox slit. Two of his squad mates had made it too.

As he withdrew his hand, the heat of an explosion washed over him – but not the one he had expected. An enemy quad launcher had roared back into life, presumably with a new, hardier crew. Whoever was manning it, they didn't seem to care where their shells struck; they ripped through Korpsman and militiaman alike.

The captain spun to face another attack from behind him. He dodged the traitor's blade, which snapped against the pillbox. As a sudden flash dazzled him, more shrapnel – metal, this time – tore a gash along his right forearm. The traitor's body shielded him from worse, being shredded in the process.

There came a series of dull crumps from within the pillbox, and smoke billowed out of its slits. It sounded as if someone had got to the quad launcher too and, at least for now, had silenced it. The Krieg were outclassing their opponents, as the captain had expected. For every militiaman that fell, though, it seemed as if two more appeared to replace them. It was usually the Krieg that swarmed their enemies, he thought, rather than the other way around.

'Keep pushing them back!' he cried through clenched teeth, a gloved hand clamped to his fresh, bleeding wound. 'Push them back and we can start to use their own defences against them.'

A Krieg squad was already crouched by the corners of the pillbox, firing along its sides. Following their example, the captain sought cover of his own. He found it behind a mass of dented, overturned drums. Diving onto his stomach, he swiped one aside to clear himself a line of sight.

His watchmaster dropped down beside him. 'Are you all right, sir?'

'I'll live,' the captain grunted. 'At least a little longer.'

The watchmaster drew a split sandbag to himself and pressed the barrel of his Type XIV heavy lasgun – 'hellguns', most called them – into it. He created a furrow that would steady the gun and thus assist his aim. His backpack battery afforded him a limited number of overpowered shots, so he didn't want to waste one.

The captain rooted in a belt pouch for a canister of synth-skin. He aimed a few quick bursts at his bleeding arm, not caring if he sealed the torn fabric of his greatcoat sleeve into it. Four militiamen emerged from a bunker ahead, but the watchmaster gunned down two before they saw him. The captain wielded his laspistol left-handed, and between them they made short enough work of the others.

'Do you have a vox signal?' asked the captain.

'Not a word since no-man's-land, sir.'

He scowled. He had hoped it was just a glitch with his personal equipment. He had lost track of his company's vox-operator. In the likely event that he had fallen, someone else should have shouldered his critical vox-caster – unless it had been blown to pieces with him.

Most of the Krieg were in good sniping positions by now, pinning down another wave of militiamen as they arrived, forcing them to sprint for cover too. Doubtless, the sight of so many traitors' bodies also dampened their fervour for hand-to-hand combat.

The captain signalled to a nearby Korpsman, who scurried up to him. 'Return to the trenches,' he instructed. 'Take a message to the colonel, or to any senior officer. Tell them we've made it through the wire. Tell them we have a foothold, but the enemy is growing in numbers. Tell them that, if they send reinforcements, then we can hold this ground. Fort A-453 can be ours.'

Another gruelling hour of fighting took a toll on the captain's confidence.

Denied contact with any of his comrades beyond shouting range, he couldn't know how many were still standing. He had started with close to a thousand, losing over half in the initial charge. He had lost count of those he had seen falling, especially since another quad launcher had entered the fray and the enemy had reoccupied a pillbox.

Bolter fire had blasted the chem drums shielding him to slag. Limping on his bad leg, he had barely scrambled out of the way in time. The captain had joined other displaced, exposed Korpsmen in a desperate assault upon an enemy trench, and, at considerable cost, they had managed to take it.

Protected somewhat from the surface guns down here, they had explored and found an entrance to the traitors' shelters. They were greeted by a hail of bullets from a dozen autoguns, holding them at bay. The captain couldn't find an angle from which to hurl a grenade without getting his head blown off.

He had no way of knowing if his messenger had made it back, if reinforcements might be on their way. All he could do was buy as much time as he could, one second at a time, knowing that any second could be the decisive one.

'It's up to us alone,' he growled to his watchmaster. 'We can hold the ground we've taken for perhaps another hour – or we can take a risk while we're still able. Instinct tells me to keep moving.'

'Agreed, sir. Should we storm the bunker?'

The captain nodded. 'Storm the bunker. On a count of one thousand…'

He had about twenty Korpsmen with him. The watchmaster despatched two squads to see if they could reach the door by other routes, or return here if they couldn't. They muttered the numbers of the countdown as they hurried away. The captain remained with the others, exchanging fire with militiamen around a trench corner, ensuring that they remained pinned and distracted. He too counted down under his breath.

At zero, he heard a warning shout. A crack of lasguns. He was round the corner with his pistol blazing before the echoes of the former had died down. He got his first good look at the large steel door, set into smooth rock at the end of a short, narrow crevice. One of his splinter groups had appeared through an opening beyond it, so that the door's defenders were suddenly surrounded.

This had the desired effect of startling some into paralysis. Others, more clear-headed, realised that with the door to their backs – bolted from the inside, no doubt – they had no option but to fight. A bullet nicked the captain's greatcoat, an instant before he ran the shooter through with his bayonet. As always, other Korpsmen had been less fortunate than him. He didn't stop to think about that. He couldn't stop to count his dead, nor wonder what had happened to his other squad or whether the traitors now outnumbered them.

Nor could he entirely trust to his well-drilled instincts as normally he would. He had to remember to favour his uninjured limbs, which threw off his rhythm. He feinted left when he ought to have dodged right, and a traitor knife was thrust towards his eye. The blade cracked but didn't penetrate the toughened metal in his gas mask's lens, and the captain caught the wielder's arm and snapped the bone.

A second militiaman blindsided him, and suddenly he was staring down the barrel of a gun – until he wasn't. The traitor was borne to the ground by the weight of a fully equipped Krieg grenadier landing on his shoulders. Three had leapt down from the rocks above the door, and their arrival quickly proved decisive. A las-beam burned through the final traitor's throat, and three bayonets sped him to the dirt.

'Apologies for our late arrival, captain,' a grenadier said. 'We stumbled upon a group of labourers, cowering but armed.' The captain nodded. He didn't comment on the fact that, evidently, two more lives had been lost.

'Do we still have a melta?' the watchmaster barked.

A Korpsman stepped forward, lugging a heavy meltagun two-handed. Directed by the watchmaster, he aimed it at the shelter door, braced himself and pulled the trigger. The captain heard the familiar, distinctive hiss of moisture in the air evaporating. It was followed, a split second later, by a terrible roar as pure heat energy met layers of tempered steel and reduced them to slag.

The edges of the door remained attached to its locks and hinges, but oozed into a glowing-white-edged hole in the middle. The Korpsman widened it by describing a circle with his muzzle, maintaining the beam. Beads of prickly sweat formed under the captain's mask.

As soon as the way was clear, he started forwards. He leapt through the hole, a dripping glob of molten metal just missing his shoulder. He expected more traitors in the bunker and wanted to catch them reeling.

A flight of ferrocrete steps descended into underground gloom. The captain took three at a time, ignoring the stabbing pains in his left leg. Reaching their foot, he dived and rolled. As he had expected, vivid bursts of light punctured the shadows, bullets pinging off the walls above his head.

His eyes adjusting quickly to the dark – the Krieg were no strangers to such conditions – he saw that he was at one end of a long, broad gallery. Doorways studded its walls, leading into deeper darkness, each of them a potential hidden hazard. The immediate threat came from half a dozen gunmen crouched behind another makeshift barricade at the gallery's far end. A few pillars offered meagre cover, so the captain gave the only order possible: 'Charge!'

His Korpsmen were crowding into the bunker behind him. Their bayonets fixed, they surged forwards. The captain, thanks to his limp, was overtaken by two of them; they crashed into the barricade and scattered its unsecured drums. He saw the labourers behind it recoiling in terror – and in that instant, something struck the captain's head like a club. Whiplash wrenched his neck and another light flashed, but this one behind his eyes. He thought he could keep running, but his muscles didn't listen to his brain. He hit the ground and lay there helpless. A shard of broken helmet landed beside him with a clatter. *Not like this,* was his first thought. His second was, *How else?*

He had been shot. Shot in the head. The captain's lifelong luck had run out on him, and finally he knew his life's purpose.

He felt his mind retreating from the pain as it intensified and there was nothing he could do about it, not even lift his eyelids. Through the rushing of blood in his ears, he heard dull pops of weapons fire, a sign that his world's war would go on without him, and then, as if from a long way away, a cry from a worried comrade.

'Captain! Captain Tyborc!'

His heart exploded in his chest, and he woke with a shuddering gasp.

Wrapped in pitch-blackness, the captain had no clue where he was. He could hear urgent shouts, running footsteps and, from somewhere above him, the muffled roars of cannons. He could have been back in his dugout, except that two Korpsmen were struggling to lift him by his armpits.

A section of the bunker roof came down on them, and they dropped him. *The bunker*... Memories flooded back into the captain's brain as he sprawled in the dirt again. His hands went to his head and found a tender, swelling bruise, but no apparent entry wound. His helmet had saved him, after all. His heart was hammering; his comrades must have given him a hefty stimm injection. That explained his conscious state, but didn't tell him how long it might endure. The powerful chemicals now surging through his system could kill him if his injuries didn't.

The Korpsmen were lifting him again. He tried to support himself, but his legs felt like elastic. Above, the cannons thundered, dislodging more dirt from the ceiling, which pattered off his shoulders. 'They... The traitors are...?'

'Shelling their own fort again, captain,' one of his bearers confirmed.

'With heavy artillery this time,' the other added. 'It looks like they're set on flattening the sector, and anybody in it.'

'They still outnumber us here,' the first Korpsman growled

with some grim satisfaction, 'so they will only further our objectives by such means.'

'But we need to get you out of here, sir. The way this place is shaking...'

'No,' the captain groaned. 'Don't risk two lives for my one. Leave me. That... that is an order.' Over all the noise, they may not have heard him; either that or they chose to disobey him, perhaps thinking him delirious. He felt a rush of resentment towards them, but dismissed it as unworthy of him.

They draped the captain's arms about their necks and hauled him along with them, trampling on the traitors' broken barricade and on their broken bodies. Along with other Korpsmen, they squeezed into an access tunnel at the gallery's end. It was narrow, rough-hewn, and at points they were forced to turn sideways for all three of them to pass. The captain tried to will his legs to work, but the effort almost blacked him out again.

He heard a tremendous crash behind him. A cloud of smoke and debris rolled along the tunnel, enveloping him. His rebreather saved him from suffocation, but he was now blinder than ever. He and his comrades hunkered down against the walls, gritting their teeth. Dust found the captain's throat, perhaps through a small tear in his mask, and he was doubled up by wracking coughs. He sucked water through a tube connected to a flask in his backpack, but not too much as it was running dry.

He didn't know how long he huddled down there, until the traitors' cannons were finally exhausted. In the ensuing stillness, Death Korpsmen picked themselves up, dusting themselves down. The captain tried but failed to stand unaided. He was helped back along the narrow tunnel, back out into the gallery. Its support pillars groaned and its floor was strewn with rubble, but it appeared largely intact.

The Krieg were regrouping here, and a couple had rooted out

lumen cubes to dispel the dusty darkness. More comrades were drawn to the light, emerging cautiously from the surrounding doorways. Each received a grateful welcome, but it wasn't long before the steady flow of arrivals ceased.

In the lumens' pallid glow, the captain saw that the gallery's far end had indeed collapsed. The steps down which he had first entered had been buried, as had the sundered surface door. Not even a sliver of daylight was still visible. Down here, he counted roughly forty soldiers, his company's survivors. He looked for one particular set of rank insignia. 'Watchmaster?'

'He went back up there, sir,' a sergeant offered, 'to round up as many of us as he could. With the vox-net down, my squad and I would never have known about this shelter but for him.'

'Then his life counted,' said the captain. 'All of their lives counted, because they brought us this far.'

He shrugged off his helpers and made himself stand ramrod straight. Falling simply was not an option. 'There may be few of us remaining, and it may seem we are trapped here, but the truth is the enemy is trapped with us. These tunnels lead deep into their network, perhaps to the citadel itself. We have proved their shells can't touch us. The traitors will have to engage us in underground combat – in which we are far better trained and more experienced than they are.'

He paused for his watchmaster to add something, but of course he wasn't there. The captain had become too used to his presence at his elbow; it felt a little odd to be without him. There would be a new watchmaster soon enough, however, and likely a new captain too.

'We hold this position, keep them busy here – keep this hole in their defences open – for as long as we are able,' he decreed. Emperor willing, that would be sufficient – but otherwise, at least they would have killed a few more traitors. Would that be enough to earn him his rest? the captain wondered.

Would the Emperor be done with him then?

The Krieg captain was found three days later.

For three days, he had fought a desperate running battle. He had kept moving, kept the traitors guessing. He had learned the layout of their galleries and tunnels and used it to his own advantage. He had pumped his laspistol dry, scavenged fresh power packs from comrades' corpses and pumped it dry again.

The enemy had sent squads of renegade militiamen with flamers, the smoke from which had made the air unbreathable, and one by one they had closed off his routes through the earthworks with demolition charges. The captain had no water left. He was down to his last rebreather filter, finding oily spittle in his throat. He had taken a knife blow to the stomach and a weeping burn to his right leg. He hadn't slept.

He had heard more explosions from the surface, but could only guess what that might mean. He might have heard faint echoes of las-fire in the tunnels, but he couldn't be sure of that either. He had just eight Korpsmen left, injured too. The traitors had inevitably pushed them back to the half-collapsed gallery, and here they were holed up, cornered but as yet undefeated. In the unrelenting dark, the captain had no sense of time. He only knew that every second mattered.

He had blocked the approaches to the gallery, nailing duckboards over doorways, setting traps with his final few grenades. The traitors had made several failed assaults already. As another explosion blew sandbags and bits of wood into the room, the weary Krieg scrambled to repel their latest attempt. Discerning shapes through a smoke haze, the captain cautioned them, 'No. Wait. Hold your fire.'

He was standing in front of the smoking doorway with a flamer, wrestled from a militiaman's arms. It was out of fuel, so only useful to him as a bluff to buy him time. By now, however, he ought to have been raked with bullets. Instead, his earpiece crackled into life, signifying that there was a vox-caster within range, and a gruff voice confirmed his instincts: *'Identify yourselves.'*

He responded, then let the dead flamer fall from his dead hands. His Korpsmen too laid down their arms at last, as a squad of Krieg grenadiers filed into the room. Never had the captain seen a more welcome sight than their skull-shaped faceplates. Their sergeant snapped to attention and saluted. 'General Durjan sends his compliments, captain.'

'How long has it been?' he asked weakly.

'It is almost dawn.'

But how many dawns? He didn't know.

The grenadier sergeant looked the captain up and down. 'You need medical attention, sir. All of you do. You are no longer needed here. We should get you to the surface and into a Chimera, transport you back behind the lines.'

'You have a safe route?'

The sergeant nodded. 'We believe we have all but cleared these tunnels by now. Do you need any help to walk, captain?'

He shook his head determinedly. 'No. Thank you, sergeant. I can manage.'

The captain suppressed a sickly groan as his eyes fluttered open.

In his drowse, he had sensed an ominous presence standing over him. He expected yet another medicae, perhaps the chirurgeon who had sewn up his stomach.

He was surprised to see a holy woman instead. Instinctively, he tried to swing his bandaged legs out of his bed, to stand to attention, but she waved a dismissive hand. 'No, please, don't rise on my account.' Though the words were considerate enough, her tone was as severe as the expression on her pale, pinched face.

She wore sigil-embellished red and silver robes, and a tall mitre tapering to two points, front and back. Whatever hair she had was scraped back and hidden beneath this. She brandished an oak staff like a cudgel. It was almost as tall as the woman herself – perhaps as tall, without her hat – and was topped by a gleaming, double-headed effigy of the Imperial aquila.

Dangling from her hempen belt was a weighty, well-thumbed, leather-bound tome, embossed with the seal of the Adeptus Ministorum.

'Can I assist you… preacher?' the captain guessed. Members of the Ecclesiarchy wore no formal badges of rank.

The woman's lips twitched. 'Confessor,' she corrected him. 'Tenaxus.' She drew a curtain round his bed, securing their privacy from the ward's other patients. 'I simply wished to ask how you were feeling.'

'I am ready to resume my duties, ma'am.'

'No medicae am I,' she said, 'but even I can see that is untrue. I'm sure you have been told you need to rest.'

'There will be time enough for that when I lie dead.'

'Ah, yes. The grim fatalism for which the Krieg are famed. Who are you, captain? Tell me about yourself.'

Though he didn't try to stand again, the Krieg man straightened his arms and dug his fists into his hips. 'Ninth Company commander, ma'am, 261st Siege Regiment, attached to 30th Line Korps.'

'The Hero of Fort A-453,' Confessor Tenaxus added.

The captain squirmed. 'I am no hero.'

'Many would disagree with that assessment. After all, you led your company to our first substantial victory in this war. With few comrades left beside you and wounds greater than most could have borne, you refused to surrender. There is talk that you may be offered the Medallion Crimson.'

'I expect neither praise nor baubles for doing my duty as I was trained to do.'

'You punched a hole through the apostate cardinal's defences and held it open against inconceivable odds. His followers are panicking, abandoning their outer defence line. You have hastened the end of this interminable conflict, potentially by years. That means more to me than you can know.'

'Any Korpsman in my place would have done the same.'

'I believe that is also untrue.'

'Just as I, in any of their places, would have done as they did. You would not be calling me a hero then, confessor. Most likely, I would be resting forever.'

Tenaxus shook her head. 'I spoke to your surviving troopers, captain. They tell me you were always the first to charge into enemy fire.'

'Someone has to be,' he responded, matter-of-factly, 'and who better than the longest-lived of us?'

'You sound as if you wish to die.'

'What is death but the fulfilment of duty?'

'Indeed, and your people embrace that philosophy wholeheartedly,' the confessor observed. 'I've seen them mounting broken skulls on their emplacements. I've seen salvaged bones laid carefully into ossuary boxes. When asked the question, most of those Korpsmen don't even know whose bones they are.'

'That is how some choose to remember the nameless dead, whose ranks most of us will shortly join.' The captain had never spoken about such matters before, never faced this sort of interrogation. He was finding it increasingly difficult to formulate answers. It made his wounded head ache all the more. 'Death,' he attempted to explain, 'is part of life.'

'The only immutable part,' agreed Tenaxus.

'It is through death that we achieve our life's purpose.'

'That purpose being?'

'Atonement.'

She nodded sagely. 'For your home world's sins.' A hint of incense wafted from her robes as she perched on the edge of the bed, the captain's air filters allowing the wholesome scent through. 'When I asked you who you were, I expected to hear a name. You do have a name?'

'Commissioned officers are required to have them, for Departmento Munitorum records.'

The confessor said no more, but she fixed the captain with an expectant stare. He remembered his watchmaster, screaming at him in the dark. The last time he had heard his voice. 'My name is Tyborc, ma'am.'

'More people should know that, Captain Tyborc. They should know who you are, and your achievements.' He recoiled from the very idea, and she noted his reaction. 'I can see how that discomfits you. On Krieg, you have no heroes?'

'To think of ourselves in such terms would be...'

'Then what of your Colonel Jurten?'

He groped for an answer to what now sounded like an accusation. Clearly sensing his confusion, his weakness, Tenaxus leaned towards him slightly. 'Colonel Jurten. The resister, when heretics seized power on his world. The soldier, whose war lasted five hundred terrible years. The fanatic, who scoured Krieg with nuclear warheads rather than surrender a square inch of it. The template against whom every Death Korpsman is measured.'

'I would never compare myself with–'

Tenaxus talked over the captain. 'No, I think the Krieg have their heroes like everybody else. Their names, I hear, are inscribed upon your mausoleum walls. You are likely named after one of Jurten's loyal followers. Their great deeds provide inspiration, an example to follow. The only difference I see between them and you is that they died, while you still live.'

The captain swallowed. 'I swear, it is not for want of–'

'That was not a criticism, Captain Tyborc. You are under no suspicion from me – and, believe me, we in the Ecclesiarchy know a thing or two about venerating the long-since departed.' The confessor sat back again, idly stroking her staff's double-headed eagle as her gaze receded into thought. 'I simply wonder if it might best serve the Emperor were the Krieg to learn to honour the still-living.'

III

The Krieg grenadier had been given no name.

A series of numbers identified him for operational purposes: First Platoon, Third Company, 19th Regiment, First Line Korps, 88th Siege Army. He also had a thirteen-digit designation that was personal to him and never changed. He only really needed to remember this when troop reassignments were posted.

Few people had ever seen his face. Like most Krieg, he rarely removed his rebreather mask. He was always aware of the weight of the skull-shaped faceplate riveted to this, a grenadier tradition. It signified that he had accepted his impending death and thus had nothing more to fear.

The grenadier's veteran sergeant had another take on it. *I wear the skull to show our enemies that death comes for them,* he always claimed. Either way, grenadier squads were honoured with the most hazardous assignments, and thus enjoyed the Death Korps' highest mortality rate.

This grenadier had endured longer than most, becoming his

squad's second longest-serving member in six months. If, against the odds, he lived much longer, he would likely be promoted. His sergeant had been giving him some leadership training, in between his duties, but this had been abruptly interrupted.

The apostate cardinal's traitors had abandoned their northern front. The rumour in the trenches was that one man alone, a Captain Tyborc, had secured this sudden victory. The First Line Korps had seized the opportunity to push eastwards, gaining more ground in one day alone than they had in the previous two years.

The 19th Regiment's objective was Hab-Zone One: a cluster of prefabricated dwellings, basic housing for Vraks' labouring class. Said labourers had been taken into the citadel and drafted, so it was believed to be derelict now. It straddled one of the two main roads that ran from the citadel to the occupied Vraks Star Port in the east, and so was an important link in the enemy's supply chain.

The air here, inside the outer defence walls, was clearer than without. The grenadier could make out the hab-zone's tall, bland structures, a few miles ahead. They would probably reach it tomorrow. For now, the Krieg spread out across the plain, digging overnight shelters. For now, he did as he had always done, what his thousands of comrades around him were also doing.

He followed his orders.

The following day, at dawn, the order to stand to arms was given.

The grenadier's freshly dug trench was really just a shallow ditch, which had flooded with rain overnight. When he stood straight, his helmet crest could be seen above the parapet. He crouched in a cold grey puddle, his hellgun readied. 'Our scouts heard engines in the hab-zone during the night,' his sergeant informed his squad. 'The traitors may be massing vehicles there.'

Behind them, the steady rumble of Krieg artillery struck up again. Mobile platforms had been wheeled up in the infantrymen's wake, some of last night's ditches deepened to serve as emplacements. Exposed as his company was, the grenadier found comfort in the shrieking of friendly shells overhead and their distant explosions. He watched as a section of the hab-zone's skyline crumbled.

The enemy responded to the provocation.

Soon, shells were shrieking out of the settlement too, confirming that it was indeed occupied in force. Their targets were the mortars, but most fell short of them. The vox-net was jammed with reports of Korpsmen shredded in their too-shallow boltholes. Colonel Adal, the 19th Regiment's commander, ensconced in a more substantial dugout near the front, had them hold fast.

Next, the traitors launched smoke bombs. They carpeted the ground all the way to the hab-zone, obscuring it with billowing white clouds. 'There's only one reason why they would do that,' the sergeant grumbled; a second later, Adal's voice in the grenadier's earpiece warned everyone to brace for an assault.

He heard them before he saw them: the full-blooded screams of charging infantry, intended to intimidate while masking their own fear. Thousands of voices. The grenadier stretched his neck to see over the lip of his trench. The dark mass of the oncoming storm loomed through the haze.

He hardly needed to wait for his sergeant's order: 'Open fire!'

The battle raged throughout the morning. Many traitors were cut down in their paths by the lasguns of the Krieg, but there were always more of them, far more than had been expected.

The grenadier ducked as a frag grenade burst outside the trench, strewing sundered sandbags over him. Barely had he raised his eyes again when a figure came hurtling towards him, howling as he impaled himself on a readied bayonet. He wore no armour, only a labourer's overalls, filthy and ragged. Through two intervening pairs of gas mask lenses, the grenadier saw a silent plea in his red-rimmed eyes.

The traitor was still flailing, lashing out with his crude blade. The grenadier pushed him up against the trench wall and twisted his bayonet in his innards. An unwilling conscript he may have been, but this earned him no quarter. 'Any one of their lives could have counted,' his sergeant had said, two years ago before their first engagement with the enemy, 'but they were too cowardly to die when the Emperor required it of them. Now they die all the same, but in shame and for nothing.'

Another traitor leapt screaming into the trench, and then two more. Expecting to find its occupants in disarray, instead they were swarmed by nine implacable warriors and prevented from bringing their guns to bear.

The grenadier's opponent went limp, wheezing up blood. Planting his boot in the labourer's groin, he wrenched his blade back out of his guts. He elbowed away an autogun aimed at his temple, its bullet striking a militiaman instead. He punched its wielder in the stomach and wrestled the weapon from him. He sprayed more bullets out above his head, hitting two more incoming bodies. He tossed the gun aside once it was empty and finished off a wounded traitor with his bayonet, sparing his hellgun's battery pack.

Someone yelled, 'Fire in the hole!' as a grenade plopped into their midst. In the grenadier's way was a howling, hopping traitor, who had taken a bullet to the knee. He swiped the traitor's good leg out from under him and pushed him onto the device, his body smothering its blast. A second grenade was deftly caught by a comrade and hurled back the way it had come, exploding with a satisfying flash.

The traitors kept coming, many bleeding, some tumbling more than they were leaping, but relentless. Their bodies piled up in the filthy water, and still-twitching fingers grasped at the grenadier's ankle and tried to drag him down alongside them. He saw a comrade falling as through cruel fortune a traitor saw an opening and thrust his blade into an exposed back. Though too late to prevent it, the grenadier avenged the death by slashing the traitor's throat open.

He fought until he was breathless, until his heart pounded, until his limbs ached, and then he fought some more. He was dimly aware, through vox-reports, that similar battles were being waged in other trenches and that several had fallen. Another squad mate was lying in the water too. But the press of foes around him was thinning out, and he realised that no new traitors had appeared in several minutes.

The last one dropped his gun, dropped to his knees, and begged for mercy. The sergeant gave him the mercy of a clean stab through the heart. The Krieg had barely a second to huddle down and catch their breaths. 'We need to–' the sergeant began, but he broke off as a deep, dark shadow slid over him.

Another figure plunged into the trench. It was colossal, and the sergeant was only just able to leap out of its way. One lumpen foot shattered a dead traitor's skull like an egg; the other buried itself in sucking mud up to the shin, so that the creature it belonged to had to tug it free.

With a psychotic roar, it leapt upon the Krieg, thrashing muscular limbs. A spinning, shrieking saw blade grafted to its right arm swiped within a hair's breadth of the grenadier's throat. A sledgehammer, wielded one-handed, thumped into the trench wall beside his ear. The creature's spittle flecked his lenses.

It was an ogryn: an abhuman mutant, ten feet tall, its immense physicality compensating for a lack of brainpower. Its very existence was an affront to the Emperor's order, but its kind could be harnessed as an unflagging, unthinking labour force. Thousands of ogryns had served the Imperium on Vraks, and now, like everybody else, they served their world's new master.

The grenadier noted the gurgling tank on this ogryn's back, the tubes punched into its neck and stomach. Other Korpsmen had seen this before: it was fuelled by a cocktail of potent stimms, increasing its aggression, dulling its mind even further. It would likely expire within minutes, its heart bursting with the strain – but, like a bomb, it would create carnage in the process.

His comrades were scrambling to evade its frenzied attacks, but its bulk in their confined quarters left them scant room to manoeuvre. He ducked another sledgehammer swipe, but was caught a glancing blow by a steel chain dangling from the ogryn's arm. He staggered, head ringing, but the creature's attention was fortuitously elsewhere in that instant.

Its saw, diamantine-tipped for cutting rock, sliced another Krieg grenadier in two, painting the trench with blood and viscera. Another comrade, finding himself cornered, scored the ogryn's chest with shallow cuts, which hardly bothered it at all. The Korpsman shredded his hands on the filthy, rusted spikes of its scrap metal armour. It shattered his ribcage with its hammer, leaving him coughing up blood on the ground.

'The flamer!' yelled the sergeant. 'Use the flamer!'

The cracks of hellguns almost drowned him out. The grenadier shouldered his own gun and worked it furiously. At least his target was difficult to miss. The ogryn clearly felt the las-beams, but brushed them off like insect stings.

Fortunately, they were only a distraction. The two members of the squad's heavy flamer team had braced themselves against the trench's narrow end. One shouted a cursory warning before they filled the air with fire. The grenadier recoiled from the searing, blinding conflagration. The ogryn, at its epicentre, let out a curdling scream – a gratifying sound – as its flesh burned, but still it wouldn't fall.

It turned its back on the grenadier, seeking the source of its torment. It spied the flamer team and bore down on them, but the sergeant planted himself in its path. The ogryn bull-rushed him, but either it was weakened or he was simply too stubborn to be moved because, incredibly, he held his ground.

He drove his bayonet into the ogryn's guts, dislodging a tube that spurted out green fluid. It had dropped its hammer and its rock saw had sputtered to a halt, but it raked the sergeant with its chains and caught his throat between its meaty fingers. It was choking him, and las-beams couldn't shake its deathly grip.

The flamer wielders hesitated, denied a clear shot by their sergeant's flailing body. He was struggling to say something, and the grenadier knew what it must be. 'Fire!' he screamed. 'That mutant freak must burn – no matter the cost!' He was surprised by how easily the words came to him.

The flamer clunked and fire blossomed once more from its innards, engulfing both ogryn and sergeant alike. A stray flame took hold on the grenadier's own greatcoat, and he dived and rolled to put it out. As the fire died down, he saw the blackened, smoking ogryn looming over him – for only a moment, before it toppled like a felled tree. The trench shook with the impact of its landing.

Of the sergeant, just a few charred bones remained. Though the grenadier would mourn him, never once would he doubt the order he had given in the heat of the moment, the one the sergeant himself would have issued. He was the senior member of his squad now, and his comrades were already looking to him to lead them.

A leader must do more than blindly follow orders, his sergeant had drummed into him. *A leader must decide how best to achieve their objectives, using all the tools they have been given. Leadership means thinking.*

In a darker tone, he had added, *But also knowing not to think too much, lest you forget that you too are still a tool of the Emperor.*

First, they tended to their fallen. Only one still lived – the Korpsman with the broken ribs – and he was beyond saving. He didn't seem to know where he was. The grenadier assured him that a monster had been destroyed, partly through his efforts. In the absence of a quartermaster, he ended his comrade's pain.

Over half his squad was gone. Four remained, himself included. He had been tuning out vox-chatter, but now he was listening again and it painted a bleak picture. Many trenches were confirmed to be in enemy hands, while fighting continued in many others. As one of his comrades stood to peer out across the plain, he drew fire from left and right.

He voxed the lieutenant in charge of his platoon, but there was no response. What had his sergeant tried to say before the ogryn's attack? 'We need to get out of this ditch!' Otherwise they risked becoming surrounded, cut off from their regiment as more trenches toppled around them.

They scrambled over the top on the grenadier's signal, using the last of their flamer's fuel to ignite scattered sandbags, creating fire and smoke to obscure their passage. Autoguns chattered, bullets whistling about their heads, but they only had a short distance to cover.

The grenadier had answered a call from a nearby trench, ascertaining its coordinates. The traitors had cleared a way through the wire to it, lining the path with their las-burned corpses. The grenadier led the charge, his three comrades right behind him. He dived into the midst of another heaving melee, announcing his arrival with a roar to strike fear into the Emperor's foes. Fear made them careless.

Driving all else from his mind, he lost himself again in the fury of combat.

That afternoon, the traitors pushed their artillery forwards.

The grenadier heard their growling engines; it sounded as if a full tank regiment was bearing down on his position. Through magnoculars, he saw the outlines of a row of squat Chimeras and what looked like a Basilisk gun platform.

The Krieg cannons barked back, of course, and more shells beat the ground between the trenches. The bone-weary infantry of both sides kept their heads down, which at least gave them a breather and a chance to tend their wounds. The grenadier started a small fire in his trench and the Krieg recharged their power packs in it, although this unapproved technique risked causing an explosion.

How many trenches had he occupied today? Was this the fifth? His squad had retaken this one from the traitors, having blasted their way into it from one adjoining. They had crawled over open ground on their bellies two more times, and two comrades had taken bullets but fought on.

It was becoming harder to know which trenches were friendly and which hostile. The voices of spotters in his earpiece sounded as confused as he was. Some trenches had changed hands three times or even more. In some places, soldiers were shooting at each other across parapets less than a hundred yards apart.

As the sun began to set, the guns subsided and a few more isolated skirmishes broke out. For the most part, however, Korpsmen and militiamen alike stayed in their holes and waited out the night. The grenadier managed an hour's deep sleep on his bedroll. Few traitors, he imagined, would be able to rest at all, which would give the Krieg a considerable advantage tomorrow.

* * *

Dawn was heralded by a lasgun chorus, as neighbouring trenches resumed their desultory duelling. Once more, though, the grenadier heard grinding engines, as the traitors' tanks rolled even closer.

He had established contact with another platoon's commander, and passed on what he had been told to his squad. 'It is clear now that the traitors set a trap for us, to lure us away from our defences. We tried to take too much ground too fast, without digging deep enough into it, and now we cannot hold it.' He wondered if, in Colonel Adal's place, he would have issued the same orders. Would he have had a choice? The colonel had to answer to his superiors too.

They were to make for Adal's command post, if they could. The Krieg flanks were collapsing, so the plan was to regroup in the middle. There was too much fire above ground to risk going up again, so the grenadier's squad took to their shovels. Another trench lay to the west, not very far away. Its status was unknown, but it might have been empty, and the grenadier thought it might connect to other trenches, which might run closer to their goal.

Hardly had they started digging when the vox-net exploded with urgent reports. A shell had torn through the canvas roof of the colonel's dugout. For a tense minute, no one seemed to know if he was alive or dead. Then his crisp voice broke into the general channel, confirming the former, but revealing that the enemy was mounting a concerted assault upon his trench. His words were underscored by las-fire.

Vraks' soft earth gave way easily to the skilled Death Korpsmen. They didn't bother shoring up their tunnel behind them. It wouldn't be needed again, nor were they digging deep at all. They burst into the other trench, finding it not quite as empty as hoped. The traitors held it, but clearly its defenders had put up a fight. Just six militiamen survived, and all were bloodied.

They must have heard the Krieg coming, but still were astounded to see them; so caked were they in grey mud that it must have seemed as if the trench walls themselves had come to life, disgorging clay golems to repel the intruders from their bounds. Few traitors put up any real resistance as the Krieg fell upon them and despatched them. They knew their time had come.

Those engines were deafening now. As the grenadier wiped the last traitor's blood from his blade, the ground trembled and dirt cascaded down the slope behind him. Crouching, staring up over his shoulder, he saw a broad expanse of metal looming over him: a dozer blade, fixed to the front of an enemy tank. More dirt flew from its chunky tracks as they nudged out over the edge, as the belly of the beast – a Chimera – exposed itself to him.

The front end of the tank hung over the grenadier's head, and he thought it might make it; its tracks might bite into the far lip of the trench before its centre of gravity rolled over the near edge and it tipped. A small chance. The gap was narrow, but still in his judgement too wide.

He started running. He screamed at his squad to do the same, but they already were – just as well, as he doubted they could hear him. Behind them, the tank's nose crashed into the ditch, bringing its walls down about itself. The Korpsmen outpaced its collapse by a hair. They ducked into a low, narrow tunnel, its wooden props splintering around them, and out into an even more shallow gully, where they lay flat on their stomachs.

Cautiously raising his head, the grenadier saw the Chimera again. Its engine was shrieking as it ploughed resolutely onwards, forcing the earth to yield before it. Painstakingly, it clambered up out of its hole, sloughing dirt from its hull as it juddered back onto an even keel and ground its way further northwards. As it left his squad behind, a daring thought flashed through the grenadier's mind.

What if we could capture it? It was an Imperial vehicle, after all, with a machine spirit that might still recognise a loyal soul. What if they could steal up behind it, out of the firing arc of its guns? A traitor sat up in the Chimera's turret. With a good enough run-up, he thought he could leap up there before he was seen coming. It was an insane risk, which would probably cost the Krieg their lives – lives that could have been better expended – but what if it didn't? What if the plan worked? Wasn't that the sort of exploit of which heroes were made?

Wasn't that what Captain Tyborc would have done?

The grenadier drew breath to give his order, still unsure what it would be – but the decision was taken from his hands. A shell streaked out of the sky towards the tank and scored a direct hit, engulfing it in flame. Its rear hatch was flung open, and eight or nine traitors stumbled out. No longer did he hesitate. 'Take them down!' the grenadier barked, as he snapped up his hell-gun and fired it.

The traitors, mostly badly burnt, disoriented, were easily cut down – all but the final two, who fled behind the smouldering Chimera. The grenadier's first instinct was not to let them escape. He hauled himself up from the mud and pelted after them. He didn't think to tell his squad to follow him, but they did anyway.

Almost instantly, they drew fire from surrounding trenches. The heaviest of it came from the west, ahead of them. Between them and the colonel. A bullet punched a dent in the grenadier's carapace shoulder plate. They dived for the cover of a shell crater, six feet deep, but mud-spattered, blood-soaked figures rose from the ground around them, emboldened by their greater numbers.

The Krieg worked their hellguns frantically, but with little hope that they could avoid being swarmed. 'Ready bayonets!' the grenadier yelled. They were about to die, but every traitor they took with them, every wound they could inflict, would increase their lives' worth. So he thought.

Salvation descended from the heavens with a shattering explosion.

Another shell tore through the encroaching traitors before most of them could even scream. The grenadier couldn't tell from which side it had come, but either way he thanked the Emperor for it. He buried his masked face in the mud as shrapnel rained down on his back. In a second, he was on his feet again.

Few traitors above ground had survived, and they lay dazed and wounded, literally shell-shocked. An enemy-held trench stretched before him, and for now no fire came from it as its occupants cowered.

His squad charged the trench with their guns blazing.

They never reached their goal.

They zigzagged across the pockmarked plain from shattered trench to shattered trench as more shells slammed down around them, unpredictable, impossible to evade but by sheer luck. It seemed that everywhere they turned, they were greeted by a storm of bullets.

They sniped back at the traitors when they could. They stormed their trenches and engaged them hand-to-hand, but only when they had to. The grenadier strove to keep them moving. Whenever they were pinned down for any length of time, the traitor forces closed on them like pincers. Their tanks continually dogged the Korpsmen's heels – and while they saved their larger weapons for the Krieg's artillery, hull-mounted lasguns took opportunistic shots at them.

They rescued the battered survivors of other Krieg squads, fighting alongside them until most of them died. The grenadier lost another member of his squad too, to a point-blank bullet fired by an enemy hiding in a half-demolished firing pit.

They struck out westward when possible, but met the stiffest resistance in so doing. They made far better progress northward, retracing their regiment's steps of the last few days. They were trying to find a way around the enemy's ever-expanding lines, but vox-reports from other squad leaders confirmed the grenadier's fear: the command post was surrounded.

Colonel Adal's voice sounded calm, resigned. *'Anyone who can hear me, fall back. Save as many resources as you can, including any wounded who will not slow you down. Most importantly, take word back to the front. Tell them what happened here. They need to know that the enemy–'* He broke off in a fierce crackle of las-fire.

'Sir,' the grenadier voxed him, 'we could still reach you if only–'

'There are roughly eighty of us left.' The colonel spoke over him as if he hadn't heard him. *'We'll hold out until relief arrives – failing that, for as long as we are able. May the Emperor be with you – with all of us.'*

The grenadier looked around the latest shallow ditch in which he crouched. His two remaining squad mates looked back at him. He couldn't see their expressions, of course. He had to assume they had heard the colonel's message just as he had. He wished he hadn't heard it. Had he not, he could have kept on trying to reach him. Had the colonel's vox-caster only failed to send as well as receive...

It wasn't worth thinking about. He had his orders. He had been in command of other soldiers for only a few hours, but already he had to say the words that no leader – at least, no Krieg leader – wanted to utter.

He had to tell them to stop fighting.

The grenadier was back where he had started. Back in the same trench he had occupied six nights ago, sleeping on the same bunk. No longer in command of anyone. His depleted squad had been amalgamated with three others, so he had a transient new sergeant, along with an acting captain.

The numbers that identified him were meaningless now. There was no longer a First Platoon or a Third Company and very little left of 19th Regiment. Colonel Adal had saved as many of his soldiers as he could, his valiant rearguard action keeping the traitors stalled for precious hours. It was said that he had faced a Hellhound tank alone. He had charged through its fire, even as his flesh was seared from his bones. With his last gasp of life, he had clamped a krak grenade to the Hellhound's hull.

The grenadier wasn't sure how anyone could know this, given that no witnesses survived, but he was certain it was true.

He had personally witnessed the last stand of his regiment's Death Riders. He had been leading wounded stragglers towards the waiting line of Krieg artillery. A six-strong squadron of genetically enhanced steeds had thundered past him in the opposite direction. Their riders had charged enemy tanks, heedless of their far greater firepower, melta-tipped lances bursting against plasteel hulls. It had been a mere delaying tactic.

An estimated eighty thousand Korpsmen had been slaughtered, all in all. Their lives had bought just enough time.

First Line Korp's other regiments had been able to pull back before they too had marched into an ambush. Though they had had to give up almost all of their ground gained, they had been well braced to meet the enemy's counter-attack. They had held them in the wreckage of their own outer defence line, preventing what could have been a catastrophic breakthrough.

The traitors had not reached the grenadier's trench.

'They have lost as much as we have,' he assured new recruits from the 15th Regiment, 'maybe even more. They threw entire battalions of tanks at us and saw the majority destroyed. Even

Vraks' armouries are not infinite. The traitors will bleed them dry eventually, whereas we are easily replenished.'

A masked officer arrived in his trench and took several Korpsmen aside to speak to them one by one. The grenadier was pumping out a flooded section of the trench when he heard his number called.

He reported to his old captain's dugout. The officer stood from a collapsible chair, head stooped so as not to scrape the roof. He wore the braided peaked cap of a commissar. The grenadier thought he must have been found wanting in some way, but the commissar extended a gloved hand towards him. Though initially confused, he recognised this as a symbol of respect, so took the hand and shook it.

The commissar gave his name as Oblonsk. 'You know,' he said brusquely, 'that your regiment has suffered heavy losses, including the whole of its command section.'

'Yes, sir. Colonel Adal gave the order to withdraw, else I would–'

'Some thought has been given to disbanding it.'

'We can do better, sir,' the grenadier protested.

'General Durjan happens to agree, and offers you a chance to prove it.'

The grenadier felt something like relief. Disbandment would have felt like dishonour – not only to himself but to his colonel and his many fallen comrades. 'I'm sure that is the right decision, sir.'

'Fresh recruits are in transit from your home world,' the commissar continued. 'The 19th Regiment will take the lion's share of them, but they will need experienced officers to lead them – including a new commanding officer, of course. One will be appointed soon, most likely from another regiment. It falls to me, to us, to shore up the 19th's command structure in the meantime.'

He reached into a side pocket of his black trench coat, and only now did the grenadier see the purpose of their meeting. He stared at the pair of fabric badges that the commissar held out to him. One bore the numbers of his regiment, his new platoon and company. The image of a winged skull leered at him from the other. 'Commissar…?'

He wanted to say there must have been a mistake; he wasn't worthy. He hadn't even held a non-commissioned officer rank. Instead, he took the badges and thanked the commissar numbly for the honour. If he sounded at all trepidatious, then this seemed to go unnoticed. The commissar had produced a data-slate and was tapping at it thoughtfully. 'You'll need a name,' he grunted. 'Any preference?'

He thought he might have taken his old sergeant's name, had he known it, had he had one. The commissar seemed to expect no answer, however, and didn't wait for one. 'Keled,' he decreed. 'I am told that a Keled served with some distinction under Colonel Jurten during the war on Krieg?'

Keled… He rolled the name about his mind. A hero's name. He didn't feel like it described him, but he would die proving himself worthy of it.

'Your new captain is expecting you at trench line R532-1442.' The commissar held out his hand again. 'It only remains for me to say congratulations, Lieutenant Keled. I am sure that you will serve the Emperor well.'

ACT TWO

THE GRIND

815–823.M41

The massacre of 19th Regiment sent shockwaves through our army. For three days, helpless in my invalid bed, I kept hearing that the whole war could be lost. I kept my laspistol within reach at all times.

The worst outcome was thankfully averted, but at enormous cost. Planned attacks elsewhere along the front had to be delayed as units were repositioned, resources diverted into shoring up the collapsing First Line Korps.

The apostate cardinal's forces had been in disarray. Now they had a chance to regroup along the citadel's second defence line, which they did. We of the Krieg are famed for our fortitude and pragmatism, but even we were becoming restless. We had already been through a wearying three-year siege, and now we faced the prospect of another, even longer.

I learned later that, in private, senior officers were expressing doubts about Lord Commander Zuehlke's leadership. Certainly, at that time, his twelve-year deadline for retaking Vraks seemed almost out of reach.

Like my comrades, I had to be patient. Still, I wondered how much older I might be before next I had an enemy to fight. I had nightmarish visions of dying in my bed, an aged, feeble husk – and, for the first time, I am ashamed to say, I doubted that I was where the Emperor wanted me to be.

Could this truly have been His plan for me?

– From the account of Veteran Colonel Tyborc

IV

Imperial drop-ships swooped from Vraks' sky like iron eagles. Confessor Tenaxus, as always, mouthed a grateful prayer for the divine power guiding their descent.

They touched down on a broad plateau cleared for that purpose. Drably garbed figures streamed from their hatches. There were vehicles too: Centaurs, Chimeras and Leman Russ tanks. They ground their way along ramps protruding from the ships' blossoming nose cones. The 88th Siege Army wasn't short of vehicles yet, though. What they needed most were soldiers to replace the hundreds of thousands lost, and one world had them in plentiful supply.

The Krieg Korpsmen swarmed down from the plateau, forming up in front of it. They may have lacked the gleaming boots, buckles, and medals of some regiments, but Tenaxus admired their precision. They moved almost as one, like clockwork. Like faceless, obedient automata.

She addressed them through a laud hailer. She had secured

General Durjan's permission to do this, knowing he would not refuse someone of her station. She kept her sermon short because storm clouds were gathering again.

Once she was done, and the general had added a few words of his own, the new recruits were marshalled by junior officers with data-slates. They were split into groups, each of which filed aboard a waiting carriage. Black locomotive engines plumed oily smoke behind them as they chugged out of their sidings. They fanned out across the Saritama Plains, each bound for a different sector of the Van Meersland Wastes. Tenaxus watched them until they were specks on the horizon.

She turned to find a Krieg captain, patiently awaiting her attention. 'Confessor,' he said, 'may I ask you a question related to your speech?'

She inclined her head in consent. She was intrigued. She was unused to being approached like this, least of all by one of the Krieg. Generally, she found them a receptive but mostly silent audience.

'You named me to the new recruits,' said the captain, and the confessor realised why his voice sounded familiar. 'You called me a hero.'

'Captain Tyborc.' She hadn't seen him since their first meeting in the medicae ward, although she had spoken of him often, recounting his great deeds with some finely judged embellishments. 'Good to see you recovered from your injuries.'

'Almost, ma'am. The medicaes still keep me from the front line.'

'That must be frustrating for you.'

'The duties I perform here are also necessary,' he recited loyally.

'Just so.' She fixed him with a shrewd glare. 'But that was not the point I made.'

'What worries me, confessor,' the captain ventured, 'is that if we encourage our recruits to seek recognition for–'

'We discussed this, did we not?' she interrupted him. 'I tell your story, Captain Tyborc, and those of other heroes, to inspire. Yes, I know how uncomfortable you feel with that label. You believe you know what the Emperor requires of you, but what if He has chosen this path for you instead?'

The captain shook his head stubbornly. 'If that were so, ma'am, then I would not be here. I would have been with them when they died.'

Tenaxus frowned. 'With whom?'

Captain Tyborc returned to the trenches two weeks later. He resumed his role as commander of his regiment's Ninth Company. He had ached to see this day for close to a year, but it didn't feel as he had expected.

Little had changed in his long absence, yet everything had. His Korpsmen turned their heads to look at him as he strode by them. Most were new recruits who could only have known him by repute, by the stories they had been told.

His veteran watchmaster greeted him with a salute, but the man behind the mask was not the same man as before, the one who had strode into battle at his side so many times. The captain asked if they had ever served together. Was he one of the survivors of Fort A-453, perhaps? One of the eight? 'No, sir,' the watchmaster replied. 'I transferred in from the Third Company ten months ago.'

'Then you must have been present for the enemy's counter-attack.'

'I was not a member of my captain's command squad then – but yes, sir, I was present. My squad and I saw it.'

'What was it like?'

The watchmaster hesitated. 'The mutant, sir?'

Tyborc had read about the incident – at least, a curt summary of it – in daily despatches. With First Line Korps collapsing in the north, three of 30th Line Korps' four regiments had been redirected to support them, leaving his own regiment to dig in and try to hold their sectors further south. An attack had not been long in coming.

The traitors had been relatively few in number, but they had a secret weapon with them. Or maybe not so secret, as Confessor Tenaxus had seemed to know plenty about it. *The steward of the citadel held certain prisoners on the Inquisition's behalf,* she had explained to Tyborc. *Heretics and psychopaths, mostly, but also those suspected of being… touched by the warp.*

There had been hundreds of such wretches, apparently, from all across the sector, chained up in Vraks' dungeons until a Black Ship could collect them.

'It was hideous,' recalled the watchmaster, 'its twisted body covered in blasphemous inkings. A severed head hung from its belt, and it was wired up to a reservoir of drugs just as the traitors' ogryns are.

'It came for us on the storm. It rode the wind, its feet never touching the ground. Lightning forked around it but never seemed to harm it – and the closer it drew to us, the colder it became, until the water in our hoses froze. Then the mutant raised a hand. It gathered lightning in its palm and hurled it like a frag grenade, over and over again. Its head snapped back, its eyes rolled back in their sockets and I don't think it could see us, but it knew exactly where to aim.'

'Command section,' Tyborc growled.

'There was no defence against that lightning. It struck down the captain, then his commissar, then on to his lieutenants and command squad. The mutant hovered right above our trench, but our las-beams couldn't reach it, as if the storm was shielding it – and all the time I could feel an intense pressure in my head. It felt like something was growing in my brain, about to burst it. I could barely stand, barely even see. All I could do was continue firing and pray that it might finally do some good.'

The watchmaster took a breath.

'Which, in the end, it did,' the captain said.

'It felt like waking from a dream. The storm blew over in a second and the mutant lay between us in the mud, its body broken, although I have no memory of seeing it fall. The traitors folded quickly after that, leaving us to count our dead.'

'I should have been there.' Tyborc clenched his fists reflexively.

His comrade agreed. 'You could have saved them.'

'No,' he said, quickly. He paused, then explained. 'I could have done no more than any of you did. I could only have died with them.'

The passing of time, weeks turning into months, did little to settle his mind.

He immersed himself in familiar activity. Morning troop inspections. Overseeing maintenance work in the trenches, which included filling sandbags, repairing duckboards and emptying latrines. Keeping his own weapons and equipment clean and in working order.

He signed off forms brought to him by junior officers: supply logistics, mostly, ensuring that his Korpsmen had a steady flow of nutrient packs, air filters, first aid kits and ammunition. There were also wastage reports – a departmento euphemism for rolls of the newly dead, lost to shells or sniper fire. He pored over every number, but knew he couldn't memorise them all. The least each of them deserved, the captain felt, was a moment's reflection from him.

Night was the busiest and often most dangerous time, when he sent Korpsmen out to work in no-man's-land beneath the shroud of darkness, laying sandbags and mines, digging earthworks, repairing razor wire.

They were constantly vigilant for the next attack – and would almost have welcomed one – but no attack came. The apostate cardinal's traitors seemed content to wait out the siege behind their near-impregnable walls.

This forced the Krieg to take the initiative. They mounted small-scale raids upon enemy lines, killing as many as they could but also gathering intelligence. Their black locomotives swept wounded prisoners away for interrogation. Captain Tyborc's Ninth Company took part in several missions, but his colonel made it clear that he was not to join them, no matter how often he insisted that he was fighting fit. He could only remain at his command post and await the survivors' return, once their best efforts had proved futile yet again.

He was heartened to hear one piece of news. First Line Korps had retaken the ground they had lost a year before. They had wiped the occupied Hab-Zone One from the map and were bearing down upon the second defence line from the north and east. Otherwise, it seemed the Krieg were making little headway. Their mighty army had come to a virtual standstill.

'If the traitors believe they can hold out long enough,' Tyborc stated to Confessor Tenaxus, 'for us to lose patience and just let them keep their spoils–'

'Yes, yes,' she agreed, 'then I'm sure they are sorely mistaken.'

She had come to see him in his dugout, wearing a gas mask but recognisable by her accoutrements of office. This time, she had asked for him by name. He didn't know why she was so interested in him. He could think of no pleasant reason.

'Unfortunately,' said Tenaxus, 'Krieg high command may not get to choose how and when this war ends.'

The captain mulled over her point.

'How about you, Captain Tyborc?' He didn't know how to answer her, what she expected to hear. She prompted him: 'Still hoping for a chance to die?'

'Confessor, I...' He had to be honest with her. He chose his words with caution. 'Would it be conceited of me to wonder if...?'

'Go on.'

'If you may have been right? If the Emperor may have another plan for me? I feel like, since I survived the fort...'

'Despite taking on the greatest risks,' Tenaxus interjected.

'And then, as a consequence of that, I was not present when...'

'When a rogue psyker wiped out your company's command staff.'

'The fate of most Krieg is to die for little gain. We accept this, as long as we know we die for something. We place little value on our lives, but also know that every life expended counts. Should I... Should any one of us imagine that his life has more value than another...'

'But isn't that what your superiors believe?'

Tyborc looked at the confessor blankly.

She expounded, 'Is that not why they hold you back?'

He shook his head. 'An experienced officer is harder to replace than–'

'And therefore, his life has more value?'

'No, ma'am.'

'Your colonel would rather you weren't shot by a labourer with a primitive gun that he can barely aim. He won't let you be cremated on your stomach in the mud by a random falling shell. He wants to see you storming the next fort or the citadel itself, pistol in hand as you wade through traitors' broken bodies – and I think, in your heart, you want that too.'

'I only want to make a difference,' he protested again. 'I do not require–'

'Captain Tyborc deserves a hero's death.'

'I don't believe that.' His heart told him that was a lie.

'While the rest of us deserve a hero's story.'

'I cannot believe that,' the captain corrected himself. 'When my time comes at last to give my life, I cannot hesitate. I cannot doubt my duty, believing it beneath me.'

'What if death is not your destiny at all?'

'The God-Emperor made us all to die.'

'Still, there are Krieg Korpsmen – many here on this planet, thanks to the years we have spent here – who have lived longer lives than you, and so clearly that was His plan for them. You could rise to the rank of colonel, even general.'

'Not a general,' said Tyborc emphatically.

Tenaxus didn't press him, but the tilt of her head betrayed her curiosity. He attempted to explain. 'Jurten never claimed a higher rank than colonel. I… Many Krieg believe…'

'You think it impertinent to outrank him. Yes, I see.' The confessor thought for a moment. 'Then General Durjan…?'

Tyborc felt a stab of guilt. 'I meant no disrespect, confessor.'

'None was inferred,' she assured him.

'There are several precedents for…' He was struggling to find the words again. 'Sometimes, the Departmento Munitorum requires…'

'It is good to know,' said Confessor Tenaxus dryly, 'that not all Krieg think entirely the same way, after all.'

It wasn't quite the judgement that Tyborc had expected to receive from her.

Five years had passed since the fort, since his last real taste of combat.

Tyborc kept himself and his soldiers in shape as best he was able. During those brief periods when his company was cycled out of the overcrowded trenches, he drilled them relentlessly and organised night-time combat exercises. Still, he worried that his instincts might dull through lack of use.

Then late one night came news of a possible development, an end to the long, exhausting stalemate. His own regiment's Fourth Company had mounted an attack, just a few miles south of his position. Their Gorgon assault transports were on the verge of breaking through the second of the traitors' defence lines around the citadel, five years after the breaking of the first. Ninth Company and others were hastily ordered to support them.

He led the way over the top. His colonel could hardly disagree that this engagement merited his presence. The shelling in this part of no-man's-land was light, the enemy having other demands on their attention. Still, the captain and his Korpsmen had a lot of ground to cover, and many would die along the way.

It was good to feel his heart pumping again.

He had made it almost halfway to the battleground – he thought he could hear the Gorgons' heavy stubbers – when his orders were suddenly rescinded. Ninth Company was to turn around and go back to its trenches. Never had obeying a lawful command made him feel so dispirited. The journey back was every bit as treacherous as the outward one, and felt twice as long to him.

The remainder of the night, he spent sifting through vox-chatter for clues to what had happened. For what had another two-score of his Korpsmen died? All he learned for sure was that news of Fourth Company's success had been somewhat premature. The traitors had repulsed their attack, so speedily and thoroughly that no other units had had time to reach them – but how could that have been so?

Eight days later, attending a regimental command meeting, he was given some answers at last.

'The attack on Sector 52-49 left few survivors,' his colonel summarised, 'and those few saw very little or can't be sure of what they saw. We have only their recollections of garbled vox-reports to go on, but most understood that the traitor militiamen had unexpected allies. Powerful allies, whose presence on Vraks if confirmed would be troubling indeed.'

'More mutants?' hazarded First Company's captain.

The colonel shook his head. He intoned gravely, 'Space Marines.'

A deathly silence greeted this pronouncement.

Finally, Captain Tyborc asked, 'How is that possible?'

'Unclear at present, but at least six, maybe more, appear to have joined in the fighting. Urgent aid has been requested from the sector's lord commander militant, firstly to identify these traitors from their colours.'

'But if they have been on Vraks all this time…'

The colonel agreed. 'Then surely we ought to have been told. Perhaps so. I also doubt they would be fighting for the apostate cardinal now, whatever… persuasions he may have inflicted upon them. That means we must consider another, even more disturbing possibility.'

He didn't have to spell it out; it was best to leave the words unvoiced. Captain Tyborc had always been aware of Vraks' proximity to the Eye of Terror. It was considered a bastion against that raging warp storm, a crucial link in a chain stretching across the Segmentum Obscurus. One more reason why they couldn't let it fall. If their war here had drawn the Eye's attention…

'Lord Zuehlke has also asked for Naval support,' the colonel continued. 'If the traitors have contacted off-world allies, we need a planetary blockade to ensure no more can land here. I needn't tell you that even a handful of Traitor Marines could turn this war against us – let alone whatever other horrors might be summoned.'

Tyborc had more questions, many more, but he kept them to himself. The colonel had told him all he had to know to do his duty. *Is this my fault?* he asked himself. *Captain Tyborc deserves a hero's death,* the confessor had said. How else could such a death be earned, other than in hopeless battle against overwhelming odds? It was as if the Emperor had seen the darkest secrets in his heart and wrenched them out into the light. As if he was – as if they all were – being punished for his shameful ambitions.

Confessor Tenaxus sighed as she stepped from the shuttle's ramp.

She had spent the past three months on Thracian Primaris, the Scarus Sector's principal planet. It was here that Lord Commander Zuehlke and the 88th Army's command staff were headquartered. She had quietly attached herself to an Ecclesiarchical fact-finding expedition and been extremely well accommodated.

Just the sight of Vraks' drab landscape, the patter of rain on her robes, the stink of its air, weighed down her heart. She wondered when she would see the back of this miserable wasteland. She caressed her staff's double-headed eagle and reminded herself that she was needed here.

In the past year, the nature of Vraks' war had drastically altered. New, more powerful players had entered the fray, against whom ordinary soldiers seemed small and all but helpless. Still, it was in the hands of these ordinary Korpsmen, these fragile but indomitable millions, that the planet's fate yet rested, and it was the confessor's duty to inspire them, whether they wanted it or not.

In three months, she had seen and heard much that had frustrated her, but also much to assist her in her crucial task.

She spent a night on a serviceable but not very comfortable

bunk in sterile, prefabricated quarters. The next morning, she rode a black train to one of the forward depots and made the long trudge into the trenches. Through the day, she addressed almost twenty groups of Korpsmen. Each group was only small, as demanded by their confines and because the Krieg had little time off-duty, but she knew the stories she related to them would spread.

They gave her their utmost attention. Some members of the 34th Line Korps, stationed at the southern end of the second defence line where it turned east towards the Srna Flats, had seen lights in the sky above the star port and were eager to know what they portended.

'The Emperor heard our humble prayers,' she assured them, 'and sent His Angels of Death to smite our foes.'

In fact, the Scarus Sector's lord commander militant had asked for help from the Adeptus Astartes, and their Dark Angels Chapter had chosen to oblige him. A battle-barge had arrived in the system unexpectedly, flanked by a pair of strike cruisers. Aboard had been five hundred battle-brothers, fully half the Chapter's complement, led by their Supreme Grand Master, Azrael.

They hadn't informed Zuehlke of their plans; Tenaxus had seen how he resented their lack of courtesy, but this she kept to herself. Their fleet had deployed drop pods and Thunderhawk gunships. They had chosen Vraks Star Port as their target. More than just a port, it was the planet's main administrative zone, once home to more than half its population. The Krieg on the ground would have to go through the citadel to reach it; the Space Marines could soar over the traitors' defences faster than their laser batteries could track them.

'The Angels set down in the Srna Flats and marched northwards,' the confessor related. 'A vast armoured column of Rhinos, Vindicators, Whirlwinds, Razorbacks, and Predators ploughed over anyone unwise enough to place themselves in their way. The apostate cardinal learned of the advance and sent militiamen and tanks to defend the star port. The Angels allowed him to do so, because it weakened his defences elsewhere – but only to a point.

'Thunderhawks swooped upon the causeways across the Balan Trench. Their turbo-lasers blasted checkpoints to rubble. Assault squads leapt from their gunships to slaughter the survivors and lay demolition charges. Each of those three causeways crumbled into the abyss. Those traitors whom the Angels had lured to the star port were now cut off from further reinforcements. They were hunted down like dogs.'

It must have been glorious, she thought, to see the Emperor's vengeance sweeping through the traitor-held city in dark green power armour; traitors cut down by storm bolters as they ran, unable to throw off the Land Speeders that pinpointed their positions to the bigger guns. Monitoring augur reports on Thracian Primaris, she had tried to visualise the scene.

'By the sixth day of fighting, the landing fields were devastated. Of the enemy's artillery, only smouldering husks remained. Buildings were torn down about the ears of the cowards who had tried to shelter in them. It is then, we believe, that the Traitor legionaries first showed their faces.'

At this point, often she heard a few intakes of breath from the normally taciturn Krieg. Alas, there wasn't much more she could tell them. 'The traitors believed themselves unassailable, but the Dark Angels wielded the Emperor's light, their noble Lord Azrael leading from the front, brandishing his mighty blade. They were also legion to the traitors' few.'

So violent had been the clash of forces that it had been detected from orbit. Details, however, had eluded the distant onlookers. Tenaxus only knew that, ten days after their arrival – and following a much more fraught and closer battle than her audience could be allowed to know – the Dark Angels had returned to their ships and departed just as suddenly. Azrael himself had sent an astropathic message to the 88th Army's command HQ, the only time he had acknowledged their presence. *By the Emperor's wrath, Vraks Star Port destroyed,* it had read. *Mission complete.*

'Xaphan has been dealt a crippling blow,' Tenaxus preached. 'He must have lost thousands – tens or hundreds of thousands – of followers, and those who remain have had the fear of the Emperor struck into them. More significantly, he has lost the star port, making him more isolated than ever before.

'Lord Commander Zuehlke has drafted three more regiments to form a fifth line korps for our army. Once they are in position, he plans to mount our largest-scale offensive yet, while the enemy is still reeling. Both he and I have every confidence that this will lead to the breakthrough for which we all pray.'

Only twice that day was she asked the question she had most wished to avoid: 'And the Traitor legionaries? What of them?'

'Pray we have seen the last of them,' she muttered.

Preparations for the fresh offensive took another two months – until early in the year 822.M41, a day and hour were set for its launch. Every line korps was to attack the traitors' second defence line in concert, placing its depleted defenders under sustained pressure. Somewhere, they had to break.

The traitors couldn't help but notice the build-up of resources along the attacking front, and so they responded with their most savage bombardment yet. If nothing else, though, long years of inactivity had allowed the Krieg to dig deep. They huddled together, protected in ferrocrete bunkers, as storms both real and metaphorical raged above their heads.

The roof of Captain Tyborc's dugout rattled as he entertained an unexpected visitor.

'I thought a brisk tour of the front lines might prove beneficial,' Confessor Tenaxus explained. 'Really, I just want to show my face. Or rather...' She indicated her gas mask ruefully. 'A reminder that the Emperor will be with every soldier who serves His cause tomorrow.'

'No need to place your life at risk, confessor. The Krieg need no–'

'So I am often told,' Tenaxus said, a little sharply. 'Never does their resolve nor their faith in the Emperor falter, and certainly no Korpsman would harbour heretical notions, nor require exhortation to report such in a comrade.'

She sighed and her voice softened. It occurred to the captain that she had been speaking to him more softly for some time now. 'In some ways, Captain Tyborc, you and I are not so different. We desire, most of all, to make a difference. On occasion, we have felt ourselves helpless to do so.'

'Tomorrow,' he swore, 'I shall make a difference.'

'You will kill many traitors, or die so that someone else may and be content with that.' Tenaxus sighed again. 'Perhaps it is I who have committed the sin of conceit, for I wish more than anything to see this damned war's end.'

'Is that not true of us all?'

'No, captain, you misunderstand me. I cannot, will not, expire before that day. My soul cannot rest until I have seen the tomb of the blessed Leonis freed. Nor before I have a chance to spit on the traitor Xaphan's corpse.'

She hadn't confided in Tyborc like this before. Nobody had. Not for the first time, he felt he was being tested. He sought refuge in an anodyne statement. 'I have faith that it will happen.'

'Soon,' said Tenaxus darkly, 'we shall know one way or another.'

'Or another?'

'One thing I am sure of – the Death Korps of Krieg would keep fighting this war for as long as they needed to win it, which inexorably they would.'

'Of course, confessor.'

'The Departmento Munitorum, on the other hand, have many calls on their resources, upon which Vraks has been a considerable drain. Should tomorrow's offensive fail to get this campaign back on schedule...'

They sat together in silence, contemplating that terrible option. The captain thought of all the loyal soldiers whose bones were already rotting in Vraks' soil. He thought of endless lists of numbers.

'Make me a promise, Captain Tyborc,' said Tenaxus. 'If ever you are offered that promotion we discussed, whether it be to the rank of general or even–'

'But–'

'Any chance you are given to make a real difference, you must take it, no matter how uncomfortable it makes you feel.'

'I... will consider it, confessor.'

'The Imperium has a need for people like you, who think as you do, at its highest levels – far more than those with little aptitude other than for political manoeuvring.' She sounded bitter.

'The offensive tomorrow will succeed, because it must.'

The confessor stood and drew her robes tighter about herself. 'I don't doubt, captain, that had you – had any Krieg Korpsman – been in charge of this war from the start, then we would have been triumphant long ago.'

The captain's goal was in his sights.

Krieg cannons had pounded the defence line for four days

straight, pulverising the enemy's forward emplacements. They had scrambled to set up salvaged guns in shell craters, behind stacked sandbags, anywhere they could as two million determined Korpsmen came thundering towards them.

Tyborc's company had been in the second wave out of the trenches, wading through the bodies of the first. He wouldn't be joining them today. He couldn't die before he knew that Vraks' salvation was secured, that his life – all of their lives – had counted. Just as his fallen comrades had doubtless believed when they had sacrificed themselves. He thought they might have been the lucky ones.

Another mad charge into enemy fire, but the Emperor as always was with him, as surely as was his veteran watchmaster at his elbow.

The thick smoke parted, and the captain saw fighting just ahead of him. His comrades had overrun a heavy stubber mounted on a tripod. Renegade militiamen were rushing them from both sides, desperate to retake the weapon before it could be turned on them. Rubble shifted under Tyborc's foot, throwing off his balance. A comrade took a bullet to the head and collapsed back into him. The captain caught her and continued to press onward, using the body as a shield. It wasn't disrespectful, just pragmatic, and the Korpsman would have been gratified to know that even in death she could serve.

He veered to intercept an incoming traitor squad, who braked as they saw him, throwing up their guns. He flung his comrade's corpse at them; reacting by instinct and in panic, they riddled it with bullets. Before they knew it – to his surprise too – his watchmaster bowled into their midst. *Not the same watchmaster as before,* he reminded himself. This one was younger than he was and evidently faster.

Tyborc was half a step behind him, even so. They braced themselves against each other's backs and picked off traitors with las-fire, their bayonets slashing out at any daring to approach them, and it was just as it had always been before.

As they thinned out the enemy around them, they drew fire from a nearby crater.

'Captain, down!' The voice crackled over his command squad's channel, so he didn't question its wisdom. He ducked as a rapid-fire burst from the now-captured stubber whistled over him to shred the crater's edge. Its occupants' heads and their autogun barrels disappeared into the hole. Barely had the stubber's chatter ceased before he was up again and leaping after them.

He landed in the midst of a dozen or so frightened traitors. He batted away their knife arms' clumsy thrusts, his pistol lighting up their makeshift shelter in strobing bursts. The rest of his command squad piled into the crater around him, until he was pinned amid a mass of slashing blades and heaving muscles. He deflected a knife thrust from his right, twisting so the blade sparked off one of his abdomen plates. He plunged his bayonet into a militiaman's stomach.

His heart was pumping and he felt a smile tugging at his lips. No longer had he any doubts, nor many thoughts at all. He lost himself in the instinctual rhythms of combat, bathing in the glow of spiritual fulfilment that came from giving himself up entirely to a righteous cause, a worthwhile cause.

This was everything that Captain Tyborc lived for – and one day, one day soon, he would die for it too. But that day wouldn't be today.

V

The sky above Vraks had been alive for some days now.

It was most evident by night, with this side of the planet turned from its sun and the gun smoke of the day's bombardments having somewhat settled. Bright energy beams flickered across the firmament, while bursting torpedoes and plasma bolts created transitory new stars.

Out in the endless void, a battle had been joined, no less fraught than the one down here. A battle in which the Death Korps of Krieg had no part to play and of which they were told little, though its outcome would affect them most of all.

Last night, a comet had streaked over their trenches, trailing flames behind it. A wounded spacecraft, plummeting to earth. Captain Fodor had followed its flight through his magnoculars. It must have come down close to the Chaylia Plateau, north of the ruined star port. Had it belonged to friend or foe? Had there been survivors of its crash?

A peripatetic confessor, preaching in the trenches, maintained that there was no cause for concern. *The apostate cardinal is losing his grip on power,* she had crowed, *so has sent a plaintive plea to other wretches like himself – renegades, pirates, tinpot warlords, mutants. Their decaying, pox-ridden vessels are being drawn to Vraks like mesmerised moths to a flame – but the only fire they find here is the holy fire of Imperial warships, in which they are consumed.*

The captain had listened, but kept a wary eye on the sky all the same.

He knew how few ships the 88th Siege Army had at its disposal. His was a newly raised Krieg regiment, the 468th, most of whose recruits, himself included, had not left the home world before. He knew how many months they had waited for transport to convey them to their first field of battle. Months wasted. He didn't doubt the confessor's word that reinforcements were starting to arrive, but he lacked her religious conviction that they would so easily overwhelm their enemies.

Of course, he would not voice such misgivings. Nor would he ever question the wisdom of his superior officers, though this had already led to the decimation of his fledgling regiment and its colonel's death in action, and now saw them thrown into another desperate battle for which they were far from prepared.

A ricocheting bullet pinged off Captain Fodor's helmet.

Thrown off balance, he lost his footing on the slippery slope. He caught himself with his hands and scrambled up behind the cover of an overturned tank: a Macharius, formerly one of his regiment's powerhouse weapons, now a smoking husk but still able to offer some protection.

The smoke with which Krieg shells had carpeted the valley was dissipating now, and he could make out the angular shapes of pillboxes above him. He relayed their positions to his mortars, which dutifully spat explosive shells over his head. Vox-chatter told him that, on his regiment's right flank, 33rd Company was caught in a lethal crossfire. At the formation known as the Mortuary Redoubt, the 31st had been hit by incendiary rounds, which sprayed out burning oxy-phosphorus gel. Both had been forced to go to ground.

The remaining Macharius found traction in the mud and brought its armour-shattering twin Vanquisher cannons to bear. It blasted a hole through the wall of an enemy bunker ahead of him. Its bolters laid down suppressive fire while its gunners reloaded their main barrels and the juggernaut continued its arduous climb.

Emerging from cover, Fodor waved his leading squads forwards, advancing from crater to crater. It was all up to him now, and he was determined not to fail. For the Emperor, and for the 468th's untarnished honour.

Was it not due to them, after all, that they had come this far?

Lord Commander Zuehlke's big push had been the first field test for his regiment, and they had come through with flying colours.

Making up one-third of the newly assembled 46th Line Korps, they had been stationed north of the Citadel of Vraks. They had moved into trenches vacated by the First Line Korps, as they had continued to push clockwise around its walls. They had had but a matter of days to make themselves at home.

The 54th Company, which Fodor commanded, had left the trenches on the third night and had soon been in the thick of the fighting. The captain himself had gained much satisfaction from his first enemy kill. Though training recruits on Krieg was necessary work, still he had always itched to serve the Emperor as he had himself been trained, and it was just as he had always imagined it to be.

How could any gutless traitor hope to match the zeal and skill with which the rawest Korpsman fought, even in a training exercise? On what world could exist a more hostile environment than his world's nuclear wastelands?

Three days of bloody fighting had stretched into five, and then a week. Tens or hundreds of thousands of Korpsmen had been slain – but to Fodor's pride it had been his own regiment that had made the sorely needed breakthrough. Their commander, Colonel Attas, had personally led a surprise night-time invasion of enemy trenches in Sector 57-50, and though his bones were shattered by a hammer-wielding ogryn, his sacrifice had opened up a gap in the second defence line, through which Krieg artillery and Death Rider squadrons had poured.

This too was only as Fodor had expected. Other regiments had been on Vraks ten years now, and though their ranks had been replenished, many Korpsmen and their officers especially must have been old and tired. His regiment was young. It was still fresh. If anyone could break the deadlock here, they could.

The colonel's fate played on his mind, however. He too had been transferred from Krieg's training camps, though he had prior service in the field. That confessor – Tenaxus was her name – had spoken much of Vraks' heroes. To Fodor's surprise, she had pointedly used their names. Would she now tell the story of Colonel Attas? he wondered. Had that been on his mind when he had given up his life?

Had an old man taken his last chance to be a hero?

They had soon been presented with another problem.

The 468th Regiment had trampled over enemy defences. They had swept through the ruins of a hab-zone, meeting minimal resistance. South of this, they had emerged into a shallow valley, two and a half miles long, to find their way blocked by a low ridge running north-west to south-east. Immediately, they had come under plunging fire from guns atop that ridge. The traitors had regrouped up there, the higher ground lending them a considerable advantage.

In the captain's view, they had two options. Digging in inside a death trap was not one of them. They had to pull back to the hab-zone or try to take the ridge. The first would be the prudent choice, given that their recent triumphs had not been without cost. Some companies were operating at less than half strength, with artillery in dire want of repair. They needed time to rebuild their forces.

The 88th Army's command staff decided on the second option.

Mortuary Ridge. That was what the Krieg had started calling it. A deceptively gentle slope, but one upon which the bones of many of them were fated to rest.

Five companies, including Fodor's 54th, were committed to the initial advance. Two more would stand in reserve – though these reserve companies would also provide artillery support. Key to this would be a pair of Macharius heavy tanks, weapons of a last resort that had been reached.

Captain Fodor had both received and given instruction in military strategy. To him, this assault appeared foolhardy. The Krieg were taking too big a risk for little gain. Their lives would be squandered to make up time lost due to previous mistakes. He saw this as an opportunity. His sole regret about his service on Vraks thus far was that he hadn't contributed more directly to his regiment's success. This time, it would be different. This time, his company had been handed the most critical assignment, and he intended to exceed expectations.

Their target was a strongpoint of pillboxes, bunkers, and minefields on the lip of the ridge. Fort C-585 was its official designation. It would not be easily captured. Were it to fall, however, then like toppled dominoes the rest of the traitors' line would surely follow. This was Captain Fodor's chance to distinguish himself.

His chance to be a hero.

He slid into another shallow crater. He landed atop five shrapnel-torn Krieg corpses: any one of his numerous squads with whom he had lost contact. The fort, his objective, was only just above him now, tantalisingly almost within reach – just as it had been for them too.

The captain yelled for his vox-operator. He bore witness as the Korpsman in question, hastening to reach him, stepped on a hidden mine and was flung into the air. He crawled on his stomach to reach his groaning comrade, whose right leg had been severed. Nothing he could do for them was worth the risk to himself; they would never fight again. The captain wrested the heavy vox-caster from the operator's back and dragged it back to his crater.

He transmitted orders to his trenches. With just a few more Korpsmen, he thought, the fort could be taken by nightfall. Short-range communications allowed him to pinpoint his leading squads. They weren't far from him. They were lobbing grenades into the traitors' foxholes. Fodor started to make his way towards them, but a fusillade of bolter fire drove him back into his hole.

He judged that the traitors were panicking as vengeance closed in on them. Krieg soldiers would have used their ammunition more efficiently. He flattened himself in the mud and waited. He received confirmation that his 13th Platoon had left their trenches and were tackling the ridge. The expected lull in the traitors' fire could hardly have been better timed.

He joined the reinforcements as they overran his position, and they took the final steps up Mortuary Ridge together, rushing Fort C-585 with their bayonets fixed. He looked forward to reporting his glorious achievement to command HQ. It felt like nothing could stop him now.

Captain Fodor led a platoon along an enemy trench, clearing their path with grenades, his laspistol blazing each time a burnt and bloodied traitor popped up in its sights. His target was the bunker he had sighted earlier, the one cracked open by a Vanquisher shell. It commanded views across the ridge's top and down its slope, but was blind to an approach through its builders' own earthworks.

For that reason, perhaps, a rabble of ill-equipped labourers had been sent to scout around it. Their response, upon running into twenty Korpsmen, was to run for the bunker's protection. A muscular, bare-armed enforcer turned them back with lashes from a barbed whip. In his other hand, he wielded a cumbersome chainsword, its teeth already crusted with dried blood.

The terrified labourers broke on the onrushing Krieg wave. Captain Fodor slipped between them, his eyes on their cruel master. The enforcer, despite his hulking build, appeared human enough. He wore a cast-iron, spiked skull mask, while the real skulls of old victims were lashed between his armour plates. The vile eight-pointed star of the Ruinous Powers was carved into his right shoulder, the scars weeping black with infection.

The enforcer saw Fodor coming and closed with him, faster than he looked. The captain got off two shots, snapping the brute's head back but barely slowing him. Enforcer and chainsword alike released matching throaty roars. The captain sidestepped a swipe of the grinding blade, but couldn't avoid its wielder's hurtling weight and was spun by a meaty shoulder slam.

He reeled into a pair of labourers, who were too startled to do much about it. Grabbing the scruffs of their necks, the captain pushed them into their master even as he bellowed curse-laden admonishments at them. The chainsword sliced through both without compunction. In his zeal to reach his foe, the enforcer batted aside chunks of his own people's bodies and waded through their viscera – and for the first time, Captain Fodor knew he was outmatched.

He had been foolish to take on this brute alone. Arrogant, even.

He wasn't alone. His comrades had dealt with the labourers, most of them, and now the enforcer found himself peppered with las-bolts. They bought a much-needed second for the captain to step back and bring his own pistol to bear.

The enforcer staggered, but rallied himself with an obstinate howl. He lunged at Captain Fodor, but a grenadier leapt into his path. The chainsword sputtered and shrieked as it bit through a ceramite chestplate and drew blood – but the Krieg soldier managed to seize their attacker in a headlock. As the enforcer struggled to throw off the determined death grip, other Korpsmen rushed him with bayonets.

The traitor succumbed to his many wounds at last. He fell to his knees and then onto his face, and the grenadier's body slumped atop him. Fodor thought about salvaging the Korpsman's dog tags, recording their number in his eventual report as posthumous recognition for heroism. Before he could act on that uncharacteristic impulse, a bullet ripped through the neck of the Korpsman beside him.

Traitors were firing out through the bunker's slits, now that their allies were no longer in the way, and he had a new threat to contend with. The captain motioned to his flamer team, who knew what to do. They targeted the gaping breach in the bunker's wall, sending tongues of flame through it to charbroil the dimly seen figures within.

The captain didn't wait to wade into the fire and smoke. He

pushed aside the thought that he was trying to prove something to his Korpsmen. He could barely see a thing inside the bunker, but any movement surely had to be a traitor and so he lashed out in its direction. The feel of his bayonet tearing into flesh and a spray of arterial blood across his gas mask rewarded his efforts.

His comrades squeezed into the bunker behind him, forcing him to choose his targets with more care. The traitors, burnt and choking even with their respirators, put up no more than a token fight. One rushed at the captain, wielding his bolter like a club, but was met by a bayonet driven full force through his stomach.

As the smoke began to clear, Fodor thought only Korpsmen remained standing – until shots rang out and he felt a sharp pain in his wrist. His fingers spasmed and his pistol flew out of his grasp. A renegade militiaman cowered behind chem drums in the bunker's deepest corner, firing blindly over them. In seconds, two Korpsmen were upon him and had eviscerated him.

The captain peeled back a bloodied glove to find a bullet hole through his right wrist. His fingers were blackened and swelling. With the adrenaline rush of combat now subsiding, he could also feel burns down his left side, where his greatcoat was half-melted and stuck to his flesh.

Gritting his teeth against the growing pain, he instructed his Korpsmen to clear space by hauling corpses outside and kicking them down the slope. He stationed snipers at every firing slit and his single meltagun by the wall breach. Having captured this enemy stronghold, now their challenge was to hold on to it.

'Captain,' a watchmaster murmured tactfully to him, 'if you have wounds to tend to, I can take command of–'

He shook his head fiercely. He remembered what Confessor Tenaxus had told them. Captain Tyborc had been even more badly wounded, but he had fought on.

* * *

The 54th Company made more gains in rapid succession.

Bunker by bunker, Fort C-585 fell to its other platoons – inspired, so Captain Fodor imagined, by his own commendable example. The traitors made a single attempt to recapture the bunker held by him. Most were cut down by the bullets stockpiled in there by their own fellows.

The remaining Macharius planted itself in the centre of the fort, a proclamation that now it belonged to the Krieg. Fodor spread the news by vox to the rest of his regiment, inspiring them in turn. Presumably, it rippled through the traitors' forces too, where it had the opposite effect – for, within hours, the rest of the 468th's stalled companies were once more on the advance.

Soon enough, they had achieved their day's objectives. They had scaled Mortuary Ridge and were arrayed across its top, the advantage of the higher ground now theirs.

Captain Fodor hardly noticed when the storm first broke. He had been on Vraks long enough to know this was a regular occurrence, and indeed black sulphurous clouds had been gathering all day. This storm, however, was the fiercest he had yet seen. Rain lashed down, obscuring his view out of his bunker's firing slits. So violent was the thunder that it rattled the ferrocrete walls.

It wasn't just thunder. The very earth was shaking. Rainwater seeped up through the bunker's dirt floor. The captain rescued his battered vox-caster from the mud and swung it, one-handed, up onto a wooden slat bench. His injured hand was bandaged, strapped up inside his greatcoat. He had refused stimms lest they cloud his thoughts, but the pain itself was a distraction. He added his voice to the vox-chorus seeking information. From outside the bunker came a flash, too violent to be lightning. All anyone could agree on was that this was no natural occurrence.

The rain eased off, the clouds exhausted from their concentrated effort. Fodor rushed back to the slits. He saw the sky criss-crossed by trails of flame and knew his greatest fear was fact: that the Naval battle above Vraks had taken a very bad turn. A mushroom cloud blossomed in the distance – he couldn't tell from which side of the newly drawn lines – the rumble of the blast reaching him seconds later.

The next vox-contact came from his company's own trenches at the ridge's base. *'Fire from the sky!'* a junior officer managed to gasp before a vox-relay blew out. At the same time, another explosion – the closest one yet – shook the bunker. Fodor ducked as debris clattered off its walls and jagged, burning shrapnel pinged through the firing slits. He couldn't make contact with anyone in the trenches thereafter. He thanked the Emperor for the ground they had taken that day, for without it the whole of his company might have been wiped out, himself among them.

He told himself he must have been spared for a reason.

A fresh outbreak of vox-chatter caused him to doubt again.

The orbital bombardment appeared to have relented, but clearly had just been a precursor to the real threat. Drop pods were plunging from the black sky, landing with such force that they half-buried themselves in the newly softened earth. Reports flooded in from east and west along the Krieg lines, to the edge of the vox-caster's range. A few witnesses were close enough to see pod hatches blowing open and unholy horrors crawling and slithering from them. None remained in contact long enough to provide a more detailed description.

A few minutes later came the first sightings of Traitor legionaries.

They were sweeping through trenches only recently claimed by the Krieg, tearing into the Imperial interlopers with motorised chain weapons. Some sergeants and watchmasters had already ordered a withdrawal, and Korpsmen were sliding and tumbling back down the ridge. *To where?* the captain thought. Not to the destroyed trenches at its base. *Back to the ruined hab-zone? Even further?*

'Hold your ground!' he snapped into his comm-bead. On second thought, he modified the order: 'Those of us who have a defensible position…'

He couldn't expect his Korpsmen, any Korpsman, to stand against an armoured Space Marine in close combat. That would be suicidal – worse, futile – to which the sudden vox-silence of one squad after another was currently attesting. *But the bunkers…* Surely their captured bunkers had to give them some advantage. Surely they were better standing firm inside them than being run down as they fled through no-man's-land?

The roar of a heavy tank engine gave him heart. The Krieg Macharius ground its way back into view through his firing slit. He saw its heavy bolters and Vanquishers flaring, but couldn't make out their targets yet. He couldn't imagine how anything could possibly withstand such incredible firepower.

'Don't be distracted,' he barked. 'Watch for anything trying to sneak up behind–' The words died in his throat.

Before Captain Fodor's disbelieving eyes, three massive blood-red figures came charging out of the smoke of the inferno. Leaping onto the Macharius' hull, they tore off its hatches with disturbing ease and reached for the crew inside it. One yanked the tank commander right out of the turret. For agonising seconds, the commander dangled, bellowing and kicking, from a clenched gauntlet, before a whirring chainaxe whipped around and through her neck.

The commander's killer held on to the severed head as the body slumped away from it. This he regarded for a moment with apparent curiosity, then flung it away in disdain. Then the Traitor legionary threw back his own head and roared in triumph – a gesture, thought the captain, more suited to the denizens of some feral backwater world than to a warrior of any honour.

With a flex of his power-armoured legs, the legionary made a prodigious leap down from the turret. His head, enclosed within a golden helmet, snapped from side to side as he sought out his next target. Behind the grille and eyepieces of his visor, a malignant light flared as he set his sights upon Captain Fodor's bunker. Though the warrior was still some way away from it, the captain didn't doubt that he could see right through the firing slits to identify his enemies within.

He pulled back from his own slit, screaming the order, 'Fire at will!'

A grenadier armed with a boltgun from a traitor pillbox took the captain's place. His pistol had cracked when he had dropped it, but in any case he would have struggled to aim any weapon left-handed. With a limited number of firing positions available, he had reluctantly accepted that others were better placed in them.

This also meant he had a restricted view of the battlefield. He demanded constant updates as his snipers emptied hotshot power packs and stepped back to reload, their places taken by eager comrades. 'More enemies incoming, sir,' a sergeant reported grimly. 'That's six altogether confirmed.'

'The bolt-shell exploded against his armour, but it hardly slowed him down!'

'Target those breaches,' Fodor snapped. 'There are flesh-and-blood creatures somewhere inside those suits, and we need to burn them before...' He looked around the bunker's crumbling walls, at the ragged sandbags patching the gash in its side, and suddenly he doubted that it could protect them at all. Rather, he felt trapped inside it. Should he have given the order to run while they still could? Too late to think about that now.

'One down!' a grenadier yelled. 'Belay that, he's... he's still moving...' Stomping metallic footsteps began to circle the bunker, and the captain heard the stuttering drones of idling chainaxes. He drew his one remaining weapon, his sabre, for the first time thinking how flimsy its blade seemed.

The sandbags stacked up in the breach shuddered with repeated impacts from without, and several burst. The impromptu barrier tumbled to reveal a huge, red-armoured figure. The Traitor legionary's bulk worked against him as he struggled to squeeze himself through the narrow aperture. The meltagun that Fodor had positioned for just this eventuality cracked and hissed, and the intruder's armour glowed as it sloughed from him.

The traitor made no sound as his charred, half-melted body collapsed into the molten remains of his protective shell. He was probably too high on whatever drugs it had been pumping through his system.

Fodor stepped back as a red-hot rivulet crept towards his toe. 'You see?' he crowed. 'They are not invulnerable. They can be killed like any of us!'

But right behind the Traitor Marine was another, still very much alive although his armour had caught the edge of the melta blast and been scorched and warped. Almost casually, he tossed a grenade into the bunker. By instinct, the Korpsmen leapt for cover as it burst in mid-flight, making the captain's head ring. Simultaneously, a grenadier staggered back from his firing slit as a chainaxe blade poked through it, to be followed by another frag grenade, which landed at his feet and rolled away from him. The grenadier leapt after it and tried to smother the blast, but some shrapnel got through and struck comrades around him.

Fodor heard but didn't see a third blast as the bunker filled with smoke, and suddenly there were enemies inside it. Two of them. He saw bullet holes in the armour of the first and, pushing off from the bunker wall, lunged at him. He aimed to thrust his sabre into one of those holes, to find the fragile heart that he knew must beat within. He could still be the hero of Mortuary Ridge.

The legionary's chainaxe swept around – the captain saw it coming, but moved in slow-motion compared to his foe – and shattered his blade. Fodor himself collided with the legionary's dropped shoulder and rebounded all the way across the bunker, landing dazed against the wall where he had started.

His ears were filled with roaring motors, clashing metal, and the strangulated cries of comrades being mercilessly slaughtered. 'The melta!' he spluttered – by now he should have heard its whine again – but then he saw it, on the floor beside its wielder's body, even as an armoured foot stamped down, crushing it.

Something landed beside Fodor with a thump, and he thought it must be another explosive. Focusing his bleary eyes upon it, reaching for it with a leaden hand, he realised that it was a masked Krieg head.

The sounds had mostly died away by now.

The bunker had slowly emptied out, but for a single Traitor legionary, whose rasping breaths and clunking footsteps Fodor could still hear. He wondered why he had been spared when his comrades lay broken and beheaded, sprawled about him. In the smoke haze, slumped in his corner, he must have been overlooked. That couldn't last.

One Traitor legionary... What if he was already injured? His mighty armour sundered? If the captain could take him by surprise... But he no longer had a weapon, and even if he had... Even if he was lucky, what difference would one more traitor's body make? Only that the rest would hear, making him the next to die, and then who would even know?

He could just see the bunker door, but its bolts looked heavy and would surely protest if he drew them, giving him away. The breach looked like a safer option. If he could reach it unheard… As long as there were no stragglers outside… He could vanish back into the surrounding earthworks. Take word back, a warning, to the front. As if they needed it. His duty was to live, he told himself, and fight again.

Hampered by his strapped-up hand, the captain dragged himself across the soggy ground and knew he was no hero.

His good hand brushed against something, which shifted with a telltale clunk. It was a pile of severed heads. His Korpsmen's heads. The traitor had been gathering and stacking them for some Emperor-unknown reason. Fodor held his breath, but it was already too late. With a faint mechanical whirring, a metal head rotated towards him. Red eyes blazed at him through the smoke.

The legionary was on him in two strides. Fodor tried to scramble away but had nowhere to go. Metal fingers closed around his neck, vice-like, and hauled him up to bring him face to visor grille with his more imposing captor. He didn't kick against him as the Macharius commander had, because he knew it would be futile.

Small bones popped in Captain Fodor's throat as armoured fingertips dug into it, choking him. His head swimming, he heard a chainaxe motor starting up, as if from a long way away. He faced death with Krieg stoicism, but his last thought was that he should at least have spat in his killer's face.

The war room was busier than ever.

Ordinates and technicians bustled about, collating reports, updating the tactical hololiths that showed the ever-shifting positions of the Death Korps' broken lines. Officers responded to incoming vox-cries and issued orders, never losing their composure even as their postures stiffened and their tones became more dour.

Confessor Tenaxus admired their equanimity. She did her best to match it, but once no eyes were upon her she knelt in a quiet corner, resting both hands on her staff's eagle head. She prayed for the strength to bear this latest setback.

The news had been confirmed an hour before. The Naval battle above Vraks had been lost. Rear-Admiral Rasiak's flagship, the *Lord Bellerophon,* had limped away, crippled. Even the arrival of reinforcements in the form of an Imperial cruiser group had failed to turn the tide. Rear-Admiral Titus Mahzur had personally taken command of the *Consul Thracii* and attempted to ram a battle-barge; pulsating lance batteries had all but disintegrated his vessel, so that only flaming debris had glanced off its target's void shields.

The Vraks System was now controlled by the enemy fleet.

At least three Traitor Marine factions had answered Xaphan's summons. So far, they had sent just a handful of drop pods to earth, and yet they had wrought devastation. They had the capability to land more, many more pods, anywhere on Vraks. The hololiths showed the Krieg starting to regroup, even holding their lines in some places, but they had lost ground hard-won over too many years. Worse still, no longer were they fighting a static battle against a contained foe. The traitors could strike them anywhere at any time.

Even here, Tenaxus thought glumly. *Even this far behind the lines.*

Perhaps she should have left while she still could. She had lost that option now. No transport ship would be able to reach her. The 88th Siege Army's supply lines had been severed. She had thought herself needed, but for what? What good were her words against the threat they all now faced? The Krieg required physical, more than just spiritual, reinforcement. They needed vehicles, weapons, ammunition to replace those damaged, destroyed, spent. They needed fuel, food, medical supplies.

Their war had also been one of attrition, one they thought

they couldn't lose, but now the tables had been turned. Now the apostate cardinal was the one who could land troops and equipment at will. What they had seen today, what they had suffered, was only the start.

The confessor could see only one path to salvation now. Once before, the Emperor had sent His Angels of Death to Vraks. If only they could have stayed longer, done more. She prayed that He might send them back again.

VI

The Korpsmen of the 19th Krieg Siege Regiment stood to attention in their trenches.

Perfectly still and silent, they listened to the voice of their commanding officer over the regimental vox-net.

He told them how they were about to die.

Colonel Keled sat stiffly in front of his vox-caster. He told his Korpsmen – the seventy thousand or so souls for whom he had become responsible – that they were being honoured. Their lives were being given purpose.

He told them of the enemy battleship that had crash-landed west of the Chaylia Plateau. Though many miles from any Krieg positions, it was behind their lines, which had made it a concern. It had been hoped that its occupants would have liquefied on impact, or burnt up in the atmosphere. The scouts despatched to confirm this, however, had returned – at least, some had – with the grimmest of tidings.

'Many of you, most, came to Vraks fresh from our camps on Krieg,' the colonel stated. 'I know you have long prayed for a chance to test yourselves in the theatre of war. That chance, our chance, has come at last.'

Eight years had crawled by since his first commission. Keled was considered a veteran officer now, though he still felt he hadn't earned the honour. For four years, he had captained a company, which hadn't advanced in all that time. In the recent battle for the second defence line, his regiment had been held in reserve.

Four months ago, he had been summoned to the general's office at the landing site. He was told that his colonel, having rebuilt the 19th Regiment after Adal's death and the massacre at Hab-Zone One, was being transferred to another in more need of his experience. So, now he was Colonel Keled, though to most of his Korpsmen he was just 'the colonel', the only one with whom they interacted. He had been referred to by quartermasters as 'Colonel 19'. A colonel whose leadership, he felt, hadn't truly been tested, but was about to be most sorely.

'Crammed aboard the downed ship,' he continued, 'were the foulest dregs of the galaxy. Mutants, beastmen, pirates. Deranged and gibbering worshippers of the Ruinous Powers.' He paused for half a second before adding, 'Traitor Space Marines. Reconnaissance tells us they set off from their crash site several days ago, and are on the march towards us.'

He said nothing to his Korpsmen about the 101st Krieg regiment, one-quarter of the 11th Assault Korps. They had been sent to intercept the oncoming enemy column. They had been handsomely equipped with Macharius tanks, along with Shadowstorms and Stormblades. It hadn't been enough.

After the second defence line's collapse, the First Line Korps had continued to push south-east, then south around the citadel.

They were now positioned almost due west of Vraks Star Port. This didn't worry them, for if its wreckage still harboured any traitors, with the causeways down they would remain trapped there. They hadn't counted on a new threat appearing in the north to flank them.

Calculations had been made, logistics run, decisions taken. With their current and diminishing resources, the Krieg could not withstand a twin-pronged attack from front and rear. Their most pragmatic option was to shorten their front line by withdrawing their eastern flank. First Line Korps would fall back to their positions of several months ago. The problem was, they lacked the time to do so, to escape with their weapons and equipment before the approaching army was upon them.

'We are to mount a rearguard action,' the colonel explained, 'delaying the Chaos-loving scum for our comrades' sake. Though we aren't expected to defeat them – they are too numerous and too well equipped – the harder each one of us dies, the more Krieg lives will be spared to balance the scales for our sacrifices later.'

The words came more easily than he might have expected. He told his Korpsmen what he would have wanted, needed to hear in their boots. Once his regiment was committed to this course of action, nothing could save them. Trapped between their enemies and one of Vraks' unbridgeable canyons, they would have no possible escape route even had they wanted one.

They needed to believe that their deaths, their lives would count.

He hadn't told them all he knew about the horrors they were facing. He had said nothing of the Chaos Titans, degraded parodies of the Imperium's own robotic combat walkers, tens of feet tall, their prodigious strides sending tremors through the earth as their turbo-lasers slashed through plasteel armour.

Nor did the colonel speak of the agile fighter-bombers whose screams had split the sky as they had flashed like lightning from the clouds, rained death upon the Krieg artillery, and soared out of return fire range within a second. His command staff, standing stoically about him, were in agreement with him. What point was there in warning them of a threat against which they had no possible defence?

It wouldn't make a difference to their actions, either way.

The attack came at dawn the following day – and, though Keled had thought himself prepared for it, still its form took him by surprise.

Having swept through the ruins of the second defence line, the enemy's foul hordes were camped out ten miles north of the 19th's trenches. The colonel had expected them to unleash an artillery bombardment and had repositioned his own units accordingly. Instead, his sentries roused him with news of an eerie phenomenon drawing in from the west.

It began as a green glow on the horizon, where the citadel squatted on its lofty perch. Steadily, the glow grew brighter and closer. Within the hour, through magnoculars, the colonel could make out dense, low-lying clouds of luminous fog rolling his way.

He sent an urgent vox-report, asking for advice, and was shortly contacted by an officious-sounding aide. *'The general understands that Vraks once served as a disposal site for forbidden chem-weapons. Command HQ has long suspected that the apostate cardinal may have stumbled upon and disinterred these.'*

Further details followed. From the gas' description, it was thought to be trimethyline-phthaloxyic-tertius, TP-III for short. Highly corrosive, if breathed in it would melt the lungs in half a minute. Given only a little more time, it could burn through flesh and, in high enough concentrations, any type of armour.

It occurred to the colonel that the 88th Siege Army might have been formed from Krieg units for this very reason. They had been raised and trained in a toxic environment. The rebreathers they wore at all times aggressively filtered and chemically cleansed their air supplies. Their greatcoats were impregnated with anti-chemical and anti-biological agents. They were far better able to withstand an attack of this nature than were Guardsmen from any other world. That didn't mean it wouldn't hurt them. The colonel wondered, but didn't ask aloud, why they hadn't been given more warning. He already knew the answer.

Nor was he remotely surprised by what he was told next.

'The general has assessed the situation, Colonel 19,' the voice of the disembodied aide pronounced. *'His orders are to stand your ground.'*

The Krieg took what shelter they could as the toxic cloud rolled over them.

Heavier than air, it cascaded through their trenches, extending sickly green tendrils into every nook and cranny. It ate through clothes and blistered skin. The cloud attacked the fabric of the Korpsmen's gas masks, their rubber air hoses, the regulator units they wore against their chests. Wherever it could create a tear, it worked its way inside. The gas claimed victim after victim, blood foaming up out of their noses and mouths as flesh was stripped away from shrieking skulls.

Colonel Keled could do nothing but pray and listen grimly as one platoon after another fell ominously vox-silent. Some of his Korpsmen, however, fared better than others. By the time it reached some trenches, the gas was not as concentrated and soon drifted away on the wind. His own coat and mask bobbled but maintained their integrity. He lived, while many others died, by the vagaries of Vraks' air currents.

It was only the beginning.

As the green fog faded, armoured vehicles barrelled out of it, tracks bouncing off the pockmarked ground. Like everything else in the traitors' arsenal, they were of Imperial design – Predators, Rhinos, and the even heavier Land Raiders – but they were filthy and dilapidated, oil spewing from clanking exhaust pipes. They looked as if they should have been on their way to a scrap world.

Korpsmen scrambled to recrew mortars whose former gunners had died or were dying. Many, they found to be irreparably corroded. As the traitor vehicles strafed the ground ahead of them with heavy bolters and lascannons, the Krieg hunkered down and fired back with whatever they could salvage.

The hatches of the ramshackle vehicles were thrust open, and creatures clambered from them. Too far away to make them out, the colonel relied on descriptions from his spotters, who weren't entirely sure what they were seeing. The creatures resembled Space Marines but rotten, decaying like their tanks. Slimy tentacles spilled out through cracks in their power armour, which was all that appeared to hold their twisted bodies together. Swarms of carrion flies buzzed about their heads.

Despite their diseased appearance, they remained inhumanly fast and strong. Charging across no-man's-land, shrugging off las-fire stings, they leapt gleefully into their enemies' trenches.

The colonel demanded reports from his scouts to the north. They informed him that the force from the crashed ship was holding still. They were waiting for their allies, sent out from the citadel by Xaphan, to clear a way for them. With the 19th Regiment destroyed, they could sweep through their trenches fresh and unopposed, to fall upon the retreating bulk of First Line Korps from behind.

That only made it all the more imperative that they hold out as long as they could.

* * *

The fighting continued all day and through the night.

The Korpsmen of the 19th Regiment resisted their stronger attackers with everything they had. They held on to their trenches as they collapsed about them; platoon commanders called down Earthshaker strikes upon their own heads, just as another Krieg lieutenant had in a story Colonel Keled had once heard.

Nevertheless, the diseased legionaries continued their inexorable advance – as yet more renegade militiamen and mutants came howling and slavering across no-man's-land to support them. The colonel had surrendered his position twice already, falling back to an older command post. He couldn't do so many more times, well aware of the chasm to his east and the monsters to his north.

He made a report, his final one, to the general's office. 'By the Emperor's grace, we can endure for one more day before exhausting our resources.' He questioned his own euphemistic language and was about to add to it, *Before we are all butchered.* At that moment, however, a Traitor legionary with a sputtering, smoking jump pack plunged out of the sky into his trench.

Up close, he was even more disgusting than the colonel had imagined. His body was covered in pustulent boils, so inflated that they had cracked his armour open. Fat green maggots bathed in streams of pus that trickled down his armoured legs. The ripe stench of decay reached Keled's nostrils even through his rebreather's filters. He suppressed the urge to retch.

The legionary swung a rusty sword, which gouged a chunk out of a Korpsman's side; within seconds, his victim was heaving and convulsing in the dirt, the wound an angry red but weeping green. A sergeant with a melta started forwards, but the colonel raised a palm towards him. The Krieg's guns had already taken their toll on their foe; the right side of his armoured suit was shattered, shedding mosaic tiles. Korpsmen were regrouping about the legionary, assailing him with las-beams, and the colonel added to the barrage with two shots from his pistol.

For an awful second, he feared he had miscalculated.

Though his exposed skin was burnt black, the Space Marine appeared to feel no pain. He shattered a quartermaster's helmet with one blow from his heavy gauntlet. His blade lashed out again and killed twice more; his second victim tore out their air tube with a howl and vomited blood, but still had the presence of mind to fall towards his killer and jam a bayonet into his ribs.

When the legionary died, it happened suddenly, his wounds overwhelming him before he knew anything about it. His armour fell apart as if it had suddenly been emptied, discharging a discoloured mass of offal. The colonel's decision to hold the melta in abeyance had cost two lives but conserved precious fuel, which could well delay the deaths of others later.

Right now, more traitors had run up in the wake of the first and came sliding down the trench walls. The colonel ordered his gunners back to their quad launchers, to discourage others. He set his sights on the fiercest-looking new arrival: a militiaman more finely armoured than most he had encountered. Better armed too. As the traitor swung his sword at the colonel, it lit up a startling bright blue. Had he blocked it with a plasteel shoulder pad as planned, allowing him to duck inside its arc, its coruscating energy field would have sliced off his arm.

He dived and rolled instead, and bowled the traitor off his feet. They wrestled in the mud until the colonel gained the upper hand. He pinned the traitor's sword arm with his knee and shot him through the eyepiece of his mask.

The still-lit power sword slid out of the traitor's limp fingers, and the colonel regarded it suspiciously. An Imperial weapon, but had it been corrupted? Would it corrupt him in turn? Tearing off his beaten opponent's gas mask, he saw no mutation on his face or in his staring eyes. He took the risk. He seized the sword. Its hilt vibrated slightly in his grasp. He felt its power thrumming up his arm, standing its hairs on end.

He stood in time to see a fellow Korpsman pinned by another pair of renegade militiamen. His new sword was lighter than it looked, and seemed to encounter hardly any resistance at all as it sliced through both their bodies.

Within minutes, the trench had been cleared of traitor scum – though the Korpsmen gave a wide berth to the festering corpse of the diseased legionary, upon which flies and maggots were greedily feasting. The colonel warned that this would be a brief respite, as if anyone had doubted it. A quartermaster brought him news that a bullet had struck the vox-caster. Its machine spirits were in their death throes, spitting sparks.

The 19th Regiment was truly on its own now – but then, the colonel thought, hadn't they always been? More worrying was that he had lost vox-contact with his other trenches. Each Krieg platoon was on its own now too.

Just as Colonel Adal had been on his own at the end.

How long had it been?

He couldn't say. The days and nights of running, fighting, hiding, running again blurred together in his memory. Had it been two days? Three? For sure, more than the one he had promised; Colonel Keled clung to that. He could be proud of his 19th Regiment. Their sacrifice, he told himself, would be remembered.

He came to with a start, not knowing how long he had slept, wedged upright at one end of a half-demolished trench. Other Korpsmen were packed in around him; he had lost track of where they came from, whether any were members of his own command squad. He didn't know how many other pockets of

Krieg resistance remained, but sounds of battle on the breeze told him they weren't finished yet.

Instantly alert, he saw why he had been prodded awake. A squad of four diseased Space Marines had discovered his bolthole, forcing him to fight again.

Between them, his ad hoc platoon had four almost-drained lasguns, two captured autoguns and several grenades. His own pistol was long-dead, as was the now-discarded meltagun, while their foes had scant need of ammunition. The diseased legionaries brandished blighted swords and axes as they bore down on their targets with intimidating speed.

The colonel ordered the use of every last available resource. There was no point in holding back now, in what he knew beyond a doubt would be his final battle, his regiment's last stand. No point waiting for the legionaries to reach them and put them to the slaughter; even less in trying to outrun them.

As Krieg grenades burst against corrupted armour, Keled screamed the order, 'Charge!' He and his Korpsmen clambered out of hiding and raced to meet their fate on their own terms.

Krieg and traitors crashed into each other, and though the former outnumbered the latter fivefold, they came off considerably worse. Plague-dripping knives cut a swathe through flesh and muscle, bathing Traitor legionaries in Krieg blood. The colonel thumbed his power sword's activation stud and felt its comforting thrum in his hand. The weapon had served him well these past few days, although its blue light was now dimming.

'Concentrate on this one!' he yelled as he landed a blow on the leading legionary, the one he judged to be the most damaged, searing a new gash into his armour. *Just one more,* he prayed. *If we can take down just one more…* His Korpsmen piled onto the monster, their blades flashing, but a servo-assisted shrug dislodged most of them, while a powerful backhanded swipe batted two more away, breaking their bones, and already other legionaries were picking off their disarrayed prey. They hacked and slashed and punched and spat, and Krieg bodies burst like cockroaches squashed underfoot.

One last thrust of the colonel's sword was parried with force enough to wrench his shoulder near out of its socket; its light flared just once more and fizzled out. He ducked the first swipe of the Space Marine's axe, but the second came down on his head before he could get out of its way. He sprawled insensate in the mud and could only wonder why he had been struck with the blade's flat rather than its edge, and why no killing blow followed.

He drifted on a dark tide of regret.

The next thing of which he was aware was hands grasping at him, taking his arms and legs, lifting him. He had to force his heavy eyes to open. Blearily, he saw the broken corpses of masked Krieg Korpsmen staring blankly up at him. The hands clinging to him were not his comrades' hands. Instinctively he tried to struggle against them, but his limbs would not obey his brain's commands.

He was being hauled towards an armoured carrier, a Rhino, cleaner than the diseased vehicles he had seen, defiled by sacrilegious symbols all the same. His captors were renegade militiamen. He saw no sign of Traitor legionaries, couldn't smell them any longer – but out of the corners of his eyes, he glimpsed other misshapen creatures, slithering and oozing across the plain, and he didn't know if they were real or nightmares conjured by his fevered brain to taunt him.

He had been dumped on the floor of the Rhino's troop compartment.

Militiamen lined the benches to each side of him. He could

just hear their guttural voices over the engine, but he couldn't tell what they were saying. Now and again, a boot would jab him in the ribs or stamp on his hand to keep him from falling into a healing sleep. What did they want with him?

His badges of rank, he thought suddenly. He had been spared because he was an officer, a senior officer, in the Emperor's armed forces. Did they think he could give them information? If so, they would be disappointed. Nothing Keled knew, no plans, no strategies, meant anything now. He was an officer with no one to command. A soldier who had seen his entire regiment annihilated once, and then had been called upon to lead it to a second, even more crushing defeat. But what choice had there been? He had only ever followed orders.

An eternity passed before the Rhino juddered to a halt and its rear hatch was unbolted and pushed open. The colonel was hauled up by his armpits and dragged from the vehicle, trailing his numb legs behind him.

He wasn't surprised to find himself inside the citadel. Its defence towers, only glimpsed through smoke before, loomed all around him. Its walls and structures penned him in. His gaze was drawn upwards by coloured light flashes across the sky: Krieg missiles, flaring uselessly off a canopy of void shields, which muted even the thunderous sound of the constant bombardment.

The Rhino had pulled up outside what appeared to be a barracks. Off-duty militiamen came over to jeer and spit at their new prisoner. Here, where the air was cleaner, they wore no respirators and the colonel saw hatred in their eyes. Sores wept and boils throbbed on their faces; it testified to how their minds were broken that they didn't seem to care.

The colonel's toecaps scraped across machine-smoothed rockcrete instead of sinking into mud. Ahead was a building that could only have been the Basilica of St Leonis. The years of neglect had not dimmed its splendour in his eyes. Though its walls were graffitied and its stained-glass windows broken, still its majestic spires dominated all about it. Beside it, the Cardinal's Palace, though equally ornate, seemed almost small and insignificant.

Somewhere inside that palace resided the apostate cardinal. The thought struck Colonel Keled like a thunderbolt. Never had he been so close to the enemy's commander. Perhaps no Korpsman had. Perhaps that was why he was here, why he was still alive. Reaching Xaphan was surely impossible – no doubt he was very well protected – but wasn't there a chance, a tiny chance, that he could find a way to hurt him? One last small act of defiance? Didn't he have a duty to try?

The colonel planted his feet on the rockcrete. He wrenched an arm free from one of his captors and threw it around the other's neck. His weapons had been stripped from him, but they had been spent anyway. He made a snatch for the traitor's autogun, tucked into his belt. He almost had it, his fingers brushed against it, but he was too weak. He felt his legs swiped out from underneath him. The back of his head rebounded from the unyielding ground, and the traitor drew his gun and aimed it down at him and fired.

The pain almost made Keled pass out again. His efforts to suppress a scream resulted in it bursting through his lips as a pitiful whine. The bullet had lodged in his left leg, above the knee, putting paid to hopes of running. It might have been best, he thought, had it killed him. He felt a rush of shame as he thought that might have been his true hope all along.

Lifted again, he was hauled past rundown hab-blocks, storehouses, offices. Alongside the palace was a gate, at which a pair of sentries quizzed his captors before allowing them through into the citadel's inner ward. This too was overlooked by both palace and basilica. A rubble-strewn roadway skirted the churned-up tiles and broken pillars of a once-elaborate courtyard. It comforted the colonel to see there had been fighting here, that at least some of this world's Imperial subjects had resisted its new master's heresies.

Past the grim grey edifice of another defence laser silo, a broad bridge spanned a deep, forbidding canyon, which he knew as the Citadel Ravine. Beyond this was the inner keep, the citadel's securest area. The colonel had studied schematics of this place without ever expecting to see it.

Overlooked by the soaring sensorium tower, the keep contained the offices and residence of the master-prefect, along with the aedificium, once a base of operations for the Imperial Inquisition. Their flags had been torn down, their markings burnt out of the walls. Colonel Keled was taken into the building through reinforced doors, which slammed shut behind him with reverberating clangs.

Rough-hewn steps descended into musty darkness; when his captors tired of carrying him, they kicked him the rest of the way down them. He was in the undercroft now, inside the dead volcano upon which the citadel sat. The tunnels and chambers down here had not been fully mapped. On this side of the ravine, they mostly comprised dungeons and interrogation cells.

No doubt Xaphan had preserved the Inquisition's torture devices.

He was almost relieved to reach his destination. A hooded guard unlocked a sliding, barred gate and thrust him through it. The only light came from a lume-globe in a nearby annex, where the guard, along with one other, was stationed. The prison cell was long and narrow. Hunched, dissolute figures lined its walls, few bothering to even raise their heads towards the new arrival.

The colonel was hauled towards a gap between two lifeless

lumps and pushed down into it. The guard took his wrists roughly and snapped manacles about them. He did the same to Keled's ankles, wrapping him in heavy chains, forcing his head towards his knees so he couldn't straighten his back. The chains' ends were buried in the ferrocrete wall.

One of his captors leaned over him and hissed in his ear, 'This is where your heresy against the Emperor gets you!' So affronted was the colonel that he choked on his retort. The traitor punched him in the face; his head snapped back but was arrested by his chains, which sent a fresh lance of pain up his spine. By the time he got his breath back, the traitors had withdrawn and closed and locked the gate behind them.

He welcomed the darkness that closed in around him.

One question continued to play on his mind. 'How?' he asked aloud, at length. 'How can they possibly believe...?'

He hadn't expected an answer, but one came in a thick, slurred voice from the bundle of rags to his right. 'They believe in the apostate cardinal. They believe him when he says their cause is just.'

'After all they must have seen...' Each word rasped across the colonel's dry throat. 'The desecration of His holy symbols, the blight, the mutations...'

'Self-delusion is all they have to cling to.'

'What do they want with us? To question us?'

'Perhaps. They have done so in the past. I hear they once dragged prisoners out of here each morning. They did not bring many back.'

'How long have you been here?'

His fellow prisoner took some time to answer. The colonel thought he might have drifted out of consciousness. Or died. 'Days. Weeks,' he said finally. 'Months. I no longer know. I am... I was a captain in the 308th Siege Regiment.'

'A colonel,' said Keled, 'in command of the 19th.'

'Sir. I didn't realise.'

'What happened?'

'We were stalled at the second defence line, sir. But Colonel Tolan told us that the new line korps had broken through in the north, so we kept pushing. When fire rained from the sky... We had no warning. We failed in our duty.'

'No,' the colonel growled. 'Our duty was to fight to the best of our ability.'

'The traitors scavenged through the wreckage. They finished off the wounded, plundered our equipment. Shrapnel had broken my ribs but missed my heart. They brought me here, but no one came to question me.'

'They know it would be futile,' Keled asserted proudly. 'They know they would get nothing. Not from any warrior of Krieg.'

'They still take prisoners away from time to time. They took my commissar... I don't know how long ago it was. Now the traitors talk of handing them over to... They call them "the Sorcerers of Nurgle". Most days, they just leave us to wallow in our filth. The guards toss nutrient packs through the bars when they remember. Our only water is the condensation that forms on our chains.'

'There must be some way we can–'

'We all think that, sir. At least for the first few days.'

'We were given these lives for one reason,' the colonel insisted, 'and as long as we still have them...' This time the silence stretched further. Through narrowed, straining eyes, he tried to make sense of the formless heap beside him. He located his fellow prisoner's head, resting between his knees beneath gloved hands, but something wasn't right.

'Your rebreather tube... Have they...?'

'What purpose has my life any longer?' the captain intoned.

'As long as we live...' the colonel began, but he didn't have an answer to the question. What if the best thing he could do now was starve himself to death? Deny his enemy whatever it was they wanted from him?

No. He refused to believe that.

He felt around the floor, as far as his shackled hands could reach. It was strewn with debris, tracked in on a thousand boots over years. His fingers closed around the most substantial chip of rock. He spent the next hour sharpening it on the wall, as the captain beside him relapsed into silence. He peeled back his fraying fatigues around the bullet in his leg. He used the rock to try to dig it out. He had thought himself inured to pain by now, but the pain was unbearable. He gritted his teeth, remembered his training, and tried again and again. He drenched his gloves in blood until he felt light-headed and couldn't risk losing any more. He tore off a strip of his fatigues and tied it round the stinging wound.

The colonel dozed, and bitter dreams took him eight years back in time, to the day of his first failure. The day he had first taken command of a squad and led them through the earth itself, but failed to reach his colonel in his hour of need. The day when he had earned his commission, and his name, by turning tail and running. By surviving.

He reached inside his greatcoat, found the chain around his neck from which his dog tags hung and teased them out. He couldn't read them in the gloom, but he could feel the letters and numbers stamped into them. The name of a hero. Now, more than ever, he knew it was no name for him.

He dreamt of a better day to come. He saw the Death Korps of Krieg storming the Citadel of Vraks, restoring it to the Emperor's glory. He pictured them finding his dry bones in its dungeons. *No,* he thought. His 19th Regiment had surely died today – for he couldn't imagine it would be rebuilt again, more likely disbanded – but the record would show that it had served with honour. It was better for all to believe its commander had died with it; no need for his true ignominious fate to be recorded. Let him just be another unknown Korpsman.

His rock might have lacked the edge to dig out his bullet, but it could serve one purpose for him. Colonel Keled scraped the rock against his tags. He kept going until he was certain he had scratched his name, and all of the numbers that had once identified him, out of them.

ACT THREE

IMPERIAL ARMOUR

825–827.M41

The arrival of Chaos Space Marines marked a new phase in Vraks' drawn-out war. Until that point, never had we doubted that patience and determination would eventually earn us victory. Now, we were losing battle after battle, forced into one humiliating withdrawal after another. We lost our grip on hard-gained ground, as our numbers were brutally whittled down.

Segmentum high command, however, had noted our plight. Lord Commander Zuehlke was summarily removed from his post, and the 88th Krieg Siege Army gained a new commander-in-chief. I never met Lord Marshal Arnim Kagori, but General Durjan described him as a devout man, hard-nosed and methodical. Someone worthy of respect.

Lord Kagori knew that, to avert a disastrous defeat, he would need more resources. He negotiated with the ruling lords of the forge world Lucius for the services of a Legio Astorum battle group: mighty god-machines to match those that had stalked from the wreckage of the crashed Chaos ship. A Naval fighter wing escorted them to their destination, through the enemy blockade around the planet. Fresh approaches were also made to the Adeptus Astartes.

Increasingly, the war on Vraks became the province of forces higher than our own. For some of us, this made it all the more difficult to see our purpose there. No longer would Krieg's fortitude and numbers be enough to win the day. When gods and monsters clashed above our heads, what did our efforts matter in the least?

What difference could our tiny, fragile lives possibly make – and who would even care to remember that we tried?

– From the account of Veteran Colonel Tyborc

VII

The Korpsmen of the 143rd Siege Regiment were lined up in their trenches. They were waiting for the order to advance, as they had many times before.

This time, however, anticipation charged the air. This time, they knew, was different. Attesting to this was Colonel Thyran's presence among them, and that of the regimental standard. Any ordinary banner, blessed in a cathedral on the home world, was sacred to the soldiers who rallied around it, but this one carried an even greater import. It served as a regimental reliquary too, for the skulls of past commanders were attached to its pole between black and red fabric flaps.

One day, thought Commissar-General Maugh, Thyran's skull would stare down from that pole too. That day might even have been imminent, but the commissar did not expect to see it. For a decade and a half, he had lived and fought at Thyran's side, and he planned to die by it.

As the appointed moment approached, the colonel mounted

his jet-black steed, which itself wore armour plating and a respirator unit. He turned to an aide and nodded grimly. The aide cocked a readied flare pistol, raised it above his head, and squeezed the trigger. A red comet streaked into the sky, and the first wave of Krieg infantry swarmed out into no-man's-land.

The 'Kagori Offensive', as scribes had already dubbed it, was the Death Korps' most audacious strike against the traitors yet. Almost all their forces on Vraks had been committed to the effort. For days, their newly restocked guns had worked like never before, burying the enemy's emplacements in debris. After years of holding back, conserving ammunition, their thunder was more deafening than ever.

After months of planning, resupplying, getting everything in place, holding the line against enemy harassment but no more than this, the Krieg were finally on the advance again. If all went well, they would reclaim every square inch of ground they had lost in the previous few years, wiping out all the setbacks they had suffered. *If all went well...*

The 143rd's role in the plan was critical. Though attacks were planned all along the front, most would serve as mere diversions. It was in the sectors held by the 12th Line Korps that the greatest gains had to be made. To that end, the heavy tanks of the Eighth Assault Korps had been made available to them.

As Commissar-General Maugh clambered over the parapet, he heard Leman Russ and Macharius engines starting up behind him. He resisted the urge to glance back – not at the tanks themselves, which he had seen in action many times, but at the even larger and more powerful machines he knew to be behind them.

The Legio Astorum had sent twenty-two Titans to Vraks. They had been judiciously held back until now, waiting for the moment when they could be deployed to maximum advantage. Now, the entire battle group stomped across the Van Meersland Wastes, bearing down upon an enemy that could not possibly have been prepared for their sudden appearance.

Forward platoons reported less incoming fire than they usually faced. In part, this was due to the shelling, including the mortar bombs that continued to streak over the Korpsmen's heads. Maugh didn't doubt, however, that the Titans' presence was also a major factor. He imagined that many traitor gunners were already running.

Three nights ago, Maugh had been drinking amasec with Thyran in their shared bunkroom at the landing site. They had just received their final briefing for the new offensive. The following morning, they would return to the trenches to brief their company commanders in turn.

'What do you think?' the commissar-general had asked. He would have put the question to nobody else, for it invited only bland approval or what some might have deemed insubordination, but Colonel Thyran knew he could answer it freely.

In Maugh's presence alone, he had removed the gas mask that, to most, was the only face he showed. 'I think it might work,' he considered.

'Pray that it does, for otherwise...'

'Lord Kagori is taking an immense gamble,' said the colonel, 'with millions of Krieg souls as the stakes – but given the situation on the ground left to him by his predecessor, I see no preferable option.'

Thyran had thought some of Zuehlke's decisions foolhardy and had said as much. Maugh admired his forthrightness. No matter to whom he was speaking – even once in a witch hunter's presence – he voiced his beliefs. If there was a chance of these being judged heretical, then all the more reason not to hide them, he had always said. Best to know and face the consequences.

'Lord Zuehlke squandered many Krieg lives,' the commissar agreed.

'This new plan will cost thousands more, but with a greater chance of success, I believe. A chance to make those lives – all those lives – count. A chance, a hope, well worth the sacrifice.'

Including, potentially, our own lives... Maugh knew his comrade well enough to know that the same thought had entered his mind. They each sipped from their glasses in silence.

'I have had a long career,' Colonel Thyran reflected. 'As a Death Rider, I fought in many campaigns, each one yielding a glorious victory. I have killed many more than my share of heretics and mutants. Should I die on Vraks, I will rest content that I spent my life as the Emperor willed it, that my service will weigh even infinitesimally against my people's sins.'

'Having seen you in battle,' said Maugh, raising his glass, 'I do not doubt it.'

'I worry for our newer recruits,' the colonel continued. 'Most have seen no other world than this one and the home world. They have grown old squatting in Vraks' dirt, waiting for a chance to earn the lives they have been given.'

He had never looked older himself, the commissar thought. When first he had seen Thyran's face, he had been surprised by his youth – though, with hindsight and a better understanding of Krieg mortality rates, he shouldn't have been. Now the colonel had age lines to match the wisdom he had always possessed. His skin was still pale from lack of sunlight, but now it was also dry and cracked. His buzz-cut red hair was greyed at the temples; his eyes were a haunted grey too, to match his greatcoat.

As far as Maugh could tell, most Krieg remained masked even around each other. The mask was part of their uniform, which made it part of them. Hailing as they did from a radioactive hellhole, they also knew how swiftly invisible poisons could spread and they were forever prepared.

The mask had other benefits too, less often acknowledged. They distanced the Krieg from each other. If they didn't know their comrade's faces, didn't have names for them, then how could they mourn them when they died? Only in a general sense. Their masks discouraged them from thinking of each other – by extension, of themselves – as individuals. They belonged to a faceless collective, no member more important than another.

The masks dehumanised their wearers. Perhaps this encouraged the likes of Lord Commander Zuehlke to value Krieg lives as cheaply as they did their own.

Maugh's job was to maintain morale, through iron discipline, within the 143rd Krieg Siege Regiment. Upon his arrival, almost twenty years ago, he had found himself more often tempering their zeal instead, advising caution. This, he had in common with every Krieg-attached commissar with whom he had since spoken. Like them, he had also come to represent the Krieg to off-worlders who didn't understand them. He put a face to them.

He had escalated Thyran's concerns about Zuehlke in a series of written reports made to various bodies. Whether any of these had reached the desk of anyone of import, Maugh had no way of knowing, but they might have made a difference.

When around the rank-and-file Krieg, he now masked himself. This had begun as a practical measure, for often they were deployed in toxic environments. It had become a gesture of respect that they, and their colonel especially, had earned from him, an acknowledgement that he was no more important than they were.

'Do you believe they're ready?' the commissar asked.

* * *

The fighting had spilled out across no-man's-land.

As the Krieg had charged enemy-held trenches, the traitors had rushed out to meet them. With their bunkers pulverised and much of their earthworks demolished, they had had little option, few defensible positions left to cling to.

Opposing waves of murky greys and browns crashed into each other and broke into chaotic tides and ripples. Screams of anger, pain, defiance rent the air as guns cracked and blades rang off each other. As masked Krieg and masked traitors thronged together, it was sometimes difficult to pick one apart from another.

Maugh was somewhat isolated from the worst of the melee. Even in such disarray, the Krieg were careful to maintain a cordon around their banner, which was hoisted by an ensign in Colonel Thyran's command squad. The colonel himself sat high up on his mount, keeping track of the ebbs and flows of the battle around him. He bellowed orders, warnings, encouragement, and admonishment as needed, knowing that his very presence would inspire his Korpsmen to greater feats of courage.

Maugh had his power sword drawn, but no traitor had yet made it close enough to feel its sting. He had picked off four so far with his bolter, choosing his shots so that more than one traitor who thought he had got the better of a Krieg opponent was suddenly and violently disabused of such a notion.

Maugh caught himself wondering how much difference they were really making. It seemed the more important battle was the one now being waged about them. The traitors had pushed their tanks forward too, attempting to shield their exposed combatants, and they met those grinding hard across the plain on the Krieg infantry's heels. Two lines of belligerent, Imperial-forged metal squared up to each other, belching fire.

None of the vehicles involved were especially manoeuvrable, so it became a matter of whose armour could best endure the other's pounding without cracking – while many of the flesh-and-blood soldiers caught in the bloody crossfire, both factions alike, found their individual struggles rendered moot. They were shredded by bolts on their way to their targets or incinerated by short-falling shells.

And then there came the Titans.

Never before had Maugh seen their like in action, and they took his breath away. He had to will his eyes not to be drawn to them, captured by their ancient majesty. Fierce Warhound Scouts bounded ahead of the pack, plasma blastguns and Vulcan mega-bolters blazing from each side of their angular snouts. Towering behind these were the even larger Reavers, their jutting heads swaying back and forth as they sought targets for their arm-mounted blasters and cannons.

Their armoured bulk itself was a prodigious weapon, each Reaver weighing in at seven hundred tons of ceramite and plasteel. Sundered bunkers and pillboxes were pulverised beneath their feet; already damaged tanks, tracks spinning in reverse as the shadows of their doom loomed over them, were unceremoniously crushed, their crews trapped in their mangled wrecks.

Grislier still were the fates of the unprotected soldiers upon whom those shadows fell; Maugh saw an entire militiaman squad stamped into the dirt, leaving little but a smear of blood to show that they had ever been. Some Krieg Korpsmen too found themselves scrambling to escape the Titans' merciless advance.

Standing out at the vanguard of the Reavers was the brightly decorated *Praetorian*, draped with kill-banners and other honours. Maugh had seen it before, from a distance, at the landing site. He had introduced himself and Colonel Thyran to its captain. The commander of the battle group on Vraks, High Princeps Drauca had cut a sullen, unassuming figure. Maugh had planned to beg a glimpse inside the god-machine, but Drauca had excused himself as quickly as he could.

Praetorian's dedicated tech-priest had been more approachable. 'A princeps spends much of his time mind-linked to a machine spirit,' he had explained. 'It requires an unrelenting force of will upon his part to maintain sanity. He becomes as integral a component of his Titan as any cog or piston. When it is struck and damaged, so too does his body bear the wounds.'

Maugh pictured the high princeps cabled up to a mind impulse unit on his bridge behind *Praetorian*'s armaglass eyes. Flanking his command throne would be a pair of junior moderati, while the tech-priest himself would sit deeper in the chest, in its engine room. Drauca would experience the input of the Titan's senses as if they were his own. Its metal limbs would feel like extensions of his limbs. He must have felt, the commissar imagined, like a god; it was a thought that made him shiver.

How can we not seem insignificant to them? Like ants, barely even worth the effort to avoid stamping on us too…

Mounted on *Praetorian*'s right arm, the six barrels of its gatling blaster spun frenetically, flinging out a storm of bullets that ripped through traitor platoons. From its left, a laser blaster pumped energy pulses into the enemy's artillery. Sitting on the carapace above its head, between its shoulders, an Apocalypse missile launcher discharged up to twenty rockets at a time, which streaked towards enemy emplacements. In the meantime, incoming fire flashed off the invisible bubble of the Titan's void shields, hardly even scraping its dense armoured hide.

'Sirs,' a watchmaster yelled out, 'on your two o'clock!'

Maugh saw it at the same time: a squad of militiamen with power swords, joined by bestial ogryns, was smashing through Korpsmen towards him. Towards the precious standard. Colonel Thyran and he reacted together as always. Even as the Krieg flank to their right collapsed, the colonel spurred his mount. It galloped at the oncoming traitors just as they least expected it, as they believed they had the upper hand. The colonel thrust the curved blade of his sabre into an ogryn's chest. He wheeled his mount around and reared it up; with a furious snort, it mauled a traitor with its hooves, cracking his skull.

The rest of the command squad fell upon their scattered foes. A heavy-set traitor with spiked armour plates slipped past them, his eyes fixed on the standard bearer, who couldn't easily defend himself without setting down his sacred burden. Maugh leapt into the traitor's path and their power swords clashed, showering both in bright blue sparks.

The traitor fought with more skill than any Maugh had encountered before; he struggled to parry each savage thrust, at the same time ducking sideswipes from the traitor's spiked elbow. In the process, he was forced to give a step and then another. No mean swordsman himself, though, he lured his opponent closer with a feint, sidestepped the heretic's overconfident lunge, and brought his blade down into the man's back. The dead traitor flopped at the commissar's feet.

Maugh hadn't come so close to death in a long time. His heart raced. He was short of breath. He had grown old in almost thirteen years on Vraks too.

He pushed the thought away. Manipulating his comm-bead, he opened a general vox-channel. 'Xaphan is desperate,' he proclaimed to every Korpsman in the 143rd Regiment. 'He began this war with millions of craven followers, but we have worn him down to just a few. No longer can he hide behind unskilled, conscripted labourers. He sends his most valued disciples against us, armed with his greatest weapons – and every one he loses is a hammer blow to his vile ambitions. Every single one.'

Engines screamed above his head, as Thunderbolt fighters

added their las- and autocannons to the holy storm of Imperial fire engulfing the enemy. Commissar-General Maugh closed with another traitor: another uniformed militiaman, wielding a plasma gun. Before she could employ it, Maugh's blade severed her gun hand at the wrist. *So what,* he thought, *if we do seem insignificant to Drauca and his Titan crews? That doesn't make us helpless.*

It doesn't mean we can't still make a difference – one body at a time!

As the first day's fighting petered out, Maugh was satisfied that his regiment had made a difference. Though others had blasted out a path for them, they had been the ones to follow it, reoccupying positions they had not seen in two years. They had cleared out miles of trenches, rooting out traitors from boltholes that the gigantic Titans could never have reached.

Returning to their old command dugout, the commissar watched as Colonel Thyran spent the evening hunched over his vox-caster. News from the other four line korps was less heartening, but this had been expected. Across the northern front, the Krieg had been held to a standstill, even losing ground in sectors where Traitor legionaries had been deployed.

Today had been a start, and a good one, but tomorrow would be crucial. Tomorrow would see Xaphan's response to today's defeats. Redeploying his resources to stave off the Titan threat would leave him vulnerable elsewhere, but what option did he have? Tomorrow, a good many Krieg would see the odds against them lessened. They would have their chances to be heroes.

For the 12th Line Korps, the converse would be true. Tomorrow, they would bear the brunt of the counter-attack on their comrades' behalf. If all went to plan, they would be facing greater hazards than they ever had before.

* * *

Maugh dived into another trench, propelled by a blast wave from behind. He landed hard, jarring the teeth in his head.

His comrades had already been here, clearing the way: traitor corpses and some Krieg were strewn about him. One of the former still had a spark of life and was dragging himself through the mud, fingers straining to reach a dropped autogun; Colonel Thyran's sabre flashed as it skewered his neck.

The colonel had left his mount behind today, having foreseen this shift to confined quarters. He had had many chances to replace his venerable blade with a dead traitor's power weapon, but had declined them all. He checked that his commissar and standard bearer were still with him, picked a tunnel and charged down it.

Maugh was grateful to spend some time underground, under relative shelter. Drauca's Titans had followed his line korps into battle once more. He had thought them absent to begin with, reassigned to some other sector, but they had closed behind him with startling speed, each stride of theirs covering tens of feet. Similar shapes had crested the horizon ahead of them, however.

The black Traitor Titans were every bit as fast and just as massive as their righteous counterparts. In very little time, they had closed to firing range, and both sets of mighty machines had begun blasting at each other with volcano cannons, turbo-lasers and Vulcan mega-bolters. The Emperor's Thunderbolts had also been met by sleek, agile enemy fighters that Maugh recognised as Hell Blades; they wheeled about each other, through the battlefield smoke, buzzing about the Titans' heads, as they duelled with their autocannons.

A grenadier squad had already been wiped out as they attempted to clamp krak grenades to a Traitor Titan's leg. The commissar had issued a general order to try nothing of the sort again without armoured support. Let the god-engines fight their own battles – for they certainly seemed to care little for the one teeming about their feet – and concentrate on surviving the fallout.

There were dangers down here too. Many traitors had also gone underground, lurking around every trench corner with grenades, knives and autoguns readied.

The command squad stumbled upon the aftermath of a sprung ambush, in which several Korpsmen had been killed, though their attackers had been dealt with too. Two survivors were trying to stem the bleeding from a bullet wound between their sergeant's ribs. Maugh glowered down at them. 'A soldier who can't tend to their own wounds is no use to the Emperor.'

The sergeant tried to pull himself together in the commissar's presence. He tried to push his comrades away from him, but one of them protested: 'Sir, if we can get him back to–'

Maugh shot the sergeant through the head.

The others got the message, especially when he turned his laspistol upon them. Had there been more people to see, he might have pulled the trigger twice more. Instead, he motioned the two Korpsmen along the trench ahead of him. He judged that they could better serve by returning to the fray than as an example to few others. Once, not very long ago, no such example would have been required. He couldn't recall the last time he had had to remind a Krieg soldier of his duty.

Thyran was right, he thought. *These new recruits are going soft – and, as their commissar, I must bear much of the blame!*

The colonel, he realised, had seen everything. 'We've been down here too long,' he grumbled to Maugh. 'Our banner needs to be displayed, so that all may see it and take pride in its presence. We need to–'

He was cut off by a colossal explosion, which drowned out his words and shook the earth about him. It had come from somewhere above their heads, but before Maugh could ascertain more, before he could catch his breath, the command squad's watchmaster tackled him, screaming, 'Down, sir!'

Instinct kept him from resisting, and they fell into the just-vacated space beneath the awning. Barely missing Maugh's head, a gigantic piece of shrapnel thunked into the trench wall where he had stood. His landing knocked his gas mask awry. He couldn't see, and his nose was filled with an acrid promethium stink.

He straightened his mask but almost wished he hadn't, as a fireball engulfed Korpsmen further along the trench, the gruesome image burnt into his retinas. The two he had sent down there were certainly among the dead. *The Emperor, too, has a dark sense of humour,* Colonel Thyran had often remarked.

Maugh joined the scorched and bloodied soldiers picking themselves up, dusting themselves down, stamping out small fires around them. He was drawn to the hunk of metal that had almost decapitated him. It had embedded itself deeply in the earth. He brushed a layer of soil from it, feeling its lingering heat through his glove. It was larger than his head, a deep black with tarnished brass trim. Picked out in veins of the latter was part of a symbol that he had seen before. A burning brazier.

He was looking at a fragment of an enemy Titan's pauldron. He turned to give the uplifting news to his comrades, but the words caught in his throat.

The regimental standard was ablaze.

Its bearer tried to beat out the fire against the trench walls; when that failed, they dropped the banner and threw themselves on top of it, rolling and thrashing until their body had smothered the last of the flames.

Concerned Korpsmen pressed around the ensign as he carefully peeled singed flaps of fabric from the dirt. Maugh pushed his way through them to get a better view. The ensign gingerly hoisted the standard again and, for a moment, he thought the damage might only have been slight. 'Nothing that cannot be repaired,' grunted Colonel Thyran, clapping the bearer's shoulder in approval of his speedy actions.

Then one of the skulls mounted on the standard shifted; its blank eye sockets seemed to leer at Maugh in mockery as it broke away from the pole and dropped. He started forwards, but although the skull appeared to him to be falling in slow-motion, still he couldn't move fast enough to catch it.

It must have been hit by shrapnel from the Titan, for already it was fractured. By chance, it struck a small, hard piece of rock, and burst along those fault lines. Landing on his knees, Maugh scrabbled for its broken pieces. Whose skull had it been? he wondered. Which of the 143rd's past leaders would accompany his regiment into battle no longer? He doubted anyone alive knew the answer to that question, only that the skull itself was irreplaceable.

Looking up, he met Colonel Thyran's opaque gaze and caught the almost imperceptible shake of his head. He realised that his current position was less than dignified, besides which others were now squatting in the dirt, combing it for bone fragments, which the standard bearer was collecting in a velvet-lined ossuary box. Maugh stood, his knees and back aching with the effort. He deposited his findings in the box, though the smaller ones crumbled to dust in his hands.

He needed to say something. 'You heard the colonel. Enough of this skulking underground. It's time we got back out there, back up on the surface. Time to show these traitors that we hide from nobody and nothing. Let this banner, battered but undaunted, fly as a symbol that, although battered too, we are made stronger by our losses and we shall prevail. For the Emperor!'

'For the Emperor!' the masked soldiers around him bellowed.

'For Krieg!' the commissar added.

'In death,' came the chorus, *'atonement!'*

The Krieg attacked the trench walls with gusto. A ladder was found to help up the standard bearer with their newly fragile charge. Maugh and Thyran joined them, ascending into a maelstrom of noise and fire. The Korpsmen ahead of them were already identifying targets – including an enemy Gorgon tank they had surfaced just behind, whose gunners hadn't seen them yet – and streamed towards them as their banner was unfurled. Maugh watched it flapping, scorched and tattered, in the wind and thought he had never seen it fly more proudly.

'I know you had your doubts,' said Maugh.

Colonel Thyran swilled amasec about his mouth, his face giving nothing away; it rarely did. He may as well have been wearing his mask. 'My Korpsmen have always exceeded expectations.'

'I hear it from other regiments too,' said the commissar-general. 'Too many thinking too much of themselves, thinking they could be the next – what was his name?'

'Tyborc,' the colonel growled.

'Fortunately, your Korpsmen have a more suitable role model.'

Thyran showed no reaction to the compliment. 'We have all had too much time to ourselves lately,' he considered. 'Too much time to think.'

'I doubt that will continue to be a problem.'

'Hmm. Perhaps.'

Maugh raised his glass. 'Here's to the Kagori Offensive.'

'To those who died to bring us to this point,' the colonel agreed.

'And the hard work yet to come.'

'To exceeding expectations!'

General Durjan had addressed his senior officers that afternoon. He had confirmed what Maugh already knew: that the Krieg had driven the traitors back to their innermost defence lines around the citadel and then cracked these too. Their Eighth Assault Korps was driving armoured columns into those cracks, prising them further open. The Legio Astorum had lost half of its twenty-two Titans, but had destroyed a similar number, close to the apostate cardinal's entire complement.

One Titan, *Invigila Alpha*, stood frozen on the plain, its weapons raised, as if standing sentry over the 143rd's newly gained positions. Its cognitive engine had been overloaded, the brains of its crew members fried, but its void-shielded chassis, scorched and battered, had endured. The Krieg had embraced it as a symbol of their undimmed defiance. The remainder of the battle group had withdrawn to their stockades behind the lines, where they would wait until they were needed again. The war was still running behind its original schedule, but only by four years now, and the general shared Lord Kagori's new-found optimism for its eventual outcome.

The enemy's blockade of the Vraks System had also been broken. Maugh had heard that, in fact, the renegade fleet had mostly dispersed of its own accord, bored mercenaries seeking fresh blood sports elsewhere. Still, a victory won through discipline and patience was as good as any other. Supply shuttles were once again arriving day and night, and the colonel had been told that his regiment's depleted ranks would be replenished in short order.

'I almost feel like things are going too well,' the commissar sighed. He sank back into his plush leather seat, letting it cradle his sore, stiff body. 'If I don't die in battle soon, I may have to retire.'

He meant it as a macabre joke, of the sort that Krieg Korpsmen often exchanged. Thyran looked at him sharply, however, for once failing to hide his surprise. Maugh grimaced back at him. 'Six days in the field, and I feel as if I have been tortured on an Inquisitorial rack. My every bone and muscle aches.'

'Perhaps it is time, then,' the colonel offered, unexpectedly.

Maugh was taken aback. 'Is that what you think?'

'You are not Krieg,' Colonel Thyran stated flatly.

'No, but I have always felt as if–'

'You have no debt to pay, and a lifetime of faultless service to your name.'

Maugh smiled to himself, realising that the words had been meant to compliment, not to insult. 'For twenty-two years, I have ordered Korpsmen to die for the Emperor. You know what they say – never ask someone to do something you wouldn't do yourself.' He drained his glass, the muscles in his arm protesting at having to lift even its weight. *Perhaps I am the one who has gone soft,* he thought.

'As you said yourself, we still have work to do.'

That was Thyran's way of saying he wanted him to stay. Maugh appreciated it, but knew better than to press the point. He broached another difficult topic instead. 'The damage to the regimental banner...'

'Is being repaired as we speak.'

'No doubt, but can it ever really be–'

The colonel interrupted him. 'When I was a ridemaster, I witnessed my commander's demise. We were clearing a hab-zone whose occupants had yielded to the Ruinous Powers, much as those of the citadel have. Somehow, one of them – some degraded mutant scum – had laid its gnarled claws on a plasma pistol. I saw the glint of its sniper scope in a ruined warehouse window. I shouted a warning, but some foul sorcery must have guided its aim that day, for its single bolt struck my colonel squarely in the head.'

'A plasma bolt,' Maugh ventured. 'Then there can't have been much left of...?'

'Eight days later, our new commanding officer paraded the regimental standard, upon which a new skull, gleaming white, took pride of place. Even in death, Colonel Henkel still watched over us, expecting us to live up to the standards he had set for us. So we were assured.'

'But you had seen his skull melted.'

Thyran nodded. 'Nor was I alone in that.'

'You chose to say nothing.'

'I chose to believe,' Thyran corrected him. 'As did we all. Against that, what did the truth matter?'

Maugh gaped at him. After all this time, he had thought his comrade could have no more secrets from him. He thought about scrabbling in the dirt for fragments of dead bone, memento mori with no value other than what others chose to invest in them. Symbols easily replaced, because what really mattered was what they represented. He thought about all that, and reacted in the only way he could.

For the first time in more years than he cared to count, Commissar-General Maugh laughed.

VIII

Rain lashed down, a constant drumbeat on the corrugated roof. Even by Vraks' standards, recent storms had been torrential. Lightning sparked between clouds that had taken on an ominous blood-red hue.

Confessor Tenaxus was filled with foreboding. It sickened her to think what might be happening inside the citadel, what Xaphan and his profane allies might be doing to make this world itself react so violently against them.

She hoped to gain some insight from the prisoner.

He sat in a comfortable chair facing her own, cradling a glass of water. He wore the uniform of a Krieg engineer, with its shorter, lighter tunic replacing the greatcoat. It was creased and soiled from his weeks of captivity. His gas mask was slung around his neck, revealing a sallow, youthful face with watery eyes that blinked frequently, still bothered by the light.

She had brought him up from his squalid dungeon, judging

that he might respond more swiftly to kindness than to torture, but she had kept his wrists and ankles manacled and her Excruciator close to hand. 'What is your name?' she asked him.

'I have no name, confessor,' the prisoner mumbled.

'That is a lie.'

'No, ma'am,' he insisted, squirming under her glare. 'As a loyal Death Korpsman–'

'That also is a lie.'

A squeal bubbled up from the prisoner's throat, but failed to form itself into a defence. Now certain of her ground, the confessor leaned towards him. 'Never have I seen a Korpsman's unmasked face before.'

'I... The air filter in my rebreather unit was spent. I merely–'

'Do you know how many Korpsmen find themselves accused of treachery?'

'Hardly any, ma'am, I'm sure.'

'Not since the days of Colonel Jurten. Why don't you tell me about him, Korpsman? Tell me about your people's hero.'

His shoulders sagged in defeat. Tenaxus nodded. 'As I thought. I did consider that you may have come to Vraks with the Arphista labour corps, but then what would you have to gain from this deception?'

'I only want what every Korpsman wants, confessor.'

'I believe you were here all along,' she accused him. 'I believe you were a labourer on Vraks, which means you must have taken up arms against–'

'Confessor, no!'

She sat back, satisfied with the prisoner's response. He still had a spark of fire in him, which was something she could use. 'What is your name?' she asked again.

'I have no name, confessor.'

* * *

He remembered his first sight of the Cardinal-Astral.

For days and into many nights, bells had rung out across the planet to herald the arrival of this holiest of men. The chapels had been packed with supplicants eager to display their devotion, while the pilgrims that thronged about the Basilica of St Leonis the Blind had seemed driven into virtual frenzies of religious ecstasy. Even such a lowly labourer as he had felt blessed and excited.

Had he been allowed, he might have joined the crowds lining the route from the star port to the citadel, camping out for days in Vraks' thunderstorms for a glimpse of their distinguished visitor. As it was, his labour gang was excused work that morning – though they would make up the hours later – and told to remain inside their hab-zone. He had joined the thousands in the streets, craning their necks to peer up at the citadel's towers.

Their patience had been amply rewarded. The Cardinal-Astral had emerged from the basilica and mounted a rocky bluff outside the citadel's walls, where a pulpit had been erected for him. From this distance, he was barely a speck to the watching workers, but still his appearance sent a thrill through them. The whispers that had reached them had been true, as Xaphan had indeed glowed with a sun's golden light.

A swarm had risen from the bluff. As it dispersed across the teeming plain, the labourers had made out cherubim with angel's wings. Three had swooped towards the hab-zone, circling above its buildings, and the Cardinal-Astral's voice had issued from their mouths, ringing loud and clear for everyone to hear.

'He spoke to us,' the prisoner recalled. 'I mean, to every one of us. He told us he valued our efforts, and it felt like…'

'He flattered you,' Confessor Tenaxus said coolly.

'It felt like, for the first time in our lives, we had been noticed.'

'What else did the apostate cardinal say?'

'He told us that we, those who toiled with our hands to keep our armies provisioned, that we were the true heroes of the Imperium of Man, for without us…'

'He told you what you wished to hear.'

'I…' The prisoner avoided the confessor's inscrutable eyes. He genuinely feared that she could read his thoughts and would punish any further lies he told her. She had warned him that his only hope, a slim hope, was to throw himself upon her mercy. He believed her, and prayed she might be merciful enough. 'Yes, ma'am, but… forgive me, how could I…? When the car– I mean, the apostate cardinal, had the hearts and minds of everyone around me, the devotion of pilgrims and priests who knew the Emperor's will better than I ever could, then who was I to doubt him?'

Tenaxus nodded, seeming to take his point.

'I think,' he ventured, 'he told them what they wished to hear too.'

He remembered how the glow around Xaphan had darkened. For hours, he had extolled the Emperor's glory, heaping praise upon the Master of Mankind's loyal subjects. Now, suddenly, he warned of dreadful trials to come, of a darkness that had already consumed worlds and was gathering around this world. He spoke of the need to fight against that darkness, and then, with a sweep of white silk robes, he had disappeared back into the basilica, leaving his audience stunned.

'You signed up for Xaphan's crusade.'

The prisoner had the decency to look ashamed. 'His War of Faith. Yes, ma'am, all of us did. He made us think we had no choice.'

'You never questioned why an agent of the Ministorum was building an army, in defiance of the Decree Passive?' He looked at the confessor blankly. She conceded with a sigh, 'Why would you?'

'My labour gang was issued with uniforms, but there were few arms spare for us. We worked through the night, hammering metal into armour plates and–'

'Who did you imagine you might fight?'

'Heretics, ma'am. Traitors. The apostate cardinal sent his priests among us. They preached that regiments of the Emperor's armies had become corrupted. They had isolated Vraks so that no loyalist force could reach us. We thought we would be fighting for the Emperor, ma'am, I swear it, always for Him, and then...'

'Go on.'

'Then something happened. Something that seemed to... At the time, we thought it proof that... Confessor, there was an assassin.'

He remembered that day, that terrifying day, when riots had erupted in the citadel's streets and in the tunnels underneath it.

The tension had been building all morning, since news had begun to spread of the assassination attempt. The general mood of shocked disbelief had given way to anger – that the Emperor's enemies had committed this atrocity upon such sacred ground – and fear, that they were closer than anyone had truly imagined. The Adeptus Arbites had stamped down hard on sporadic violent outbreaks, but the order they upheld had felt febrile.

With hindsight, the parading of the assassin's corpse had inflamed emotions further. 'I didn't know what I was expected to do,' the prisoner confessed. 'I had been drafted into the Frateris Militia but given no orders. I was simply returned to my work duties, told to wait, but now... now the very threat against which we were recruited was here. The enemy was inside our gates.'

'You were unprepared,' said Tenaxus.

'Yes, unprepared, and that was why...'

He didn't know who had suggested it: that they couldn't wait any longer, they needed to arm themselves. For everyone's protection. He did remember voicing his agreement, but then, before he knew it, he was being swept along by the tide and any second thoughts would have been futile. 'By the time I reached the armoury, the gates were standing open.'

'Opened freely?' Tenaxus enquired.

'I... didn't know, but no one tried to stop us. The garrison stood back and let us in, let us take what we wanted.' He had acquired an autogun quickly enough, but had faced fiercer competition when it came to ammunition. Too many were snatching up more magazines than they needed. He had elbowed three labourers aside to lay his hands on just a couple, and taken a punch to the face to keep hold of them.

Snapping his first magazine into the breech, he had enjoyed a sense of strength and purpose. It was odd to remember that now, because he had felt nothing like it since. Even then, it had drained away quickly. So, he had had a gun, but what did he intend to do with it?

'Back outside, on the surface, there was panic and confusion. I tried to break it up, but no one listened to me, and what could I do? I couldn't tell who was fighting for what cause, and nor could anybody else. Was I to shoot my colleagues? The Arbites were already in retreat; a baying mob was attacking their precinct. I tried to make my way to the basilica. I thought I could protect the holy shrine, at least.'

The confessor's pinched face softened slightly.

'There were bodies underfoot, some alive but wounded. I saw the Battle Sisters of the Order of the Argent Shroud. They had come to Vraks as Xaphan's honour guard and we trusted them, thought they were here to save us. The crowd parted for them, but then someone... someone yelled that they were traitors too, and...'

'Impossible!' Tenaxus spat, hardening again.

'They fired their weapons, those red bolters.'

'With cause, no doubt.'

'There were innocents... People clutching at the Sisters' robes, pleading with them, falling at their feet in supplication, but they... It was a massacre!' He shuddered as the images flooded his mind anew.

'Can you swear they were not fired upon first?'

'I couldn't swear to it, no, but–'

'It would only have taken one or two agents in the crowd.'

'I see that now, confessor,' the prisoner agreed, 'just as I see the failed assassin was likely also an impostor.' He had hoped to regain her approval, but this time discerned no reaction from her at all. He didn't pause to wonder why.

His mind was trapped back in that day. He relived his terrible paralysis, a soldier with no training, not knowing what was expected of him. Gas grenades had been set off and militiamen had strafed the precinct square from the citadel's ramparts, not seeming to care who they hit. His indecision saved him. Had he taken half a step forwards, he would certainly have died.

He didn't know, would never know, who if anyone had given the order, but suddenly, booming peals of thunder shook the very world and fire and metal rained down from the sky, from the citadel's high towers, its vaunted defences turned inwards upon its own inhabitants.

By instinct, he ran blindly, ears filled with screams and explosions, his nostrils with cordite and the stench of death. He didn't get far before he fell and lay trembling, hands over his head as running feet stamped down around and over him. He lay for what felt like forever, until his deadened ears cleared and he realised the bombardment had mercifully ceased.

'They razed the precinct square,' he reported, choking on the words. 'Hundreds of people... and the Arbites, none of them survived. Only those, like me, who had been on the edges of the crowd, who made it far enough in time.'

'What of the Battle Sisters?' asked Tenaxus, sharply.

The prisoner nodded. 'A handful, yes. I saw... Disciples, the apostate cardinal calls them. His inner circle, his most trusted followers. Militiamen like us, but they have all the best equipment. I don't know where... They appeared as if from nowhere. They dragged the Battle Sisters, the ones still alive, from the wreckage. Their armour had protected them, but they were dazed and wounded. Some put up a token struggle, but they were chained and hauled away.'

The news seemed to pain the confessor.

'I never laid eyes on them again. As far as I know, they're still in the citadel's dungeons. The Cardinal-Astral came out onto the palace steps to announce that they had been impostors, infiltrators, under whose sway the Arbites had fallen – as had the master-prefect and his staff.'

'You believed him, of course.'

'By the time the rioting was spent, by morning's light, we had no hope but to believe. The citadel was Xaphan's. He had the support of its steward, its priests, the officers of its militia, and anyone who raised a doubt against him...'

'You let fear sap your faith.'

'You have to understand, confessor. What we feared most was to think that our own actions... That we may have spilled innocent blood. We had to put our faith in Xaphan, had to do as he commanded, because the only other option... If we were right about him, then the Emperor would surely smile upon us. If not, then it was too late for us already. We were… I was already damned.'

The Krieg had made it easy to believe.

For long months, years, he had dreaded coming face to face with them. He had dug and maintained earthworks, hard physical work of the type to which he was accustomed, only now with the threat of shells screaming overhead and nights spent in pitch-black, airless bunkers. He had stood on the firing steps of cold, muddy trenches, gun barrel resting on a sandbag, trying not to shiver as rain dribbled down his neck, but the citadel's artillery had held the invaders at bay.

Until the day it didn't.

Until the day that tens of thousands of those dark-clad, ghoulish figures had come charging across the Van Meersland Wastes towards him.

His heart had leapt into his mouth. He had almost turned and run; it was only the threat of the enforcers' whips that stopped him. He had pumped the trigger of his autogun instead, spraying out bullets without taking time to aim them. There were targets everywhere he looked, in any case, and he hardly even cared if he hit them or not, only that they were deterred from coming closer.

In that, his efforts had seemed doomed to failure.

He saw Korpsmen falling, some certainly dead, but their numbers seemed only to increase. Some were close enough now for him to see their skull-shaped faceplates, to see that they were everything he had been told they were. Remorseless, faceless, brainwashed drones, obsessed with death. It was easy to believe they had been turned against the Emperor. Far harder to imagine they had ever truly served Him.

'I thought I'd die that day,' he admitted to Confessor Tenaxus, 'but I thought – I believed – I would die in the Emperor's service.

When the Krieg withdrew at last, when they just seemed to melt away, I believed He had answered my prayers.'

'How many of His soldiers do you think you killed that day?'

The question cut straight into his heart. 'I heard they had reached some of our trenches, slaughtered everyone inside them. I believed what I'd been told – that they were monsters, that we had to defend ourselves against them. I… I didn't know what monsters were. Not then. Not yet.

'It was about a year ago,' the prisoner continued. 'We were told the Krieg were digging, like cockroaches, trying to reach us from below, so we had to dig too and intercept their tunnels.'

Tenaxus nodded. One of Lord Marshal Kagori's strategies had been to open up a new front in Vraks' war, a subterranean front.

'My squad spent months underground. I jumped at every shadow, every sound. I thought I might go mad, but somehow I learned to… I don't know…'

'You mentioned monsters.'

'We were redeployed to one of our deepest armouries. Our officers knew the Krieg were coming – we'd detected the vibrations from their drilling machines – so the complex had been cleared, and we set an ambush inside it.'

Tenaxus winced, recalling the incident in question.

'They blasted their way in with breaching charges. They… We thought ourselves prepared, but the size of the explosions… I don't know how many militiamen we lost in that one moment, just smeared against the walls by the sheer force of the shockwave or… A pair of storerooms collapsed. There were people buried in the wreckage, and I saw–'

Tenaxus was losing patience. 'Tell me about the monsters.'

He braced himself and swallowed before, in a hollow tone, he told her.

* * *

He remembered muzzle flashes in the darkness: the shotguns of the first wave of Krieg invaders, the heavy stubbers manned by his own people. In their staccato lights, he saw bodies piling up in the armoury's corridors. He heard the explosions of grenades, their smoke only further obscuring the situation.

A shower of masonry on his head, on the air tank on his shoulders, dislodged him from his assigned position, fearing a roof collapse. He wasn't running, he told himself, only relocating. If any enforcer had seen him, he wasn't sure they'd appreciate the difference, though perhaps they might appreciate the fact that he had only run into greater danger.

Before, at least he'd had a barrier between him and his enemies, flimsy as it was. Now, they were everywhere he turned. Ducking round a corner from a rattle of bullets behind him, he recoiled from a squad charging towards him. Shotguns barked, their pellets ripping through two of his comrades; he pushed one into the fire to shield himself as he leapt for the narrow opening to a sap tunnel, and only later thought to question whether she had actually been dead.

He fumbled with his autogun, but a Korpsman was already in the tunnel entrance. He thrust his arm-mounted blade towards the dark figure's head, but the stock of a shotgun deflected it. He knew that if he ran, bullets would pursue him along the confined tunnel; he had foolishly trapped himself.

He attempted a bull-rush instead, and was surprised by the ease with which the Korpsman gave way. They tumbled out of the tunnel together, into a chaotic scrum. Warm bodies stumbled and reeled into him, threatening to crush him, and he couldn't make out which were friendly and which wished to kill him. Flailing elbows jabbed him in the ribs and head. He continued to wrestle with the one foe of which he was certain – mostly, just straining to keep that shotgun pointed away from him – and gradually he realised something. He was stronger than the Korpsman. He was winning.

With a rush of elation, he knocked the weapon from his opponent's hands. A swipe of his blade drew blood from the Korpsman's arm. Red, human blood. He had been so afraid of the Krieg for so very, very long, but they were only human after all. Just as he grasped the implications of that thought, something hard and blunt struck him in the small of his back and knocked him off his feet.

His autogun, taking the brunt of his landing, broke. He tried to stand but was trampled down again. Helpless on his hands and knees, he was struggling to breathe and thought he must have used up too much oxygen. He thought about wrenching out his air hose, but with dust billowing and flamers flaring everywhere, he doubted it would help him. His mind raced with all the ways he could have been about to die, until he realised that the melee was thinning out around him.

A giant metal foot crashed down beside his ear. A giant metal figure loomed over him, stooping down towards him. Giant metal fingers closed around the scruff of his neck and plucked him from the ground. Red lights flared behind the eyes of a red metal visor. Then a metal arm flexed and almost casually flung him aside, with enough force to wind him as he struck the tunnel wall. He had been identified as friendly, but also as an obstacle in the armoured giant's path.

The giant had pushed his way along the tunnel, almost filling it, his stooped head scraping its roof. Shotgun pellets had burst against his chest in vain, as the dark figures of the Krieg had backed away from him in fear, but not quickly enough. His chainsword had roared into action.

'You must have been aware of the legionaries' presence,' said Tenaxus.

'It was no secret,' the prisoner agreed. 'Our priests spoke often of Lord Arkos and his promise to summon powerful allies to Vraks, and in time they informed us that he had been true to his word. They told us he would save us, only I…'

'You had doubts about these "allies".'

'As time went by, the apostate cardinal made fewer appearances in public, with less to say each time. His priests spoke more often of Lord Arkos, and then… and then there came another, even worse…'

'What of the basilica?' the confessor urged. 'It still stands?'

'I… I assume… I haven't seen inside the citadel for months. I don't remember when I last saw the apostate cardinal, or heard that anyone had. Or even Lord Arkos, since the trait– I mean, since the star port fell. I always feared he might have died there, but we were told nothing and none of us ever asked questions. I suppose I should be… I *am* glad to think he must be dead, but at the time…'

He shuddered at the memory of that one-sided battle in the tunnels. In a way, he had been lucky that it had been cloaked by darkness, but the sounds and the smells and the strobe-lit snapshots of it had haunted his sleep since.

The red-armoured Space Marine, his saviour, his shield, had been joined by two battle-brothers, emerging from the shadows, and another, he had belatedly grasped, cutting off the Krieg's retreat. With a savagery such as he had never seen before, they had waded into their trapped prey, eviscerating them with whirling swords and axes, and he had been relieved, but that feeling had soon soured in his stomach.

He had seen screaming, kicking Korpsmen hoisted by pairs of giant gauntlets and rent limb from limb. He had seen legionaries smearing their visor grilles with their victims' viscera, and one had daubed a profane symbol in Krieg blood across his chest.

Mechanically augmented howls of barbarian rage had rung in his ears, his nerves had been wracked by gleefully bellowed curses, and the lies to which he had so desperately been clinging had melted away in the heat of that horrifying moment, as he had seen his so-called allies for what they truly were.

Drawing his knees up to his forehead, he had wept into the coarse fabric of his uniform fatigues. He didn't know how long he had stayed like that, thinking an enforcer might find him and end his anguish with a bullet to the head, wishing he could find the courage to end it for himself.

The Space Marines – the Traitor Marines, he ought to call them now – had moved on, leaving a charnel house behind them. A dropped and broken lumen cube spat fitful light upon the rotten fruits of their depravity. Turning his head, revolted, he had caught his breath at the sight of a Death Korpsman, like him slumped against the wall, mere feet from him. Scrambling over to the body, he had confirmed that it was dead; its neck was broken.

For the first time, he had been properly face to face – or rather, face mask to face mask – with his purported enemy. This Korpsman hadn't worn a skull faceplate as some of them did, just an ordinary gas mask. Even this had put him in mind of a skull with its blank expression and dead, staring eyes. Was it really any different, though, he wondered, from the mask he wore himself?

It occurred to him that this might well have been the Korpsman with whom he had wrestled, each of them desperate to kill the other. He had no way of knowing. He had found himself reaching for the mask, although he wasn't sure why. Perhaps to replace his own failing respirator with the Krieg's rebreather unit? His hands had trembled as he had peeled the mask back.

'And?' the confessor had to prompt him. 'What did you see?'

'I saw...' He considered his response. 'I saw a man exactly like myself, and I thought… In that moment, I thought I could have been him, how much better that would be, and then… and then I thought I could still be…'

Tenaxus pursed her lips in disapproval. 'So, you stripped the uniform from a dead Imperial soldier. You condemned him to rot in anonymity, his fate never known.'

The prisoner squirmed again. 'I… Yes, I did, confessor.'

'And for what purpose? To prolong your own wretched life?'

'I don't know. Maybe. I hadn't time to stop and think, I just… I wanted out of that situation. I wanted to be anywhere else and maybe… maybe to be anybody else.'

'You saw that your pathetic band of traitors was losing this war.'

'On that day, ma'am, down in those tunnels, it didn't feel that way.'

Another point she had to grant him. The Krieg had been repulsed that day, though not for long. Renewed attacks upon the armoury had also failed, but had given the infantry of the 471st Regiment, part of the new 46th Line Korps, a chance to advance upon it above ground. They had been permitted to employ chem-weapons, something that ought to have shocked her. She wondered if her prisoner even knew that corrosive gas had been pumped into the armoury, how he might react if he did.

Perhaps he would just be relieved, as was Tenaxus, that its remaining defenders had been eliminated, the Berserkers of Skallathrax included.

'And where were you during those subsequent battles?' she demanded.

'I was with the Krieg, confessor, having fled the tunnels with them.'

'You were hiding among them, in their clothes.'

He shook his head, vehemently. 'Fighting with them.'

'Against your old comrades? Old friends?'

'I wasn't placed on the front line. I never had a target in my sights.'

'But if you had?' Tenaxus pressed him.

'I would have pulled the trigger,' the prisoner mumbled. She fixed him with a sceptical glare. He insisted, 'I would have. Those people weren't my friends. I don't know what became of my friends. We started wearing respirator masks, stopped using names. We hardly talked at all, because we didn't know who might be listening. I fought alongside men and women who... I might have known them once, but now...'

'They were traitors. Say it!'

'They were traitors. Even those who may have doubted, as I did. They still fought for the apostate cardinal, whatever their reasons.'

'And they deserved to die?'

He bowed his head in resignation.

'How did you do it?' the confessor asked him. She believed now that he could tell her little of strategic value – she had always suspected as much – but still she was curious to hear how his story ended. 'How did you pass among the Krieg, unnoticed, for so many months?'

The prisoner shrugged. 'I suppose I... kept my head down, hid my face. I did as I was told. No, that isn't quite... I followed the herd. I tried to do as everyone around me was doing, for fear of standing out. If I am truly honest, confessor...'

'I expect nothing less.'

'Rarely in my life have I done anything else.'

'With one notable exception,' she reminded him.

'Apart from that one day,' he agreed. 'One moment. The one

time I made a decision for myself, and I... I don't regret it, even though...'

Tenaxus raised an eyebrow.

'Most of the days since, I have spent digging. We've been trying to reach the curtain wall around the citadel, and sometimes the enemy lays mines in our path or they break into our tunnels or they shell our positions, and I live every day in terror, knowing that I could be killed in the blink of an eye, knowing I can't escape because I've nowhere left to run to.'

For the first time, he looked Tenaxus in the eyes. 'Confessor, you accused me of defecting for some personal advantage, but believe me, little in my life has changed. Only one thing. No longer do I doubt that I am fighting for the Emperor, and maybe it's too late to save my soul, but at least I know that every shot I fire, every thrust of my spade into this world's earth, is an action taken in His service.'

The prisoner slumped back in his seat again, as if unburdening himself had physically exhausted him. Tenaxus considered his case for a long moment. Thought to be the sole survivor of a Death Korps engineer platoon, he had been reassigned to one whose members had no reason to know him. His new watchmaster reported that, for months, no fault had been found with his demeanour. Suspicions had only been aroused when his squad had crewed a Hades breaching drill, and his lack of training with such had been exposed.

'What is your name?' she asked the prisoner again.

'I have no name, confessor.' She was about to remonstrate with him when he elucidated. 'I gave up my name, because I had brought shame upon it. I have only a number now, and even that is not my own.'

'You took up arms against the Emperor.'

'Yes, ma'am,' he confessed freely.

'This cannot go unpunished.'

'No, ma'am.'

Unexpectedly, the confessor smiled. 'However...'

He stepped blinking out into Vraks' grey daylight, a prisoner no longer – at least in no formal sense. His equipment – his stolen equipment – had been returned to him, including his weapons. A Krieg rebreather mask concealed his face.

Dog tags were slung about his neck, bearing a number he had stolen too, but still he knew he could bring honour to it, as had those who had borne it before him and the many who would bear it long after.

He straightened his back and marched towards the locomotive depot. He was ready to die for the Emperor, and thereafter rot in anonymity. He only prayed his worthless life could make a difference, that he could atone for a fraction of his sins against the Master of Mankind.

As Confessor Tenaxus had said when she had pronounced this death sentence upon him, 'I believe you will make an exemplary Death Korpsman.'

IX

At 714826.M41, thirteen years into Vraks' twelve-year war, the curtain wall around its citadel was finally breached.

The breakthrough occurred in the Sector 57-44 mine to the south and west. To the north-east, Colonel Tyborc was woken by the shock wave, which he later learned had hurled Korpsmen from their bunks and collapsed some of their dugouts. By the time it reached him, hundreds of miles away, it barely had the strength to rattle his plasteel helmet, which hung from a nail beside his head.

That morning, even so, he and his command staff raised a glass to the 88th Siege Army's grand achievement, though they didn't actually lift their masks to drink the contaminated water.

The following months saw repeated attempts by the Krieg to force troops through the breach, which of course was fiercely defended. Colonel Tyborc followed their progress in daily despatches, frustrated by every costly failure. Another million Korpsmen died during that time, more numbers for the rolls of the dead, but at last came news that, with aid from the Legio Astorum and the Red Scorpions Chapter of the Emperor's Angels, their objective had been achieved. There were Krieg inside the curtain wall, at last, with the citadel itself firmly in their sights.

It all seemed a long way away from his current position.

For two years, Tyborc's 261st Regiment had been at a standstill. To the south, a swathe of the Van Meersland Wastes was infested by disease-afflicted mutants, among whom walked equally blighted Traitor legionaries. The 19th Regiment under Colonel Keled had perished there beneath a shroud of toxic green gas, since then the Krieg had stayed clear of the area that they had now labelled the Green Hell.

The bulwark against such filthy horrors was the battered First Line Korps, but the positions into which they had been consequently forced were untenable without rearguard support. The 30th Line Korps provided this, but the price was that four regiments were tied down here, achieving very little.

On this side of the citadel, the curtain wall stood unbroken, a ferrocrete shield six storeys high and a hundred feet thick, bristling with parapets and firing towers, but for the most part, unless a fortuitous breeze cleared the smoke clouds around it for a moment, Tyborc couldn't even see it.

He was summoned to a briefing of his line korps' command staff.

He wondered how many times he had ridden back to the landing site – and how many times of late it had only been to learn that nothing much had changed. This time, however, felt different. It had been hardly a week since the last command meeting, during which the general had hinted that change was in the air.

If this was indeed the case, then Tyborc felt that he would welcome it, whatever form it took.

Stepping from his carriage, he was struck by the presence of an unusual number of power-armoured figures, bedecked in holy relics. Attended by bloated retinues, they thronged the spaces between the Krieg's well-worn temporary structures. On the chests of a few, he saw the Imperial aquila brandishing a rod and axe: the symbol of the Ordo Malleus. *Daemonhunters!*

He felt a shiver down his spine.

A daemonhunter led the briefing, while General Durjan stood to one side, remaining mostly silent. In itself, this variation in procedure made Tyborc apprehensive. Inquisitor Lord Thor Malkin was an ancient man, his shrunken body dwarfed by his suit of artificer armour. Half his face had been replaced by metal and bionics; Tyborc wondered if the rest of him, buried inside his ablative shell, had weathered his years any better.

He spoke in a dry voice, brittle like old parchment. He wasted few words, which Tyborc appreciated. He spoke of the need to close the 88th Siege Army's ring of steel around the citadel, which meant sending forces into the plague-infested sectors and scouring them clean. Acknowledging the daunting nature of this task, he assured the Krieg that they wouldn't face it alone. The Emperor, he said, would be with them. *The Emperor,* Tyborc thought but didn't say, *is always with us. Is that all?*

That wasn't all. 'Effective immediately,' proclaimed Malkin, 'each Death Korps regiment on Vraks will have an inquisitor attached to it, whose will in all matters must be obeyed without question. Said inquisitor may also, under circumstances deemed by his or her sole discretion, take formal command of said regiment and lead it into battle.'

* * *

Confessor Tenaxus answered some of Tyborc's questions.

He had been seeing more of her since his promotion, since he had been spending more time behind the lines at his regimental headquarters. She was a confidante to him, a comfort when his own thoughts gave him cause to worry.

'The Ordo Malleus is concerned,' Tenaxus told him. 'We have all seen the signs in recent months: blood in the sky, bones rising from the earth – pilots have glimpsed a second sun between the clouds, casting a baleful glare over us – and readings from the Emperor's Tarot have confirmed it. It is feared that something dark and terrible is being stirred on Vraks.'

'Something daemonic?'

She stiffened at the sound of the word, but answered, 'Indeed.'

'Whatever it is–' Tyborc began.

'Please,' she interrupted him, 'spare me your hollow bravado.'

He blinked at her, surprised. She passed a hand over her red-rimmed eyes and sighed. 'This war was meant to be won in twelve years. Thanks to our gains made since Lord Kagori's arrival, he was able to procure an extension to that deadline, but not easily.'

This sounded like good news to Tyborc, all the same. 'To the bureaucrats of the Departmento Munitorum,' Tenaxus continued, 'Vraks is no longer a priority. They agreed to resource our campaign for five more years – of which now four remain – but only at the most basic level.'

'Then the ordo...?'

'May be our only hope, which is why the lord marshal has indentured the 88th Siege Army to them. The sundering of the curtain wall by Strike Force Ainea was, you might say, his final gasp. The apostate cardinal called for a War of Faith, and now he has one, Emperor grant that he lives to regret it.'

'Or dies soon in agony, for nothing,' the colonel growled.

The confessor's lips twitched. 'Remind me, Colonel Tyborc, how long have you had command of your regiment?'

'Two months and thirteen days, since my predecessor's death.'

'For who better to lead them than the hero of Fort A-453?'

He shook his head emphatically. 'I was our longest-serving captain, that is all. The longest-lived.'

'And yet, no sooner have you settled into your new post than you find it usurped from you.'

'I... You have helped me understand, confessor, why–'

'You would hardly be human,' she assured him, 'if you didn't feel a little slighted.'

'I would hardly be Krieg if I questioned my orders.'

'Even the Krieg's stubborn loyalty may not suffice to save us from what is to come,' said Tenaxus with a sigh. 'I fear that time is running out.'

Tyborc received more orders over the following weeks, as plans were finalised.

The push would be led by the 263rd, with two tank regiments supporting them. They would swing around First Line Korps' positions and plunge into the plague-infected sectors. On their heels would be the 262nd, with the 269th – to which Inquisitor Lord Malkin had attached himself – behind them.

Tyborc's 261st Regiment would be the last to move, with the least distance to cover. Sweeping up behind the others, they would occupy and hold the ground gained by them in the north before bearing westward towards the curtain wall. They were expected to take the fewest casualties, face the fewest horrors. He wasn't sure how to feel about that; a part of him was relieved, another part ashamed of it.

On more than one night, he dreamt of daemons. He woke in a sweat, heart racing, mind racing too with images of glaring eyes and gnashing fangs and writhing tentacles that he couldn't bring into focus and didn't care to. He hadn't really dreamt before, certainly not like this, and it unsettled him. He looked out for Tenaxus at the landing site, craving her sage advice, but didn't see her.

He saw a good deal of Thor Malkin. Despite his decrepit state, the inquisitor lord appeared indefatigable. Tyborc gathered that his heavy-looking armour contained actuators that mimicked muscle movement, but still it must have taken an immense force of will, focused through a neural interface, to move it as surely and dexterously as he did.

According to Tenaxus, Malkin had come out of retirement to fight one final battle here on Vraks. This made Tyborc think about his own advancing age, which was still no age in comparison. He saw little prospect of dying any time soon, of being allowed to rest, but this didn't trouble him as once it had.

At 273827.M41, the 263rd Krieg Siege Regiment, along with the Seventh and 11th Tank Regiments, began its advance, in the wake of the usual barrage from the guns of 30th Line Korps. Colonel Tyborc followed their progress as best he could, from the bunker that currently served as his command post at the front.

Vox-reports were often vague, confused, with creeping green mists adding to the ever-present smoke to obscure the senses of combatants and spotters alike. As the enemy launched its inevitable counter-barrage, their shells spewed yet more smoke and TP-III gas into the atmosphere, creating a fresh Green Hell in which many squads found themselves engulfed and were soon lost.

Progress was made, nevertheless. The Krieg tanks, sealed against the poison gas, surged forwards. They drove disorganised traitors back before them, despite some attempts at resistance and some

tanks being lost. They encountered the acid-eaten corpses of renegade militiamen, no more immune to their own gas than were their foes; the more intact showed symptoms of virulent diseases.

By nightfall, six miles of ground were captured. The next two days told similar tales. By day four, however, Krieg Korpsmen were reporting encounters with hideous mutants, many so deformed as to be unrecognisable. They may have been humans or ogryns or something else entirely, but all were covered in painful-looking pustules, screaming in equal parts anger and pain as they attacked.

It was on this day that Inquisitor Lord Malkin himself took to the battlefield in his bronze-plated Land Raider, *Mae Virtus*, equipped with laud hailers through which his presence was continuously, loudly proclaimed.

It was also on this day that several squads, usually in their final messages, reported encounters with Traitor Marines, as had been expected, and with other things, worse horrors than most of them could find the words to describe…

On day five, Colonel Tyborc and the 261st Regiment marched into the Green Hell themselves. They met little opposition but for a few already wounded Chaos spawn, slithering in the mud. These were quickly hacked and burnt to death by disgusted Korpsmen, the colonel himself never having to fire his pistol.

They occupied a new set of trenches, relatively intact, and began the laborious process of clearing them of bodies and bringing their big guns forward. A fortuitous thunderstorm that morning had dampened the mists, but as a cold evening drew in, green tendrils re-formed, probing into their dugouts.

The vox-caster squawked into life: a platoon commander reporting an attack upon his trench. He gave the coordinates, and Tyborc worked out that he was close. He led his command squad through the unfamiliar network, encountering dead ends and having to change course twice. Charging along a painfully narrow communication tunnel, he found his way blocked again, by a hulking figure this time.

Immediately, he knew it wasn't human. Its back was turned to him, muscles rippling as it lashed out at a foe he couldn't see, presenting a broad target to him. He shot the creature three times on his approach, then thrust his bayonet into its back. With a howl, it smashed down the Korpsman in its path and rounded on him.

It was, as the colonel had assumed, an ogryn, but it looked as if its skin had suddenly outgrown it. Its face had slid down its head, eyes staring from its chin, jaw merging into its sagging chest. His second bayonet slash cut its flesh but, as far as he could judge, no vital organs – and, with a sickly gurgle, another fold of skin flopped down to seal the gash.

The ogryn swung a massive hammer, with chips like bite marks in its wooden head, at Tyborc. He couldn't say it was holding the weapon exactly, more that fluid extrusions of its flesh were wrapped about it. He ducked a blow that punched a hole into the tunnel wall. The rest of his command squad couldn't find a way past him to the creature. He fired another las-beam, point-blank, into its undulating gut. He must have hurt it, but compared to what it was already suffering…? The ogryn, he suspected, this degraded Chaos spawn, was far beyond pain.

He couldn't let that hammer hit him, but in the cramped tunnel, nor could he dodge it forever. He tackled the ogryn, its foul flesh oozing over him, threatening to suck him in; a swollen boil burst in his face, pus spattering his lenses. His wrist was caught by a slimy, whip-thin tendril. Never had he been gladder of the uniform that sealed him off completely from the outside world.

Teeth gritted, he pushed his arms into the mass, his pistol with its bayonet attachment clutched in both hands. He jerked the blade in a frantic sawing motion – and finally, blessedly, he felt the strength leaving that foetid, misshapen body. The ogryn sagged against him, almost smothering the colonel in its folds. He extricated himself from it with a shudder. Its flesh had ruptured, overripe offal spilling from it as it hit the tunnel floor with a wet slap.

Another figure stood revealed behind it. A gun was aimed at Tyborc's head. He recognised the weapon first and then the wielder. A Krieg Korpsman. She must have taken her hammered-down comrade's place in the tunnel mouth. Her bayonet was draped with ogryn entrails, which meant she had probably just saved Tyborc's life. Still, she kept her lasgun levelled.

'Colonel Tyborc… Is that you?' the figure asked.

'Do I look like a mutant freak?' he snapped.

He bulled his way forward into a larger trench, in which there was more fighting. He saw a Krieg mask and greatcoat pinned against the wall and he snapped up his pistol, but as he was about to fire, he realised that his target was masked and coated too, and all at once he saw the reason for his comrade's suspicion.

Krieg Korpsman was battling Krieg Korpsman. Colonel Tyborc thought madness must have claimed them. Then another masked figure rose in front of him, dragging itself up from the mud, and he saw the gaping hole in its chest where its heart should have been and knew it couldn't possibly have been alive.

It lunged at Tyborc, hands outstretched towards him, gnarled talons bursting through the fingers of its gloves. He readied his bayonet against it, but his current watchmaster interposed himself between them, protecting his commander. The creature, blasted by a hellgun, staggered but caught itself and lunged again. Like the mutated ogryn, it didn't appear to feel pain.

It buried its head in the watchmaster's throat as if to bite him, as if forgetting the rebreather mask it wore. It hesitated, its body language suggesting bestial confusion, and Tyborc and two grenadiers set about it with blades. They hacked and slashed at it, driving it back into the ground, but no blood came forth from its wounds and it struggled on with undiminished strength.

The dead, he thought. *Our own dead have been returned to life as a weapon against us!* The one thing upon which a Krieg Korpsman could rely, and now even that was stolen from them. *How many have died in the Green Hell?* he wondered. The 19th Krieg Siege Regiment, four years ago; more in the past few days.

'Break its bones!' he ordered, and his squad stamped and hammered at the zombie's arms and legs until they shattered; even then, it writhed and thrashed in the dirt, still trying to stand up.

Another zombie came lurching towards them, and this one had lost its rebreather, exposing its face. A bloated red face, foaming at the nose, skin peeling from it, white eyes staring blankly from black sockets. Though revolted, Colonel Tyborc was almost relieved. Better, he thought, to see these monsters for what they truly were, rather than to imagine...

'These are not our comrades,' he barked into his comm-bead. 'These are daemons who make mockery of their noble sacrifices, and they must be destroyed if our comrades are to have their well-earned rest.'

His command squad piled upon the unmasked zombie, methodically breaking its bones as they had the other. Tyborc brought his pistol butt down on its skull, but with a burst of ferocity it thrust its head forward and clamped its teeth onto his left arm. Larger and sharper than they ought to have been, they chewed through the fabric of his coat. He had to break the zombie's jaw with his gun butt to dislodge it. It had left a mark on his arm, but failed to break the skin.

The colonel wiped away a green gobbet of burning saliva, as his comrades continued to pound on his attacker. Confirming his narrow escape, a breathless voice burst over the regimental vox-net: *'Don't let them break your skin. They are diseased! They–'* The voice dissolved into wracking coughs.

All along the trench, more monsters in Krieg clothing were tearing off their gas masks, as if only just comprehending the impediment they caused. They were baring their teeth. Tyborc called for a flamer team, but one was already burning fallen zombies, until their blackened bodies stopped kicking at last. This was some small comfort to him, as he had begun to fear nothing might still them.

He picked off a few more at range before another came at him. This zombie was missing its right arm and its head lolled on an almost-severed, blood-encrusted neck. He punched the creature hard enough to complete its decapitation; its head ricocheted off the trench wall like a scrumball. The body flailed around blindly for several seconds, still lashing out at everything, before it tripped over a splintered crate and landed on a blazing pyre.

The Krieg were getting the measure of these monsters now, and had the edge over them. One squad were lighting torches from the flamer fires, so that they could burn bodies without using up more promethium.

Suddenly, however, yet more bodies dropped into the trench: a second wave of zombies, in an even worse state of decay. Their clothes had rotted and green skin sloughed off their bones, erasing the distinction between loyalist and traitor. One landed close to Tyborc with a jolt that broke its brittle hips and sent it sprawling; he snatched up a shovel, the better to bludgeon it with. As more of its bones broke, one hand shot out and seized his ankle, which the zombie tried to drag towards its mouth; it took four shovel thrusts to sever its hand at the wrist, and even still its clawed fingers remained locked around his boot.

Almost seven million Korpsmen had died on Vraks, perhaps half as many traitors – and what about the native labourers in the years, in the decades, before that? How rotted did a corpse have to be before it couldn't be defiled in this manner? How long before the dead here outnumbered the living?

Perhaps, the colonel thought, they did already.

The battle raged for twenty more minutes. The Krieg, with their superior discipline, dexterity and firepower, retained the advantage, but too many fell all the same. Tyborc bore unhappy witness to a grenadier's fate as, dodging one zombie's claws, they stumbled into another, which tore out the soldier's throat with its teeth before anyone could stop it. More common were the Korpsmen who, having suffered even the shallowest of scratches, all too quickly succumbed to burning fevers and could no longer stand but were doubled up by agonising spasms.

One of the last zombies pushed its way through Tyborc's command squad – their instinct was still to surround him with a ring of steel in battle, despite his protestations – and lunged for him. He backed away from the snarling, spitting creature, firing, and felt his foot crunching through bone.

The zombie never reached him: his watchmaster leapt on its back, a brawny arm around its throat, and others thrust smouldering torches into its flesh. He tried to forget that it was a Krieg body they were burning, a Krieg voice howling and wailing in bitter frustration as its purpose was denied.

He had stamped through the ribcage of the zombie he had

fought earlier, the one whose fingers still clung to his ankle. He stooped to extricate himself from both, and noticed something he had not before: the tatters of a grey Krieg greatcoat hanging from the wretched skeleton and, on one ragged epaulet, a mud-caked badge of rank. A colonel's badge.

A pair of dog tags dangled from a chain around its neck. Unable to stop himself, Tyborc reached for them. He turned the tags over in his hand and tried to make out the name and numbers stamped into them. He couldn't – not only because they were filthy and tarnished, but because a deliberate effort had been made to scratch out the information. He couldn't help but think that might be for the best.

On day six, Tyborc's regiment was instructed to hold its ground.

Trojan support vehicles arrived unexpectedly, carrying supplies. Their cranes lowered heavy wooden crates into the trenches. Stencilled onto them in black were skull symbols over crossed bones, a dour warning of hazardous contents.

He persuaded some Trojan drivers to take sick Korpsmen back to the landing site with them. Basic first aid and a night's sleep had done some victims of the walking corpses more good than it had others. He feared that some couldn't wait for an in-demand Samaritan medical transport.

One such was his watchmaster. As he was hoisted away on a makeshift stretcher, he found a reservoir of strength and seized the colonel's wrist. 'Sir,' he wheezed, 'if I… If I don't make it…' Tyborc resisted the reflex to say, *You will. You can beat this.* It would have been just another platitude.

'Don't let me be buried,' the watchmaster begged him, 'not in Vraks' soil. Do not let this place steal my death from me.'

He squeezed his comrade's hand and nodded grimly. The watchmaster looked relieved as he was loaded into the back of the waiting truck. Tyborc wondered if he would see him again. How many watchmasters had he outlasted now? It shamed him that he had lost count.

He turned his attention to the crates. Prising one open with a crowbar, he was unsurprised by what he found inside. Chemical shells. Collaring a junior officer, he had him arrange the crates' unpacking and dispersal of their contents around his artillery units. By the time a messenger from command HQ arrived that afternoon, the colonel already knew what he would say.

He was surprised by his commissar that evening. Newly promoted to his post, he asked Tyborc a question he did not expect. 'What are your thoughts on this, colonel?'

'It wouldn't be the first use of such weapons on Vraks,' he answered guardedly.

'By the enemy, yes, but–'

He silenced the speaker with a firm shake of his head. 'Sometimes,' he growled, 'it takes fire to fight fire.'

The commissar mulled over what he had just heard, but then argued, 'Chem-weapons were outlawed for a reason. Our mission is to save this world. If we... If this bombardment goes ahead, then swathes of its land will be poisoned, inimical to human life for centuries to come.'

'The land is already poisoned,' Tyborc pointed out, 'and at least it will be the Emperor's land again.' He was thinking of his home world and suspected that the commissar, who had never set foot there, knew it, for he questioned him no more.

Confessor Tenaxus would have questioned him further, he thought. She would have drawn out his nagging doubts. He wished she were here, so he could talk the matter over with her. *As if it matters what I think,* he told himself for the thousandth time. *The decision is not mine. But if it was...*

* * *

He was never called upon to fire the chem-shells – though had he been, of course he would have done so. Other regiments did. They blanketed no-man's-land in a toxic soup thicker and greener than ever before, and then, in their impregnated greatcoats and rebreather masks, in their tanks, they advanced through it.

'I worry,' Tyborc's commissar confided in him, 'that some of the… things we have seen may suffer no harm from our poisons – as they did not from their own – but even thrive on them.' It was a doubt that had occurred to him too.

During the night, two more diseased Korpsmen had passed away. Their bodies had been burned at dawn, but they were only two of many. He prayed that, by seeding the Vraksian earth with chemicals, they could at least hasten the decay of those who lay within it – otherwise, he feared, their unwilling deeds in death may outweigh those of their lives, and what hope for his world's atonement then?

I would have done it, he decided. *I would have given that order, as Colonel Jurten once did, and would have known that the Emperor was with me.*

By the day's end, he had begun to doubt again.

The Krieg had identified an underground armoury – thought to be the traitors' last outside of the citadel – in Sector 59-44, and had made it their highest priority. An Inquisitor Vokes had taken command of the 262nd and was leading the assault, with support from the freshly deployed 61st Tank Regiment.

Initial vox-reports from the front were full of promise, but that soon changed.

'What did you hear?' asked Confessor Tenaxus, eyes narrowed.

'That foul creatures spilled from the armoury,' said Tyborc, 'with single eyes and horns on their heads, limbs shrivelled but stomachs distended. And they were plastered head to toe with dirt and had clouds of flies around them. And more than one report mentioned their voices. They had a sort of droning chant, which somehow wormed its way into the ears, into the mind and…' He shuddered, afraid to picture the scene too well.

'I have heard tell of such creatures,' Tenaxus acknowledged.

'Are they…?' He stopped himself from speaking the word, remembering her reaction when last he had.

'Mortal beings once,' said the confessor, 'afflicted with some ungodly rot.'

'Does that mean…?'

She anticipated the colonel's question. 'It cannot affect the strong of mind. Nor, in this case, the bones of the dead. Only traitors who, having consorted with the unclean, have paid an excruciating but just price for it.'

'There were also… engines,' ventured Tyborc. 'A lieutenant described it as if the traitors' tanks had been possessed and now walked on their tracks, their front ends splitting open into mouths with gnashing metal teeth.'

'Had I known of General Durjan's orders…'

'The chemical bombardment?'

'I would have advised against it.'

'Though surely the general had Inquisitor Lord Malkin's support?'

Tenaxus sighed. 'He knew the dreadful risk he took, and in some ways it was rewarded. In others…' She trailed off. Tyborc didn't press her further, but waited, eager to hear more if she deigned to share it with him.

'It is confirmed,' said Confessor Tenaxus at length, 'that the barrier between realms has been broken on Vraks.' The news, though not unexpected, felt like a hammer blow to Tyborc's heart. 'We believe that vile sorcerers used our own falling chem-shells to complete some manner of poisoning ritual.'

He understood only some of her terms of reference, but it

was enough. He focused on the most salient detail. 'Then the breach must have been in...?'

'Sector 59-44,' the confessor confirmed.

'And something came through it?'

'Many things, of which you have described some.'

'There was something else.' He swallowed dryly. 'I don't know what it was, only that it was... bigger than the others, more horrifying still, and that no Korpsman who saw it up close could begin to describe it before...' He swallowed again and shook his head. 'None of them survived.'

Tenaxus corrected him: 'Some did, but their minds were broken.'

He opened his mouth to defend his comrades' honour, to protest that such a thing was simply impossible, but he knew it to be a lie.

Tenaxus leaned across the desk between them and lowered her voice to a conspiratorial whisper. 'There were indeed daemons on the battlefield that day, Colonel Tyborc, and you should thank the Emperor that you saw nothing of them and heard little more.'

'I heard enough to haunt me to the end of my hours.'

'You should also take heart, because there were angels too.'

'We... did wonder if it may have been so.'

'Neither your general nor the inquisitor lord made their decisions lightly.'

'No, ma'am, I'm sure they didn't.'

'And they had prepared for the worst.'

'For hours,' Tyborc recalled, 'we lost contact with the 262nd Regiment. Then, just as we... as I thought all was lost, we heard from their commander again. He reported the traitors' armoury secured, and that was all. Later, I saw the rolls of the dead, Inquisitor Vokes' name among them. I saw Colonel 262 only this morning. He refused to be drawn on that day's events. If I knew no better, I would say he feared to speak of them. All he would tell me was, "The Emperor was with us."'

Tenaxus nodded, lips twitching. 'There are secrets He must keep from us, for everybody's good.' And that was her last word on the subject, which Tyborc reluctantly accepted.

He clung to the hope of angels offered by her, but kept one secret to himself.

He had intended to tell the confessor of his dreams, which had been worse than ever lately. *For what,* he thought, *if the daemons who assail my mind in sleep are real, and what if my doubts have unlocked a gateway for them?* He too was afraid, and ashamed to say the words.

Instead, he resolved to fight the daemons, fortify his mind with prayer and drive them from his thoughts forever. For wasn't he a Krieg Death Korpsman, after all? An heir to Colonel Jurten? Nor was he just some nameless soldier either. He was Colonel Tyborc, of whom the lower ranks and even priests spoke in awe.

He was a hero.

ACT FOUR

WAR OF FAITH

827–829.M41

Under the firm hand of the Ordo Malleus – and Inquisitor Lord Hector Rex, whose willpower matched his giant stature, effectively our new commander-in-chief – the course of the war was radically altered.

There had been upheavals in the enemy camp too, as the testimonies of captured traitors told us, although the full story would only be divined by our telepaths later. The apostate cardinal, Xaphan, instigator of this conflict, had reaped the bitter fruit of his actions. His first and closest ally among the Traitor legionaries – Chaos Lord Arkos the Faithless, his own position weakened since his humiliation at the star port – had inevitably turned on him and imprisoned him.

The new master of the Citadel of Vraks was Zhufor, head of a Traitor Space Marine warband known for very good reason as the Skulltakers. Through a combination of threats, bribery and displays of strength, he had united disparate traitor factions under him – even besting the Berserkers of Skallathrax's commander in a savage, un-armoured death duel.

No longer were we striving to save a world. The fate of Vraks seemed hardly to matter any longer, in this clash between two powerful and utterly inimical forces, each pledged to eradicate the other. Some things, however, didn't change. The outcome of the war would still hinge upon the Krieg's best efforts. An Imperial victory could only be built upon our bones.

I first met Inquisitor Lord Rex when he sentenced me to death.

– From the account of Veteran Colonel Tyborc

X

Many were the heroes of the war on Vraks.

Many were the names of fallen Korpsmen inscribed upon Krieg's mausolea to inspire those millions who followed in their footsteps and also mark the incremental progress of that blighted world towards its far-off absolution.

But many more in number were those Krieg who died unnamed, whose fate it was to be forgotten, each in their own ways heroes too.

One such, whose story was unearthed by Confessor Tenaxus, was dubbed by her the Hero of Hangman's Hill.

She knew neither his name nor his number.

She only knew his rank, which was lieutenant – by virtue of a battlefield promotion, she had to assume. No paperwork for this had been filed, likely because of the death of his company commander.

As a member of the still-young 468th Siege Regiment, he must have played a part in the big push of five years ago, breaking through the traitors' second defence line at the cost of Colonel Attas' life. He must have sheltered at the base of Mortuary Ridge from the orbital bombardment of the battleship *Anarchy's Heart*. As an acting lieutenant, he had served in his regiment's 15th Company, leading its Fourth Platoon; before that, Tenaxus couldn't say.

As demanded by the lord inquisitor, the Krieg were tightening their cordon round the Citadel of Vraks. In their sector to the north, however, our unnamed hero's regiment had found its approach stalled by difficult terrain.

For months, they were pinned down in bleak grey, craggy hills, battling their way from one concealed, grimly defended bunker to the next. Approaching the range's southern tip, they had been harassed by traitor guns within the curtain wall. An engineer company had been sent to build a temporary road so that much-needed artillery support could reach them. They had blasted through rock, laid asphalt strips, but under unremitting fire they had perished in their hundreds, and so progress had been achingly slow.

The new Colonel 468, tired of waiting for his tanks as his regiment was whittled down around him, had decided to wait no longer. Under cover of the night – by which his predecessor had achieved his final, greatest victory – he led an infantry assault upon the first of three defence laser silos.

Though set up to defend against attacks from the sky, the silo's guns had been retrained, and searing energy beams lashed from it, adding to the deadly hail of the usual bolter and autogun bullets. The Krieg, of course, had not flinched from the storm, and very many had been slaughtered, but dawn had found them standing over traitor corpses in the silo's rubble, and so their appalling casualty rate was judged to have been worth the gain.

A few nights later, they had launched a similar attack upon the second silo, with similar results – and, a few nights after that, upon the third. With each attack spearheaded by a different company, our hero must surely have been in the thick of one of them. He must have seen comrades scythed down or blasted into oblivion around him and must have fought on undeterred, spared by the Emperor's grace perhaps because He had decreed a higher purpose for him.

He was probably a watchmaster or quartermaster at that time. Along with the rest of his company, he must have looked up with some trepidation at their next seemingly insurmountable challenge, jutting into the sullen sky above them.

Point 202. So it was marked on their tactical maps. The final obstacle between them and the curtain wall. Enemy forces had massed atop it, and they too had been busy in the night. They had erected gibbets on the summit and hung the bodies of Krieg prisoners, taken in nocturnal raids over the past weeks, from them. Some bodies were in wooden cages, others left to twist and rot slowly in the breeze.

By all accounts, it was a display of such morbidity as to be worthy of the Death Korps themselves – for which reason, its orchestrators should have known that it would not deter them in the slightest. Rather, it was now that Point 202 received its new, macabre but evocative, name.

The Krieg's mortars pounded the northern slope of Hangman's Hill. Lacking the power to reach all the way to its summit, their main goal was to lay down smoke cover for what was to come.

At the firing of a signal flare, 15th Company sprang into action. Already they were under strength from recent gruelling months, with most platoons down to only four squads or fewer, but this didn't dampen their zeal.

They attacked the hillside with their lasguns blazing. The enemy responded with las-fire and bullets of their own. They sent grenades rolling and skipping down the hill, bursting into deadly clouds of shredded rock and metal.

Was our hero among them at this time? Tenaxus didn't know, but she suspected not, considering how this first attempt turned out.

A few squads made it to the top. Too few. They set about the traitors with their blades and took more lives than they lost, but failed to dislodge gunners and grenade launchers from their advantageous positions, failed to clear a path for those behind them. As the sun began to set, their writhing silhouettes were framed against a backdrop of glowering red.

Lower down the hill, the company captain lay dying. A sniper's bullet had punched through his helmet, into his head. A current of scree had swept him over a sheer outcrop, and now he was sprawled out in the open where no medic could get to him without also being shot down.

His deputy put a whistle to his lips and blew the signal for withdrawal. Had he waited too long, in the hope that the captain could somehow be saved yet? Tenaxus had the impression that some of his subordinates thought so, though never would they have said it aloud.

Regardless, the Krieg by all accounts had remained characteristically bullish. They hadn't been defeated, only slowed. They had reduced the traitors' numbers, but replenished their own from the 468th's other companies. When they made their second attempt upon Hangman's Hill, it would be against odds that had shifted just a little in their favour – and not one of them doubted that there would be a second attempt, for what else were they to do?

More than one Korpsman quoted Captain Denos, 19th Company's commander. *To retreat is defeat,* he was reputed to have said.

Advance! Advance! In our death lies victory. This left an impression on Tenaxus, as the maxims of the Krieg tended to be drawn from the long-dead-and-buried rather than from the still-living.

In the end, there were three more assaults upon Hangman's Hill.

For a second and a third time, the Krieg were repulsed and scores of them lost their lives, but they took solace in the knowledge that their foes had also bled.

Nor, as far as their spotters could tell, were the traitors reinforced, which wasn't surprising. Though they had received little news from elsewhere along the front, they had heard of Krieg units making sweeping gains, finding outposts empty, vehicles and equipment abandoned. Where renegade militiamen had been found cowering, many of them had simply surrendered.

Though the traitors atop Hangman's Hill were more stubborn than many, the officers of the 468th Regiment felt sure they would break too. How could they not, when faced with wave after undiminished wave of implacable attackers? Could they really still be more afraid of their leaders in the citadel behind them? If so, then that was something the Krieg would have to change.

As for our unnamed hero, he must have transferred into 15th Company around this time, and surely joined at least one failed assault. He may have distinguished himself in this battle, for it was likely in its wake that he received his unsanctioned promotion – bestowed upon him by an inexperienced captain requiring a deputy, having neither time nor ability to comb through records and work out which surviving comrade ought to have been next in line.

Once he had donned his new lieutenant's badges, few of the Krieg themselves could have told him apart from their previous wearer.

Tenaxus only knew that, when they made their fourth assault upon Hangman's Hill, the one that would ultimately prove to be successful, this rookie but valiant lieutenant fought at the vanguard of it.

They launched their final assault at night.

Partly, this was to take the hill's fatigued defenders off-guard, a strategy that had lately worked well for them. Partly, it was because their mortars had run dry of shells and couldn't provide them with cover, so the dark would have to do.

The dour silhouette of Hangman's Hill loomed before the young lieutenant. He could no longer see to its top, couldn't see the bodies exhibited there, their numbers having grown in recent days. He knew that as long as he climbed, though, he would be heading in the right direction. He also knew that somewhere on the hillside was the regimental banner and, although he couldn't see it, its presence inspired him.

He hauled himself up the treacherous slope, its surface giving way beneath his boots, sliding him back one step for every two he took. He didn't think about how far he had to go. He did as he had always done, as Death Korpsmen did: he advanced one step at a time and tried not to stumble over his predecessors' corpses.

His company fanned out across the hillside, using the landscape to their best advantage, darting between rocks, ducking into hollows. Whenever the lieutenant saw a muzzle flash above him, he aimed a las-beam at it. For once, he didn't have to conserve ammunition. He salvaged power packs from three dead Korpsmen in his path, tossing most of them to comrades.

'Keep firing,' he barked at them, repeating their captain's instructions. 'Don't let up for a second. Tonight, we take this blasted hill at last, or else by dawn our bodies hang upon it and we add to our world's shame!'

Undercutting his words, a grenade burst nearby without warning, shrapnel tearing through his greatcoat. He half-dived, was half-thrown, to the ground, turning an ankle in the process. His left arm stung. It was bleeding, but the cut looked shallow.

As the lieutenant raised his head ruefully, two Korpsmen dropped beside him, offering assistance. Irritably, he waved them away. He was an officer now, frustrated with himself. He had to do better.

His ankle protested as he tried to stand. He judged that it wasn't strained or broken, though. He was halfway to the summit; he could see a jagged line where black sky met blacker earth. He propped himself against a rocky ledge and strafed that line until his power pack was dry, then slapped another into place.

He was being left behind by his platoon. He tested his weight on his ankle, which fortunately had calmed enough to bear it. Limping only slightly, the lieutenant ploughed onwards and upwards.

Approaching the crest of Hangman's Hill, his platoon found themselves ambushed.

Instead of waiting for their attackers to reach them, traitors came bounding down the slope with feral howls, spraying bullets out before them with abandon.

Having not expected such a brazen move, half a dozen Korpsmen were caught in the open and shot down. Others leapt for cover and sniping positions, while more – those with no better option – simply charged on through the onslaught, frenetically working their own triggers.

Still lagging behind his comrades, the lieutenant was almost bowled over by more than one Krieg or traitor body rolling and bouncing past him, bones snapping with each impact. The gunfire around him lessened as the two small but determined forces closed swiftly with each other. Detaching his bayonet from his lasgun, wielding it like a sword, he rushed to join them.

Among the traitors, he identified one, more muscular than most, barking orders at the rest, clad in barely scuffed carapace armour. At his shoulder, a filthy, cringing wretch hoisted a tattered banner, blood-red and black, a mockery of the Krieg's own standard. The lieutenant couldn't make out the intricate symbols stitched into it and dared not look too hard as they made him feel uneasy.

He felt the ragged cloth were somehow radiating hate, which battered him almost like a physical force, at the same time stoking the fervour of the renegade militiamen; a pair of them rose up before him, keeping him from their presumed leader, and the eyes behind their masks were red and crazed.

One fought with a long-bladed knife; the other was unarmed, but swiped at the lieutenant with a matted, hairy claw, which he barely saw coming in time. He winced as he was pushed back onto his bad foot. He parried a knife thrust from the first militiaman, seeing that his gas mask had split at his temple and a stubby, twisted horn of bone was poking through.

It didn't surprise him that these traitors bore the marks of their foul heresy. It only spurred him into fighting harder.

One of them, the one with the claws, sprang at him and bore him to the ground, where they wrestled, the mutant trying to pin the lieutenant down, his main concern to use it as a shield, keeping it between him and its comrade, who had drawn a laspistol and was looking for a shot at him.

Talons raked his chest, but he managed to swat the mutant's arm aside and slit its throat. Disgusting black blood welled up from the wound and spattered on his lenses. He pushed the mutant's twitching body off him, exposing himself for the second it took him to clamber to his feet, less smoothly than he would have liked. By the Emperor's grace, a fellow Korpsman had engaged the horned mutant with the pistol, which now had its back to him. The lieutenant thrust his blade between its ribs, glad to find that its heart was still where it ought to have been.

Whirling in search of his next opponent, he saw a scrawny figure draped in rags. Rather than a full face mask, it wore a respirator over its nose and mouth, exposing mottled skin and wisps of dark hair sprouting from an egg-shaped head. Though Korpsmen and militiamen were brawling closer to it, the creature ignored them, glaring past them at the young lieutenant.

Its white eyes caught his gaze and trapped it. The creature raised an emaciated finger, pointing directly at him, and he felt fear like he had never known before – an existential terror. He had been birthed only to suffer and die and be forgotten, and how was that fair? He wanted to turn and run and not stop running until he had outrun everything he ever was, outrun himself.

He overcame the impulse with thoughts of the heroes of Krieg. He muttered their names to himself, from Colonel Jurten to Captain Tyborc and Colonel Attas, and the sound of those names bolstered him – for his life was only worthless if their lives had been too, which would make atonement unattainable.

His mind clearing, he remembered being warned that the enemy had witches among them, an entire coven of them. One was worming its way into his mind with blasphemous lies, but his training allowed him to resist such warp-spawned violations. The lieutenant thought about what mattered, what he knew to be true – the Emperor and his people's debt to Him – and, though his arm felt leaden and too heavy to lift, through force of will he raised it and yanked on his lasgun's trigger. And just like that the fear was gone and the real world that had somehow slipped away from him suddenly snapped back into focus.

He had shot the psyker in its shoulder. It wailed as it clutched a skeletal hand to the burn, as a pair of Korpsmen took advantage of its weakness to rush it with their bayonets. He saw now that it was already badly wounded, in no state to resist them. He set his sights upon the traitors' leader, now tantalisingly within reach.

No one got in his way this time; few combatants remained from either faction. Only as the lieutenant closed with his opponent and found that he didn't fight alone did he know that his faction was winning.

The arch-heretic fought as if possessed – perhaps he was, from all the rumours circulating in the trenches – shrugging off cuts and blows that would have felled an ogryn. Along with his fine armour, Vraks' armouries had gifted him an energy-charged flail. Its striking head sizzled as he swung it on a gleaming chain, its spikes rending greatcoats, cracking armour plates, and scattering the Korpsmen that assailed him from all sides.

A glancing blow sent our hero reeling, and a sergeant in his eyeline sustained a shattered jaw. Two Korpsmen fell and didn't stand again and more were badly wounded. The lieutenant's chest felt tight; he thought he might have cracked a rib. He looked for an opening and threw himself at the arch-heretic again.

He managed to pin a brawny arm, stilling that deadly flail – for only a second before, with fanatical strength, the traitor wrenched himself free, but a second long enough. The traitor disappeared beneath a writhing mass of Korpsmen. When the lieutenant, thrown free from the scrum, next saw his body, it had been roughly hacked to pieces and, with a final sigh, it collapsed into a heap of bloody meat.

Beside the arch-heretic's mutilated corpse lay his standard bearer, burnt black by a Krieg flamer, shreds of his hateful banner strewn about him. The lieutenant took inordinate pleasure in grinding them into the dirt with his boot heel.

* * *

Fourth Platoon's survivors collected around him.

They were only a handful in number, but those heroic few had outlasted their enemies, which was all that mattered.

Still limping, he led them the final few steps up Hangman's Hill, unsure what they would find atop it. The company vox-caster had been lost weeks ago, denying him updates from its other platoons. No withdrawal had been sounded within his earshot, however, and the clamour of battle had subsided.

The lieutenant passed an overturned heavy stubber, the bodies of its traitor crew beside it. He was cautiously hopeful as figures loomed ahead of him, then gratified to see that they were masked by Krieg rebreathers. They were already cutting comrades down from the makeshift gallows.

A few more steps and the Citadel of Vraks rose up before him on its mountaintop, its spires and towers black against the still-dark sky. Its curtain wall stretched across the valley floor between them, and he looked down upon its parapets.

The final barrier between the Krieg army and its goal. The lieutenant's mind rested on that thought for a moment, and it dulled the pain he must have been in.

'Sir,' said a voice at his elbow. He turned to the speaker, a watchmaster. 'Sir, you are the ranking officer.'

'Surely not,' he said. 'What of the captain?'

'I saw him fall to bolter fire, along with his command squad.'

He looked around, scanning his comrades' shoulders for badges of rank. There had to be someone here with more experience than he. Another battered squad attained the summit. A pair of them cradled the regimental banner between them, doubtless salvaged from the body of its bearer. More rank-and-file Korpsmen. Others were closing in around him, looking to him.

They were his responsibility.

His first instinct, the same as theirs, was that he needed orders.

He picked a relatively unscathed Korpsman and despatched him back to the trenches to report the success of their mission to the 468th's commander.

The regimental banner was brought forward and offered to him. Nonplussed, the lieutenant took it, and at the very moment that he did, Vraks' sun broke the eastern horizon and bathed the scene in hues of pre-dawn crimson.

The Hero of Hangman's Hill. This was his moment.

At least, that was how Confessor Tenaxus imagined it had happened.

She had put the story together from accounts of wounded Korpsmen in the medicae huts. By the time she travelled to the trenches to relay it to the Korpsmen there, she found that many already knew it, the story having sped ahead of her.

Versions of it echoed back to her, each with its own embellishments. The story seemed to exercise the Krieg imagination even more so than her tales of other heroes. She wondered why this was, especially considering her failure to name the Hero of Hangman's Hill. She concluded that his very anonymity was appealing to his comrades. He could have been any one of them, doing his duty, by chance finding himself in the right place at the right time to become something more, someone to be remembered.

She wondered where he was now. Still camped out on the slopes of Hangman's Hill, waiting for an order to march on the citadel itself? The Krieg had completed their road at last and rolled their cannons forward. Though they were still beset by traitor fire, no longer were there spotters at Point 202 to guide it.

No doubt they had buried, or burnt, the bodies of their dead, restoring them to rest. There were versions of the story in which the young lieutenant had died too, succumbing to his wounds only hours after his great triumph. If that were indeed the case, then perhaps it was even for the best.

She remembered discussing the Krieg's heroes with the then-Captain Tyborc, on a medicae ward a seeming lifetime ago. *The only difference I see between them and you is that they died, while you still live.*

When my time comes at last to give my life, he had said to her, years later, *I cannot hesitate. I cannot doubt my duty, believing it beneath me.* She had waved his doubts aside, believing him incapable of understanding. Since then, she had come to see him as a wiser man than anybody knew.

It might be best, she thought, if that young lieutenant wasn't seen again, if he never returned from the front to claim credit for his actions, never carried the weight of his comrades' expectations, never had his name tarnished by potential future failure.

Best if he rested where his story ended, in the dirt of Hangman's Hill; in that way, in some way, he could represent them all.

Tenaxus had taken another shuttle flight to Thracian Primaris. Hardly had she left its space port when she learned that her trip had been in vain.

She had failed to procure a meeting with Inquisitor Lord Hector Rex, nor any member of his command staff, in large part because they were busy preparing to relocate to Vraks itself. Hastily pulling whatever strings she could, she had beaten them back there by a day and a half.

Her first sight of the lord inquisitor, therefore, came as he disembarked from his ornate landing craft, surrounded by a retinue of warriors, servitor-scribes, and one pale, dark-robed, white-eyed figure whom she took to be an astropath. Even Lord Marshal Kagori followed him meekly down the ramp.

Rex himself was impressively tall and broad, clad in fur-trimmed robes that only added to his muscular bulk. Dark hair framed a craggy face crazed with battle scars. His deep blue, piercing eyes possessed an intense quality that made the confessor feel they could strip layers of her soul away, even at such a distance, through the crowd that had gathered to greet him.

He wore his badge of office, the 'I' symbol of the Inquisition, on a heavy golden chain about his neck. A tiny creature hovered at his shoulder, with feathered wings fluttering: a cybernetic cherub, likely a psychic familiar.

It was an impressive entrance, putting her uncomfortably in mind of the last revered holy man to arrive on this planet. Today, it was the Proctor-General of the Scarus Conclave; last time, it had been the Cardinal-Astral of the Scarus Sector.

For six weeks, Tenaxus had worked to secure a meeting with the lord inquisitor. Whispers had reached her ears that the Ordo Malleus, which Rex represented, was at odds with the Ordo Hereticus over his plans for Vraks; the confessor felt that her own body, the Adeptus Ministorum, ought also to be heard.

She was granted her audience, but not with Hector Rex. Inquisitor Lord Malkin towered over her in his suit of armour, and she regretted taking the seat he had offered her. Malkin himself didn't sit. She wondered if he could in the armour, if a chair could bear its weight. She imagined it supported his aged muscles well enough.

She opened by stating her credentials, which he waved aside. 'I have too much to do and too few days left ahead of me to waste time on formalities,' he told her, not unpleasantly.

Tenaxus nodded. 'Very well, my lord.'

Malkin had been interrogating prisoners, especially those who had deserted from inside the citadel. Having done the same herself, she hoped to share their findings, but Malkin revealed that he had already read her reports to the Ecclesiarchal Palace.

Though taken by surprise, she pressed on boldly: 'Of course, there is much that, for the sake of prudence, may not be written in reports. The presence on Vraks, for example, of the Ordo Malleus' Chamber Militant.'

She expected a reaction to that statement, but was disappointed. The inquisitor's expression was inscrutable. 'Was there something you wished to ask me, Confessor Tenaxus?'

She cleared her throat. 'There has been much talk of the lord inquisitor's plans for Vraks and, having been here since–'

Malkin interrupted her. 'This war has dragged on more than long enough – you wouldn't disagree with that? – and the cost of past delays has been extreme. Regrettable as it may appear to some, our response must be equally extreme. The time has come to take decisive action.'

'I understand, my lord.' She tried again. 'But having been here since the war began, observing its progress, I feel I have earned–'

'Then tell me,' Malkin growled, 'how many rifts have opened here? How many horrors of the warp have already slipped through? Too many to be happenstance, I'm sure you must also agree.'

'You concur with my assessment that there may be–'

'Sorcerers on Vraks, making offer of the blood of millions spilled on its battlefields to feed the insatiable lust of the Ruinous Powers.'

Tenaxus swallowed. 'If that is indeed so, my lord, then–'

'They must be destroyed!' The servos in Malkin's armour whirred as his gauntlet made a fist. 'Even if this world and everything on it must burn.' He had cut to the heart of Tenaxus' concern and clearly knew it.

'The 88th Siege Army was formed to save Vraks,' she protested.

'Since which time, the situation and our mission parameters have changed.' Malkin fixed her with a challenging glare.

'My lord, this is a shrine world, a required stop on the Devotion to the Ten Thousand Martyrs of Scarus pilgrimage route. Surely there must still be a way to–'

His dark augmetic eye flashed dangerously. 'Lord Rex is well aware of the value to the Ecclesiarchy of Saint Leonis' remains.'

'They are beyond value,' insisted Tenaxus.

'But let me ask you this, confessor – is the preservation of one dead saint's bones worth the real and imminent risk of an entire sector falling to Chaos?'

'What price would you place on faith, inquisitor?' she responded, stubbornly.

'Millions more lives could be lost if we dare to hold back.'

'I assure you, the Krieg would gladly make that sacrifice.'

'Lord Rex will not,' the inquisitor declared, and he turned his back, signalling that the discussion was over. 'The decision is made,' he informed the confessor in a low, rustling voice. 'We will strike the Citadel of Vraks with every weapon, every force we can muster. We will bury the traitors and their blasphemous allies in its rubble – and if that means your basilica too must be pounded into dust, then so be it.'

Tenaxus waited at the landing plateau for a shuttle.

Fifteen years, she thought bitterly. *Fifteen years have I languished here on Vraks, and what has it availed me? I can't save the holy shrine. I have failed in my duty, failed the memory of my blessed forebears, failed the Emperor Himself.*

Vraks' sulphuric rain beat down upon her head, fitting her mood. *Now, all that remains is for me to return to my ministry, to make my own confession…* She drew her cloak tight about herself and clutched at her staff's double-headed eagle.

She couldn't help but think about Hangman's Hill.

She couldn't drive the image from her mind, the one that every Korpsman she had questioned had described to her. The young, unnamed lieutenant, filthy, bloody, tired, but standing at the summit, standing proud, being handed his regiment's banner, unsure what to do with it at first but then finding his resolve.

He had taken four steps towards the highest point he saw, where he had planted the Krieg's flag in the ground. This land, he had declared, with a corona of sunlight around him as if to signal the approval of the Emperor, was Imperial land once more. He pledged his life and the lives of the Korpsmen he now commanded, at least in that moment, for that day, to its defence.

Such a small gain in the scheme of things, that tiny scrap of ground, and yet…

The shuttle was coming in to land. A Krieg platoon was waiting to unload tanks of water from it, fresh from the reservoirs of Paeleos VIII. Tenaxus could leave Vraks behind forever, shake its grey dirt from her boots. She longed with all her heart to do so, but knew she would never forget.

She thought about that tiny victory, how much it had meant to the Krieg. For them, it seemed to be a symbol of everything that truly mattered: that they did not surrender. They didn't run away. When they were knocked down, they picked themselves up and fought on, and died in the knowledge that even the smallest difference they had made had been worthwhile.

For weeks, Tenaxus had preached to them about the Hero of Hangman's Hill. She ought to have listened to the story herself. It struck her that the shame she was feeling was not only due to her failure.

By the time the shuttle had set down, she was no longer waiting for it. She had turned and strode back to her quarters. Taking inspiration from the Death Korps of Krieg, Confessor Tenaxus had resolved to fight on.

XI

Commissar-General Maugh rarely found himself surprised, least of all by the colonel alongside whom he served.

For twenty-two years, he had been attached to the 143rd Krieg Siege Regiment, which for most of that time had been commanded by Colonel Thyran. Despite their different backgrounds, the two soldiers had found much in common.

When the colonel issued orders, Maugh knew what they would be, for even if there had been no discussion beforehand, they were the orders he would have given. Whenever the colonel took to the battlefield himself, his commissar was there to watch his back and vice versa.

Until this time.

With the breaching of the curtain wall around the citadel and the arrival on Vraks of Hector Rex, it had seemed as if victory was within reach at last.

Then had come news that some Death Korps regiments were

to be withdrawn, the Departmento Munitorum in its wisdom feeling them better employed in other arenas. From what little Maugh could discern, the Ordo Malleus being famously tight-lipped, Lord Rex had protested this decision strenuously, only to be undermined by the Ordo Hereticus for its own opaque reasons.

So it was that, at 253828.M41, the depleted First Line Korps was disbanded. The survivors of its three remaining regiments tramped up the loading ramps of drop-ships and, one company at a time, were whisked away. Lost also was 19th Bombardment Korps, taking with them fully half of the 88th Army's heavy artillery, and most of Eighth Assault Korps, leaving only one of its tank regiments behind.

The lord inquisitor had redrawn his plans accordingly, with 12th Line Korps required to take up much of the slack created by the absence of the First. This meant redeploying to the trenches vacated by them, ensuring that the ring around the citadel remained unbroken, albeit now somewhat thinner.

It also meant inheriting their mission objectives. Specifically, Third Regiment had been poised to strike at the curtain wall's main gate, in Sector 579-459. Lord Rex considered this key to his long-term strategy, for with the gate captured, the traitors couldn't hold the wall itself. The attack, therefore, would go ahead as planned, and 12th Line Korps would provide a regiment to make it so.

That honour had fallen to the 143rd. The surprise for its commissar-general was that Colonel Thyran had assigned him to lead the assault.

He would do so from inside *Landwaster*, a Leman Russ tank that he had commanded in several battles before. The Krieg had given it a fresh coat of paint for the occasion. It was a dull but solid grey, with crisp white regimental markings. Five skull decals along its turret had been preserved and refreshed, each representing an enemy tank destroyed by its Demolisher cannon.

The Demolisher was one of the Astra Militarum's most powerful line-breaking tools. A single shot from it would shatter the traitors' gate, if only Maugh could get it close enough. Its short range was its only drawback. *Landwaster*'s front armour had been reinforced to protect it from its own gun's blowback.

Maugh entered through the tank's side hatch and climbed up into the turret. His primary gunner, younger and more agile, scrambled up the vehicle's side and dropped into place beside him. His driver was already running through last-minute cogitator checks, while two sponson gunners and a loader rounded out the six-strong crew, squeezing into the cramped compartment below him.

Fine-tuning the vox-caster beside his head, he sent an instruction to the driver, who fired up the engine. Maugh felt its power thrumming through his seat, through his bones, through the armour-plated plasteel hull around him.

Hunched over his auspex surveyor, he took readings off the distant curtain wall, which told him little. Krieg guns had been pounding it all morning, shrouding it in smoke. The heat flashes of its defenders' weapons did appear to have lessened in frequency, perhaps only because they were now harder to detect.

It was up to him to judge when those defences would be weakest, choose the opportune moment for his tank squadrons to push forward. It was his responsibility alone. Thyran wouldn't be joining him on the battlefield this time, despite this mission's paramount importance or perhaps because of it.

The projected casualty rate was brutally high. Too high to risk the early loss of the regimental banner. *Even if,* Maugh thought dourly, *it can be replaced more easily than anybody knows.* Hence the colonel held the banner back for later, for when both it and he could truly make a difference. Still, he needed someone to lead the charge, someone he trusted implicitly to represent him.

The moment had come.

So the commissar's instincts told him – at least, that there would be none better. He ordered his driver to advance. He didn't vox the other tanks. Instead he stood up in his turret, letting their crews see him and know him to be with them. He signalled to them with a sweep of his arm and heard their engines also roaring into life, almost drowning out the thunder of the guns.

Landwaster juddered over blasted ground strewn with shell casings and studded with craters. Maugh had to cling to the turret's rim or risk being pitched from it. He knew he should take shelter, but he couldn't resist a look behind him first.

Spread out in a V-formation with him at its point was an inspiring display of armoured might: Chimeras, massive Baneblades, Leman Russes, an ancient pair of Ragnaroks straight from Krieg itself, whatever Colonel Thyran had been able to lay his hands on, and stomping up behind these, two Reaver Titans of the Legio Astorum, as breathtaking to the commissar as when he had first set eyes upon them.

He didn't think he had ever felt prouder.

If I don't die in battle soon, I may have to retire.

How long ago had he said those words to Thyran? They echoed through Maugh's head now as his senses returned to him slowly.

He was face down in the dirt. His left shoulder ached and, as he tried to lift his head, the pain flared up so strongly that his mind retreated from it, back towards the comfort of oblivion. He clenched his teeth, willing himself to stay awake, alive. He lay and focused on his breathing as he gathered up the fragments of his memory.

He remembered being head down in *Landwaster*'s turret. Aware of the rest of the world only through his surveyor and vox-earpiece. The ping of bullets off the hull, some too close by his ear. The answering chatter of his sponson-mounted bolters. His primary gunner, pressed up against him, waiting eagerly to bring the big Demolisher to bear.

He remembered the shrieks of missiles overhead as the Titans to his rear emptied their pods towards the curtain wall. He saw the heat flare as a Chimera on his right flank was struck by an enemy shell and blown apart. As the wall's cold expanse drew inexorably closer, a gap appeared in it, created not by the Krieg assault but because its huge, armoured main gate was rolling back.

Pouring through it came a great mass of infantry and tanks. Maugh made a slashing motion to his gunner and *Landwaster* was immediately bucked by the Demolisher's recoil, its front end lifting off the ground, slamming back down again. Scores of traitors were consumed in that first blast; Maugh yelled down to his loader to speed up, even as he was shouldering a fresh shell up into the breech.

Still, by the time his cannon roared again, its targets had had time to fan out and were surging towards him. His surveyor had highlighted shapes among them that it was unable to label; they read as machinery but scuttled like spiders on multiple twisted limbs. Maugh had not needed to name them to understand they had to be destroyed, and he had had his gunner target a cluster of them.

He had ordered his driver to brake and let his infantry – just two of the 143rd's twelve companies for now – sweep past him. The enemy tanks blazed too, and their guns wiped out whole Krieg platoons before they even met the oncoming horde. Maugh had mouthed a silent prayer of thanks to the Emperor that, this time, he wasn't among them on the ground but was cocooned in Imperial armour.

That prayer turned to dust on his tongue as *Landwaster* juddered into motion once again.

There had been no warning of the shell that tore through his turret. Suddenly, Maugh had found himself in a world of fire and smoke and noise and pain. His control runes had half-melted into his gloves as his gunner's headless corpse had slumped against him. For a dizzying moment, he wasn't sure if the tank was even upright, but instinct had guided his fumbling fingers to the turret hatch release and he had pulled it. He had scrambled up through the hatch, flames licking at his boots.

The last thing he remembered was leaping from *Landwaster*'s roof as the flames caught its ammunition stores and it exploded. The searing blast had caught him in midair and thrown him. A shrapnel hail had overtaken him and he had felt an intense stab of pain as a large, hot, twisted plasteel dagger had punched through his shoulder, pushing out a gout of blood, and then…

He heard the rumbling of guns, but in the distance. His comm-bead had been jolted from his throat and Maugh couldn't find it. He tried to call for help, but he could form no sound but a pitiful whimper, which no one was around to hear. The battle had moved on while he had slept.

He had been left for dead.

He managed to twist his neck to see the burning wreck beside him. None of *Landwaster*'s crew could have survived. No one but him. It must have been assumed that he had been cremated with them. Had his body been discovered, then a quartermaster would have been summoned. Maugh would have had medical

assistance or, were this considered futile, then his equipment would have been salvaged from him. He felt his power sword against his hip.

If I don't die in battle soon... Lying helpless on the ground, feeling a deep, cold numbness gnawing its way through his limbs, Maugh thought of Colonel Thyran. *Perhaps it is time, then,* he had said, and suddenly, Maugh knew what he had previously only suspected and tried to deny. He knew he had been sent out here to die, and he knew exactly why.

His colonel had believed he was doing him a favour.

The sounds of battle brought him round again.

The first thing Maugh felt was burning shame, because his will had failed and oblivion had claimed him. The second, which he fiercely denied to himself, was disappointment, because his suffering was not yet over.

The pain from his shoulder was duller than it had been, easier to bear. His body, he suspected, was going into shock. He pushed himself up onto his right elbow. Though black smoke swirled about him, through it he could make out writhing, ghost-like figures. He couldn't tell which were Krieg and which their foes, but the third thing Maugh felt was hope that this time they might find him.

He realised how unlikely that was. The traitors had the upper hand against his comrades, to have pushed them back this far. The main gate wouldn't fall today, but very many Korps-men would. Perhaps, he thought, that was why he hadn't died yet – because he was still needed, because he could still make a difference.

The main thing Commissar-General Maugh felt was resolve.

With his good arm, he levered himself to his feet. The pain was excruciating, not only in his shoulder but lighting up his every nerve; it was all he could do to hold in a scream, which he did although no one would have heard it. He drew his sword, gripping it in two hands as if to draw strength from it. He straightened and brushed down his proud black uniform, though it was scorched and caked in mud and blood. He took one faltering, jerking step forward, then another.

Each breath felt like sandpaper in his lungs, his racing heart felt as though it would give out at any moment, but somehow he stayed upright. He stumbled on towards the writhing ghosts, willing one of them to see him – any one of them, friend or foe; it would be up to the Emperor to choose.

One of them did, at last.

A figure came stomping through the smoke towards him. A giant of a man made even larger by his blood-red, skull-adorned plate armour. In one hand alone, he hefted a massive, whirring chainaxe; the other was encased in a red-glowing, sparking, spitting power fist. He fixed his prey with a crimson, blazing glare through a face mask of interlocking fangs.

Even in full health, even with a command squad behind him, Maugh would have found this a daunting opponent. In his current condition... He thanked the Emperor for him. He thought of Colonel Thyran, poring over a report, learning that a random shell fired without even being aimed by some unknown, snivelling traitor had taken his commissar's life. Now, instead, he would be told that Maugh was slain in single combat with a blood-ravening Champion of Chaos.

A story worthy of him. He knew it should not have mattered, but it did.

The duel was entirely one-sided and brutally short. A single chainaxe blow smashed Maugh's sword from his hands and knocked him down. The power fist lashed out and caught his head before he could roll away. The last sound he heard, before his skull was crushed, was his killer laughing in his face.

The battle for Gate 579-459 had entered its fifth bloody day.

The gate itself had fallen on the first, vaporised by the Titan *Aeacus Ultra*'s melta cannon. The traitors, however, steadfastly defended the breach, no matter how many Krieg came rushing at them to be cut down or beaten back.

Colonel Thyran had sent his final company into the fray this morning. He had no more forces to commit.

Aeacus Ultra had been forced to retire two days ago, crippled by the neutron laser of a Valdor tank hunter, but the enemy was clearly tiring too. As was so often the case where the Krieg were concerned, this would be a war of attrition.

The colonel was holding one last card in reserve, and that was his own command squad. He had assembled them in a front-line trench, where he monitored reports and waited for his moment. The decision would be his alone. He had thought to discuss it with his commissar, but something had stopped him.

His new commissar…

The voice of one of his spotters crackled over the vox-net. *'Sir, I see him.'*

'Are you certain? Can anyone confirm?'

'Hard to see… He's surrounded by traitors in Terminator armour, just as he was before, but yes, sir, this matches our reports.'

Thyran nodded to himself. He glanced at his commissar beside him. In his crisp black uniform and Krieg rebreather mask, he resembled his predecessor closely, apart from the lack of a general's badges. His record was just as immaculate and, having served with various of the 143rd's companies since before Vraks, clearly he knew the Death Korps of Krieg, which was why the colonel had asked for him. He could trust him. He hadn't truly spoken his mind to his new commissar yet, though, nor shown him his face. He didn't think he ever would.

Nothing has changed, he told himself, but everything had changed.

'Colonel,' the commissar prompted him, 'the enemy's leader has taken to the field. For the sake of the regiment's morale–'

'Agreed,' he interrupted. 'As I planned.'

He blew his signal whistle and was first to mount the scaling ladders.

A traitor charged screaming at the colonel, whirling a flail about himself.

Thyran stepped to him when the traitor expected the opposite. With a deft thrust of his sabre, he skewered the militiaman's wrist, so that his weapon flew from his numbed fingers into his own face, shattering his nose. The traitor reeled, stunned, as the sabre flashed again, carving an X into his exposed chest.

A grenadier leapt forward to finish off the traitor with a bayonet. Not that this had been needed, at least not in Thyran's judgement. Though he had held his rank for many years now, more than he had once thought possible, still he was a Death Korpsman at heart. He had learned the motions of collating, strategising, and, worse, politicking around holo-maps in airless rooms, but it was only in the thick of combat that he felt truly alive.

It wasn't exactly as it had been before, of course. He missed his steed's back between his knees. He had left it behind as, with the ground churned into mud by days of intense shelling, even its splayed feet would have struggled to keep their balance. He also had to acknowledge that he was treated differently to other Korpsmen. His comrades, always aware of his position thanks to the banner he fought under, protected him above all others. *They're protecting the banner,* he told himself, but it was a hollow distinction.

His commissar who wasn't Maugh yelled, 'Tighten up the line there and keep your damned eyes open. The next time an enemy gets so close to your commander, I'll have the squad that let him pass them flayed!'

Thyran kept his command squad moving forwards. 'Does anyone have eyes on him?' he demanded into his comm-bead. 'Where is he?'

He hadn't believed the reports to begin with.

After all this time, it seemed too much like wishful thinking that the leader of the traitors on Vraks had shown himself, that at last the 88th Siege Army had a chance to engage him directly and destroy him.

He had ordered his spotters to get closer, to provide more details. By day's end, he had been furnished with a fuzzy pict-capture, which he had sent back to HQ for verification. That same night, he had been contacted by Inquisitor Lord Malkin himself, who had confirmed it.

Blood-red Terminator armour. A wizened face, skin stretched across its skull, pulling its lips into a rictus grin behind a mask of fangs. This had to be the lord of the Skulltakers, the Bloodreaver, the Impaler, the Butcher and Despot of Vraks; these names he had earned, and many more. This had to be Zhufor.

For the next three days, however, he had not been seen again. Colonel Thyran had fretted in his dugout, afraid that he had missed his chance. Until today. Until now.

A monstrosity reared up before him on metal spider legs.

The inquisitors had been calling these 'daemon engines': perverted machines fused together from the scrap of destroyed guns and tanks, animated by obscene, bloodthirsty spirits reputedly trapped inside their chassis. This one had a melta cannon lodged in its leering mouth, and it breathed fire.

It blasted the front end of a Chimera to slag, but the simultaneous last gasp of the Krieg tank's battle cannon widened a crack in the monster's hull, from which emerged a gout of flame. With a tortured shriek, the engine's metal face twisted into a parody of pain. A Leman Russ strained forward to leverage its weakness, but was swarmed by militiamen and ogryns.

The colonel barked an order to his squad. He pelted towards the daemon engine. It appeared to be recovering, straightening its five or six legs to make itself taller. Its neck twisted, tilting its bestial head down towards him, and he saw a flash in the barrel between its jaws. The colonel yelled a warning as he dived and rolled between two metal legs, hearing the vicious hiss of the melta behind him, feeling its heat on his back. He was under the daemon engine now and, reaching up, he clamped a magnetic krak grenade to its sooty underbelly.

Then he ran again, his command squad re-forming around him. He hadn't time to ask how many charges they had managed to plant. A rapid series of explosions blew out the knee joints of three of the daemon engine's legs, tore open its stomach, and brought it crashing to the ground, where it continued to thrash and spew bullets from a distended limb, but coughed up only oily smoke.

Militiamen fell under the Leman Russ' tracks as it entered weapons range to pound the monster with its cannon. Having done a quick count of his squad, Thyran was already trying to get his bearings, working out where Zhufor had been sighted last.

'That was a bold move, colonel,' his commissar muttered in his ear. 'We could easily have lost you, or the standard.' He couldn't tell if this was meant as praise or criticism. Had the speaker been Maugh, then he would have been able to tell.

Too many thinking too much of themselves, the commissar-general had said, *thinking they could be the next – what was his name?* What would he have thought if he could see his old comrade now?

'I'm not trying to be a hero,' Thyran growled, as much for the benefit of his old commissar as for his new one, but even as the words were spoken, smoke parted on the breeze, the melee about him shifted, and, as if the Emperor Himself had cleared a path for him, he locked eyes with his target at a distance of a few hundred yards. For an instant and no longer.

Zhufor, like the colonel himself, was well protected: a blood-red iron curtain of armoured warriors closed before him swiftly – but bearing down on them was the remaining Imperial Titan. Though four days of fighting had tarnished its bright blue and golden livery, *Astor Tyrannis* still cut a swathe through the traitor scum.

A score of missiles streaked from its Apocalypse launcher, and Zhufor's Blood Cult scattered as an inferno rained down upon them. To Thyran's disappointment, they emerged from the smoke of it undaunted, returning fire with double-barrelled combi-bolters, and several charged the mighty Titan, running its las-blast gauntlet to swipe at its feet with powered mauls and axes.

Thyran started forwards, but even he baulked from plunging headlong into such a conflagration. *Let the Titan deal with Zhufor!* He himself had voxed its princeps with the Chaos lord's location. The absence of a response had felt pointed, but his message had clearly got through. *It won't reach him,* the colonel thought. *The Titan might destroy his bodyguard, but Zhufor will escape!*

For the second time, a path appeared before him, and Thyran, who had thought himself unflappable, stood astonished at the sight of the Chaos lord determinedly striding towards him. The Traitor Marine batted his own allies aside with his chainaxe, seeming not to care about – or even to delight in – the wounds he inflicted upon them.

It had not occurred to Thyran that when he had seen Zhufor, so too had Zhufor seen him and judged him worthy of his personal attention. He was torn for a moment between his need for vengeance and his duty to his Korpsmen. Would he be a hero or a fool who died for nothing and took his squad, his regiment, down with him? What would Maugh have said?

Then he saw the skulls adorning Zhufor's armour, as if in mockery of his sacred banner, and, mounted upon Zhufor's back, fingers gripping his broad shoulders, he saw a body, relatively fresh but stripped of its flesh to its gleaming white bones. A crisp black uniform, not yet beginning to rot. A peaked cap bearing the Imperialis winged-skull symbol; a commissar's cap.

Thyran planted his boots in the mud and held his sabre ready.

He instructed his squad to stand back. Before they could protest, he added, 'My job is to keep that monster pinned here as long as I am able. Yours is to hit him with flamers, meltas, hellguns, everything we have. As soon as you have a shot, take it, even if it means shooting through me. I don't expect to survive this fight, but I do expect my honoured comrades to make my death mean–'

An explosion stole his speech from him, flinging him to the ground.

His ears were dead, his head swam, and he didn't know what had just happened, only that he had to get back on his feet before Zhufor made it to him or die on his back. His squad mates strewn about him were likewise picking themselves up, apart from a couple who weren't moving.

Looming through the smoke was another daemon engine, with a mortar extruded from its stomach. Thyran heard the clunk of the weapon reloading, but judged that its target was the Titan, that its last shell had fallen short by chance and even then only the periphery of the blast had caught him.

He had more immediate concerns – or so he thought, until his commissar beside him gasped and stiffened and he saw that a harpoon had shot out from the engine, impaling him through the thigh. Worse, attached to the harpoon was a rusted, mucus-dripping chain, which the daemon engine was now reeling in, dragging its prey towards it.

The commissar struggled, but was yanked off his feet again, pulled through the mud on his back. The colonel joined his quartermaster and standard bearer in hacking at the chain, but it was a melta blast from his remaining grenadier that severed it. As his quartermaster tended to the writhing commissar, the colonel whirled around to face a huge red figure – not Zhufor, but one of his Terminator guards.

In contrast to the Chaos lord, there was no indication that this one had ever been human; any biological parts it may have retained were interred deep within the armour. With his command squad broken, Colonel Thyran expected to die, and for far less than he had intended.

Then he saw that the Terminator was missing an arm and, with it, its main gun. Fluid spurted from the ragged stump; he couldn't tell if it was blood or oil. The rest of its armour had also been cracked like an egg, smoke seeping from it, and all down its left side it had melted and recongealed into a formless mess. The Titan's guns – perhaps those of Thyran's tanks too – had critically damaged this monster, but sheer belligerence wouldn't allow it to die.

It swung a chainaxe at him, but its melted teeth had spluttered to a halt and the Terminator's one arm lacked the strength to effectively use the heavy weapon as a bludgeon. Flinging it away, it lunged at Thyran with an electronically modulated roar; sidestepping it, he thrust his sabre into the red armour's inner workings, releasing its machine spirits in a glorious display of incandescence.

The Terminator roared again and lashed out with a massive fist. Though its injuries slowed it, it was all Thyran could do to evade its barrage of clumsy swipes. If one of them connected, he knew he would likely lose his head.

Inevitably, a desperate dodge overextended his stride and the treacherous ground gave way beneath his heel. As he fell, as he tried to roll away, a melta blast cleaved the air above him, close enough to singe his greatcoat. Contrary to his orders, which had technically only applied to Zhufor, his grenadier had been waiting for a clear shot at the Terminator's head.

It was the final straw for even that raging juggernaut, which toppled backwards and slowly sank into its own impact crater. The colonel, back on his feet, looked desperately for Zhufor, but Krieg and traitors alike had filled the gap between them and he saw no sign of him. He realised that his Blood Cult too had disappeared, but for a few mangled remains.

Swallowing his frustration, he broadcast over the regimental vox-channel. 'The Butcher of Vraks has fled the field,' he announced. 'Our goal is ours for the taking now, with just one final push, with just a few more noble sacrifices...'

The battle went on well into the night.

Colonel Thyran was exhausted, as his Korpsmen must have been too, but with Zhufor's withdrawal he felt that victory was close. He also feared that, were he to let up now, he couldn't muster up a force sufficient for a sixth attempt tomorrow.

The Emperor rewarded his persistence, as He always did.

Gradually, Thyran came to realise that the shadowy shapes around him were only those of friends. The booming of the Titan's guns, and those of his own tanks, were dying away for want of targets.

Finally, a lieutenant voxed him, his platoon having reached the rubble of the curtain wall gate to find it undefended. The remaining traitors had followed their despot's lead and slunk away into the darkness.

Within minutes, the colonel had attained the site himself and had his banner planted there. The empty eyes of his predecessors' skulls looked down on him in mute approval. He imagined that Commissar-General Maugh was among them, in spirit if not in actuality.

He voxed command HQ, telling them simply that the gate was theirs. For now, nothing else mattered. There would be time to count the cost tomorrow. He would need to shore up his squad, of course. He had left his commissar propped up against a burnt-out Leman Russ with a harpoon through his leg, clinging to consciousness, waiting for a stretcher. Even if he had survived, he would be out of action for some time, but he was easily replaced.

Against all odds, the colonel himself had suffered no more than bruises, scratches and strained muscles.

For the next few days and weeks, he stationed himself at Gate 579-459, as Krieg forces poured in to expand and fortify their stronghold there. He wanted to be seen among them, wanted them to see him as no different to any other Korpsman, though he knew this wasn't true and that they knew it too.

He thought a great deal about Maugh. More than once, he overheard his name being spoken in reverential tones. The commissar-general's heroic sacrifice was talked about, remembered, and the colonel found himself glad of this, though perhaps he ought not to have been. Would Maugh have approved?

He wondered if he might die as well when his time came.

He felt as if he had missed his chance, but that somehow this might have been for the best. *Fortunately,* Maugh had told him, *your Korpsmen have a more suitable role model.* A leader who would give his life for his regiment, for Krieg and for the Emperor, without seeking glory for himself.

Just, he told himself, *like any other Korpsman.*

XII

By the end of 829.M41, the 88th Krieg Siege Army occupied trenches all around the base of the Citadel Mountain. The long war was almost at an end, and Inquisitor Lord Hector Rex was determined to finish it.

He had driven his army of Death Korpsmen to exhaustion and beyond, bringing them to this precipitous point. He had kept up the pressure on their beleaguered enemies, allowing them no time to regroup after a series of setbacks. Now, he had the citadel's three main gates in his sights.

His tacticians told him that the taking of those gates would necessitate the bloodiest battle of the war yet.

The only way up the mountainside for an armoured vehicle was a service road, which wound a winding path up the eastern tip past weapons pits and sniper holes, and which by now had undoubtedly been mined. It would be up to infantry companies, therefore, to make the climb alone, and in many parts it was too steep even for them, limiting the routes available to them, funnelling them towards the traitors' waiting guns.

Not for nothing would the Krieg come to know that blasted hillside by the pithy sobriquet 'the Murder Slopes', for it would come to claim the lives of close to a million Korpsmen, among them the vast majority of the 261st Siege Regiment, thereafter disbanded in disgrace.

For Veteran Colonel Tyborc, said regiment's commander, the Murder Slopes would prove to be the site of his life's greatest shame.

He received his orders from the lord inquisitor himself, in the incongruous surroundings of a warm, quiet, well-appointed stateroom.

Though Tyborc was a man of stature, Lord Rex towered over him effortlessly. His eyes penetrated Tyborc's soul and made him fear that he had been summoned into his presence to be judged. Perhaps he had been.

'Your service record is impressive,' the venerable daemon-hunter growled.

'Thank you, my lord,' said Tyborc.

'The hero of Fort A-453, I am told.'

He didn't demur. 'Some call me that.' By now, it was a simple fact.

'Then hardly one to flinch from what the Imperium requires of you now.'

Lord Rex outlined his plan concisely, unapologetically. He provided more data on a slate and holo-crystal, which were handed to the veteran colonel by a servitor-scribe. Not that there was much more to be said.

Death Korpsmen would attack the Murder Slopes in waves until its defenders were worn down, and Tyborc's regiment would lead the charge. It was not necessary to spell out what this meant for them; all present knew it well enough. The lord inquisitor fell silent, awaiting a response. His cherub familiar, rarely still, settled on his shoulder, fixing the Krieg man with its own burning glare.

Tyborc felt a deep sense of relief.

For the first time in too many years, his path was clear to him. He knew what he had to do. He had to fight for the Emperor and die for Him. Just that.

Nor would his life be wasted. He had seen and heard enough of Hector Rex to trust that he had a sound strategic mind. He had impressed Tyborc often, not least with his humility and courage. Since he had come to Vraks – as neither Zuehlke nor Kagori had done while in post – he had taken up arms on several occasions. He had fought in the dirt like everybody else. Now he was doing something else his predecessors never had: he was looking a Krieg colonel in the eye as he sent him to his death.

So, the only response this colonel gave was a simple, crisp salute. Then, with the lord inquisitor's approval, expressed by a curt nod and with what Tyborc perceived to be a softening of his forceful gaze, he turned and marched out of that quiet room to meet his Emperor-ordained fate.

For the next few weeks, he was kept too busy to doubt.

The 261st moved into new positions in the forward trenches, closest to the Citadel of Vraks. Here, they had to dig deep as Imperial guns thundered over their heads day and night, almost suffocating them beneath a shroud of smoke.

'The citadel's greatest defences,' Tyborc briefed his senior officers at their regimental HQ, 'are its nigh-on-invulnerable void shields, fed by geothermic heat wells sunk under its foundations. The shields' only weakness is that enough sustained force applied to them will in time exhaust them.'

The 21st Bombardment Korps had been charged with achieving that goal, in the service of which every Death Korps regiment had been required to turn over the bulk of its ammunition stores. He let this news sink in for a moment.

'Then, sir,' a captain ventured, 'when our infantry attacks the Murder Slopes...'

'It will be without the benefit of covering fire,' he confirmed. 'Regrettable, but that is how it has to be. Unless those void shields fall, we die on those slopes for nothing, for the citadel gates will remain impregnable to us.'

In many other areas, Colonel Tyborc stressed, Lord Rex had proven generous, blessing them with additional resources. 'Our three leading companies will each advance in fifteen Gorgon transports. These will sweep over two thousand Korpsmen past the traitors' few remaining outer defences.'

'Until the slopes become too steep for them,' his commissar added.

Tyborc tacitly acknowledged the point. He had chosen three companies to spearhead the advance, to be first to give their lives. The soldiers in the room were waiting to hear their assignments, waiting for their fates to be pronounced. He knew that, once it was, they would accept his decisions without question, without rancour.

He told them what they wished to hear.

He wished he could have led the charge himself. Once, he would have done so, but Fort A-453 felt a very long time ago now, and like the army in which he served, he had come a long way since then.

Now Veteran Colonel Tyborc had a more onerous duty.

He monitored the first wave's progress from his dugout. Hunkered down behind a trench wall, he listened from what felt like an unbearable distance as the rolls of his regiment's dead grew inexorably longer.

'Sir, First Company captain reports that their Gorgons have run into a minefield!'

'Seventh Company under fire from a camouflaged Earthshaker!'

The plan, as devised by Lord Rex, was simply to attack the citadel's three main gates at once. First Company marched on the Cardinal Gate from the north, but five of its Gorgons were reported destroyed within minutes. Tyborc winced as another pair were blasted into slag, fired upon by a defence laser silo as they attempted to back up out of danger. The armoured chassis meant to protect their passengers instead became their funeral caskets.

From the west, Seventh Company approached the less-defended Lower Gate. From here, they intended to proceed along the narrow Pilgrim's Road to the St Leonis Gate, which served the basilica and palace. Their captain had fallen out of vox-contact, however, and shortly the worst was confirmed.

The news from 15th Company was better, though they too were under heavy fire. Tyborc had made the Great Gate, at the citadel's eastern tip, his primary target, committing the most resources to it. The other two attacks were little more than diversionary in nature. If he could take the Great Gate – or just make it close enough for the regiment behind his own to take it – then that would be sufficient.

For him, no other day in Vraks' war had felt longer than this day.

'Enemy infantry sighted to the north!'

'First Company reports another Gorgon lost, sir.'

How many of First Company had even reached the Murder

Slopes? Fewer than half, by his reckoning. Now, militiamen were pouring down the hill towards them and, having the advantage of higher ground, were cutting a swathe through them with las-beams and bullets. The company commander's voice came spluttering over a vox-channel: *'Colonel… need to call in the second wave now… being overwhelmed here… Do I have your permission?'*

'Seventh Company pinned by laser fire from the Southern Bastion, sir!'

In the south-east, 15th Company had lost over half its Gorgons, and thousands of disgorged, unprotected Korpsmen were scrambling up the Murder Slopes into curtains of fire. For a short time, Tyborc hoped they might attain the first loop of the service road above them, but they were losing their lives to the traitor guns too quickly, for too little progress.

Soon, 15th Company also launched its second wave ahead of schedule.

The routing of First Company, in the meantime, was complete, with few Krieg boots having even left impressions on the hillside. His heart heavy, Tyborc voxed his 19th Company commander. The battle for the Cardinal Gate was passed to him now. No transports were available to him, so his Korpsmen had to charge on foot across open ground. Tyborc prayed that, even so, they might endure longer, make it further, than their predecessors had.

He checked his chrono and was even more disheartened to see how little time had passed. *My time will come sooner than I thought…*

The longest day ground on, bloody minute by interminable minute.

Each wave of faceless Korpsmen teemed up from underground

to clamber over the bodies of the wave before, being cut down in their turn, adding to the charnel piles. Inch by agonising inch, life by life, they crawled closer to the all-important gates. Nowhere near close enough.

Several times, the sky flared with multicoloured lightning, telling Tyborc that the citadel's void shields were being overloaded one by one. Spotters reported that where Earthshaker and Bombard shells now struck, they were no longer fizzling uselessly but rather smashing into storm-worn granite walls. He chafed at an opportunity that, at present, he was ill-placed to exploit. How long before the traitors repaired at least some of their generators?

As the longest day faded at last, the longest night drew in. By now, Tyborc's 19th Company had followed the first into oblivion, and the Fourth looked more than set to join them. Not a single one of his platoons had achieved its objectives, with most still mired at the hill's foot.

He voxed a measured report to Inquisitor Lord Rex. He took responsibility for his failure, but stated that as long as there was the smallest chance of victory, he would fight on. The terse reply said no more than he had expected: *'You have your orders, Veteran Colonel Tyborc.'*

He had been holding back his strongest force, his combined grenadier squads. He also had one final armoured column, which he now set into motion. Atlas recovery tanks rolled up the citadel's approach road, their dozer blades sweeping mines from it. As they wended their way up the mountain, in their wake came a dozen Leman Russes of the Fifth Tank Company, with more grenadiers on foot behind them.

'This is it,' the colonel muttered to his veteran watchmaster.

This was indeed his last, most desperate hope: that, after breaking three infantry companies upon the rocks below the

Cardinal Gate, he had at least lured the majority of the traitors there; that a sudden, powerful assault upon the Great Gate might take its defenders by surprise and give him what he craved, one final laudable achievement for his regiment – and for himself – before the end.

Tyborc would lead the grenadiers' charge. He would take the 261st Regiment's banner out onto the battlefield with him. For the final time. If Confessor Tenaxus was right, then it would inspire his troops to know that a hero fought among them. It might make a difference. Perhaps it was even for this reason that he had been chosen.

Or perhaps Lord Rex had just wanted him humbled.

He opened a general vox-channel to his Korpsmen. He didn't know how many could still hear him. He wanted to tell them that, even in defeat, they made him proud. Today, it had been Tyborc's solemn duty to watch as his regiment died. Tonight, his body would rest alongside them and that would be his honour. In the end, he could think of no more appropriate words than those of the Krieg Litany of Sacrifice: 'In life, war. In death, peace. In life, shame. In death, atonement.'

It was simply that, this time, the numbers were against them.

The ground around the citadel was a charred pit of swirling black smoke, through which Tyborc could barely make out his own command squad, barely see the Krieg corpses upon which he couldn't help but trample.

This meant, at least, that he made it to the mountainside unharmed, though gunfire crackled through the miasma around him. Nor could his scattered Korpsmen have seen his unfurled banner, but at least they would know it was there. *At least they will not have to see it burn…*

Tyborc launched himself upon the lower Murder Slopes,

knowing speed was of the essence. The traitors, having seen the wave of grenadiers surging towards them, began to concentrate their fire upon them. Having planned to make his last stand in front of the Great Gate, now he would be content to make it halfway there.

He heard thunder rumbling behind him. He had dragged his final few field ordnance batteries forward to provide what support they could for him. He heard thunder rumbling above him too. Another storm was about to break.

To the west, Seventh Company's attempt to crack the Southern Bastion had failed, forcing them to fall back again. To the north, Fourth and 20th Companies had beaten back renegade hordes to climb a little further, but an enemy strongpoint buried in the mountainside had frustrated their advance, a dozen squads having already fallen in their attempts to reach it.

To the south-east and above, Tyborc's tank commanders reported that they were being blasted by lascannons from the citadel walls. His Atlases and three of his Leman Russes were now just smoking wrecks; the remainder pushed onward and, as the service road swung back around, they came into sight of the Great Gate's towers and were able to loose off a few shots at them.

He had almost reached the road himself when the citadel's guns unleashed a renewed salvo. Exploding shells sprayed brightly blazing phosphor, which not only burnt through the Krieg's body armour but also lit up their positions for further shots. All across the Murder Slopes, they ducked into cover where they could, though many could do little more than flatten themselves against the obdurate rock.

Tyborc's squad hauled las-seared corpses from a weapons pit and flung them down the mountainside, clearing room for themselves. Even so, his watchmaster's back was sprayed with blazing, sticky gel and he had to be helped out of his melting greatcoat before he was too badly burnt.

With a series of terrific crashes, a massive hunk of metal came bouncing down the slope, skidding perilously close by Tyborc's too-shallow recess before coming to a smouldering rest. He made out scorched Death Korps decals on the mangled chassis of a Leman Russ. He voxed his tank commanders but only one responded, in the process of abandoning her vehicle. *'Burning wrecks blocking our ascent,'* she managed to gasp out. *'Can't force a way forwards or back with the units we still have.'*

The phosphor shells stopped falling minutes later – not even Vraks' armouries were well stocked with such rare chemicals – but Tyborc suspected they were only a precursor to a concerted counter-attack. The voice of a grenadier watchmaster on the service road confirmed it. *'Colonel Tyborc, the gate is opening…'*

In the estimates of tacticians, both Death Korps and Ordo Malleus, roughly half a million Vraksian traitors remained ensconced inside their lofty fortress. What they could only guess was how many allies, the Lost and the Damned just like themselves, had been drawn to them and joined their cause in almost two decades. Some of those off-world allies revealed themselves now.

A mass of blood-red Traitor legionaries streamed through the citadel's Great Gate, accompanied by armoured vehicles and sundry combat walkers. The designs on their armour marked them out as belonging to several disparate factions, but eager thralls all to the Chaos god of Blood and Skulls.

Tyborc told his Korpsmen, 'Stand your ground!' The gates were a lost cause to them now, as perhaps they always had been, but retreat could not be countenanced. They could still hold their gains, however modest these had been, until the next regiment advanced. They would still die for something, which was all that had ever been required of them.

Perhaps, he thought, the wrecks of his own tanks would slow the enemy down. He was already hearing, though, that Traitor Marines had left the road, along with many of their vehicles. A platoon to the west of him had been annihilated as a Predator plunged down the slopes towards them with its autocannon flaring.

Rain and hail lashed down as lightning set the sky ablaze. The very mountain trembled and Tyborc, recalling that it had once been a volcano, felt like it might suddenly erupt.

Starting to make out nightmare shapes above him – some humanoid, others decidedly less so – he gainsaid his own order: 'Stand your ground if you can. Fall back to the traitors' old defensive placements, dig in behind their walls if you must, but don't let them retake what we have bled for.'

'Sir,' his watchmaster interrupted. 'One o'clock!'

A red-armoured figure dropped from the raging sky, landing a short way from the colonel's squad, throwing up rock dust with its impact. It didn't appear to have noticed them yet in their hollow, but it would at any moment. A pale, scarred, dark-eyed head rotated towards them, blood crusted around a mouth filled with teeth filed to razor-sharp points.

'Aim for the eyes!' Tyborc yelled as he fired his laspistol, the crack of its discharge joined by his comrades' weapons in a raucous, percussive chorus. The traitor had made a mistake in eschewing a helmet, the colonel thought, for even Krieg hell-guns struggled to penetrate power armour, but they burnt flesh with ease. *As long as they can do it quickly…*

His target launched itself into the air again. Tyborc followed the arc of its flight, but his next two shots went wild, to his frustration. A ton of metal crashed back down to the ground, much closer to him now, and that exposed head snapped back as if a beam had nailed it. A raw scream burst from the Traitor legionary's throat, but more of rage than pain.

'Keep shooting! Put him down!' the watchmaster yelled, an edge of fear to his voice that Tyborc hadn't heard before.

The legionary thundered towards them, broken skulls and rusted chains beating a tattoo against his chest, a bloody axe brandished in each gauntlet; Tyborc felt an urge to run himself, but knew it would be futile.

He took a slow breath, stiffening his muscles. He watched as the traitor's head loomed larger in his sights. It was indeed burnt, the skin a livid red to match his armour. One eye was closed and weeping pus. Tyborc had one final shot at him, so had to make it count. As calmly as he could, he squeezed his trigger.

His shot punched through the legionary's good eye. Another barrage of las-beams scoured his face, stripping skin away from bone.

He kept on coming, forcing Tyborc and his squad to scramble out of his way as he dived – no, toppled – towards them. He sprawled across the weapons pit's low parapet, demolishing it. Face down, he thrashed about, though whether still alive or simply animated by his armour's cogitators, Tyborc couldn't tell. A close-up shot to the legionary's half-melted head put the matter beyond doubt.

'If that was it,' the veteran colonel opined, 'if that was our lives' final achievement, then we have earned the right to die with pride.'

Undercutting his sentiment, he heard an engine roar, looked up, and saw a blood-red Vindicator tank ploughing a furrow towards them. A Demolisher cannon barrel peeked over the top of its broad, flat dozer blade. Tyborc opened his mouth to give instructions, but realised he only had time to bark a single word: *'Run!'*

He heard the Demolisher's own bark as he stumbled down

the hillside, felt its searing heat on his back as the pit he had only just vacated erupted into flames.

Across the Murder Slopes, death and confusion reigned.

Platoons and squads were scattered by the oncoming wave of blood-red armour, driven ever further backwards. Veteran Colonel Tyborc felt a dismayed twinge as he set foot on level ground and realised that not an inch of the Citadel Mountain would be reclaimed for the Emperor today.

He looked for his next defensible position, having been uprooted from the last three, but saw none among the corpses and the ruins of traitor emplacements. Somehow, his command squad had remained together as their platoon had scattered, and they sheltered behind the few remaining Krieg guns at the hill's foot. Medusa and Earthshaker crews worked frantically, reloading and firing shells over their comrades' heads at the red masses on the slopes above them. They scored a few palpable hits, including one that blew a Predator apart.

'At least the traitors will know they've been in a fight,' Tyborc consoled them and himself.

His voice was drowned out by the storm. Thunder rumbled even louder than the guns, and the smoke-filled sky was the same blood-red as his enemies' armour. Jagged bolts of lightning lashed the hillside, and he prayed for some to fry a Traitor Marine or disable a tank, but in his heart he knew that his God-Emperor had no power over this phenomenon.

Lightning struck again, directly in his eyeline, dazzling him, but as his vision cleared, the colonel made out a new figure crouching up on the slopes, as if having ridden the bolt itself to earth.

He tried to dismiss it as a trick of the smoke, because it was like nothing he had seen in the waking world before, its presence here so wrong that it made his brain scream and his skin crawl. It had the height and build of a Traitor legionary, and their blood-red colouring too, but was unclad. Long, twisted horns sprang out of each side of its head. Its eyes were like smouldering coals; a long, black tongue unfurled from its maw like a whip.

It wielded a glowing, flame-licked sword seven feet long. It sprang down the Murder Slopes sure-footedly on black, clawed feet. It was coming for Tyborc, as its ilk had come for him so often in feverish nightmares.

He was looking at a daemon.

One of many… Creatures like it were appearing all across the slopes. Breathless reports filled Tyborc's earpiece, though the storm interfered with his vox-caster, drowning most of them in static. An account made it through of a daemon materialising in the midst of one luckless platoon, cackling madly as its blade cleaved through multiple Korpsmen with each energetic swipe.

'Fall back to the trenches,' he ordered. 'We can hold them there!' *Brave words,* he thought, but what they really needed was some form of intervention.

As Tyborc raced through smoke and mud, he gasped out an appeal of his own on a general vox-channel, for anyone who could relay it back to his commanders, to Lord Rex. Failing this, he found it inconceivable that the Ordo Malleus' augurs hadn't already sensed such a violent disturbance in the warp. Where was Inquisitor Adso, nominally attached to the 261st Regiment, from whom the colonel hadn't heard in months? What of the ordo's enigmatic Chamber Militant, rumoured to be watching Vraks from orbit for just such an eventuality as this?

The daemons were faster than the Krieg.

Some were mounted on fire-belching steeds, more machine than animal, with brass armour plating and horn-like blades protruding from elongated snouts. Tyborc glimpsed their squat shapes as they stampeded past him, his eyes itching at the symbols of the Blood God etched into their metal hides. They ran their prey down squad by squad, trampling them into the dirt, as their laughing riders' burning swords lashed out to claim one Krieg head after another.

Some squads found daemon steeds between them and the trenches, beating them back, allowing the unmounted daemons and Traitor Marines from the slopes to fall upon them from behind. Tyborc heard his Korpsmen's screams as, in their hundreds, in their thousands, they were gleefully ripped apart.

He felt he had been running forever and had just as far to go, until the ground dropped away and he fell more than jumped into his most recent command dugout. Recovering himself, for an instant he felt relieved to be out of the carnage, not to fear the sudden impact of burning hooves against his back. He hopped up onto a broken firing step and steadied his laspistol on a sandbag.

As if a mere trench wall can protect me…

Other squads had also reached the trenches, but with little artillery remaining to deter them, the daemons were leaping in after them, continuing their massacre, and Tyborc was starting to hear from his regiment's commissars that a good many Korpsmen were reaching the trenches but not stopping.

His commissar screamed into his comm-bead, 'Your orders are to stand and fight, do you hear me? Failure to obey is a capital crime. Your lives, as of this moment, are worth nothing, but you retain the choice to die with honour!'

Tyborc couldn't believe what he was hearing. For the first time in his life, he was paralysed, not knowing what to do. No part of his training nor of his long experience had prepared him for this eventuality.

The same was not true of his commissar, who continued to bellow: 'Any Korpsman presenting a back to the enemy will be summarily shot. I expect each commissar and, in the absence of such, platoon commander to carry out this sentence. The Emperor expects us all to do our duty!'

Tyborc's grenadiers, his most experienced troops, were lining up around him, around the banner that somehow still gave them heart. From elsewhere, however, through his earpiece and without it, he was hearing a very different story. More Korpsmen dropped into his trench, a short way from him, and though some froze at the sight of their colonel and his squad, the rest fled screaming through the earthworks, admonishments futile against their abject panic.

He almost couldn't blame them.

He had known his regiment would die tonight. He hadn't expected a bloodbath such as this. He had told his Korpsmen, believing it himself, that their lives could make a difference. He had told them they could be heroes. He hadn't prepared them – how could he have prepared them? – to face such warp-spawned horrors, and a part of him wondered if Hector Rex had wanted it that way.

Had he known all along that this would happen?

How many Korpsmen had been slain already? How many at their own officers' hands? Tyborc's commissar was hailing his counterparts in other platoons, but raising few. Many of these too had surely perished, but how many more had joined their charges in heedless flight? The Krieg had always known themselves to be every bit as stoic as any Commissariat agent; the point appeared, in an upturned way, to have been proven.

Soon, however, they would meet another obstacle. They would reach the trenches occupied by the 269th Regiment, whose officers had encountered no daemons and would see only

Korpsmen – Tyborc's Korpsmen – routing without orders to do so. He didn't know how they would react – the situation would be beyond their experience too – but he feared the very worst. The thought of Krieg fighting Krieg sickened him to his stomach, while any of his Korpsmen surviving such a conflict would face execution or, at best, consignment to a penal legion.

Veteran Colonel Tyborc burnt with a sense of injustice.

At last, he knew what he had to do.

He opened a general vox-channel and gave his regiment its final order. 'Run,' he told them. 'Run as fast as you can and stop for no one. Save yourselves if you can. Don't die for nothing.' Then, when he had finished speaking, he closed his eyes, shut out the tumult around him, and took a deep, cleansing breath, for now he knew his destiny. He knew how his story ended.

When he looked again, his commissar was aiming a laspistol at his head. The only surprise was that he hadn't pulled the trigger yet. His hand was shaking. Tyborc stepped down from his firing step. He said nothing. *Let them spit on my body and vilify my name if it spares even one of my soldiers, if they can blame me alone for leading them, leading all of us, to this…*

A fresh commotion behind him made him whirl around on instinct.

A daemon was hacking its way along the trench towards him. One by one, his grenadiers threw themselves into its path or tried to wrestle with it, blunting their bayonets on it, most losing their heads to delay its advance for mere seconds. They were dying to protect him, despite his instructions to the contrary.

'Colonel Tyborc!' came a strangulated cry. Whirling again, he followed the frozen stare of his veteran watchmaster and those of his command squad's other members. He gaped out over the trench's low lip and, in a blaze of lightning, he saw a daemon larger and fiercer still than any of the others.

It must have been thirty feet tall, with iron barbs studding its muscular, blood-red body. A pair of black, membranous wings unfurled from its back as it took its first ponderous step forwards, and the earth itself burst into flame where its cloven foot stamped down.

The daemon threw back its hideous, doglike head to emit a resounding howl, which made Tyborc feel as if his ears would burst and his brain shortly after. He recalled the reports he had heard from inside the Green Hell, of a monster too horrific to describe. *None of them survived,* he had said of the Korpsmen who had seen it, but Tenaxus had corrected him: *Some did, but their minds were broken.*

He never made the decision to run. He just found himself running. He raced along communications trenches and sap tunnels. He had no destination in mind, no possible future; he could only try to put as much space as he possibly could between him and his nightmares, all the while knowing that he could never truly escape them, for wherever he ran to, they would be there waiting for him.

Veteran Colonel Tyborc ran – and his grenadiers and his command squad, including his commissar, ran with him. His regimental standard had slipped from its bearer's hands – or perhaps he had let it go deliberately, not wanting to taint it with their shame – and it lay on the trench floor behind them, being pounded by the storm, sinking slowly into Vraks' mud.

ACT FIVE

THE EMPEROR TRIUMPHANT

830.M41

Fourteen million Krieg Korpsmen died in the retaking of Vraks.

Against this, the dishonourable fate of the 261st Siege Regiment barely merits a footnote, buried in the archives of the Departmento Munitorum and rarely acknowledged without. The Death Korps regiment whose morale failed them. The regiment that broke. My regiment. The record implies that some manner of psychic manipulation may have triggered this unprecedented conduct. I know better.

In the years since Vraks, Krieg high command have clamped down more tightly than ever upon displays of what they term 'egotism' in their ranks. I hear that, in some units, even senior officers will answer only to their numbers.

They are reminded that Colonel Jurten required no reward, no recognition for his historic achievements. He died a lonely, miserable death before his war was won, not knowing if he would be remembered as a hero or a villain, a saviour or a zealot, a wise man or a fool, or not at all.

Locked out of that world now, I see it more clearly than I did.

I see how the stories told to the Krieg, my people, condition us to think ourselves unworthy, to see ourselves as somehow less than human. I also see why this is wholly necessary, for how else could we accept our appointed role – more vital than ever in such fraught days as these – in the Emperor's never-ending wars?

How else could we ever find redemption?

– From the account of Veteran Colonel Tyborc

XIII

For ten days after the disbandment of the 261st Krieg Regiment, Confessor Tenaxus locked herself inside her spartan quarters. She communed with the Emperor, self-flagellated, and questioned her life's purpose.

'I believed in the Krieg,' she said aloud. 'I believed them unshakable, as many assured me they were. Should I have examined them more closely?'

She had asked to speak to the regiment's deserters, but had been denied. Inquisitor Lord Thor Malkin had informed her that, officially, there *were* no deserters, only soldiers following questionable orders. The few survivors had been dispersed across the remaining regiments of the 30th Line Korps.

When Tenaxus had questioned this decision, the inquisitor had simply scowled and stated, 'We can ill afford to lose warm bodies capable of holding lasguns. As ever, the Krieg will atone for their sins with their lives.'

She had persisted: 'What of Veteran Colonel Tyborc?'

What if death is not your destiny at all? she had asked him, planting a seed in Tyborc's mind that she had nurtured and watched grow. Against his protestations, she had built him into something more than he had been. Was she to blame, then, for his failure to live up to his own legend? What of the many Korpsmen before whom she had exalted him; what were they thinking now?

'His fate is in Lord Rex's hands,' Malkin had stated flatly.

She emerged from her seclusion to find little changed.

A pall of gloom hung over the landing site. Tenaxus could sense it, though others would have denied its presence. Krieg and inquisitors alike busied themselves with preparations for their next assault, for they had nothing else to occupy them.

Little doubt remained of what had only been suspected: that the traitors in the citadel, through their heretical dark arts, had created a portal into the immaterium. It was spoken of plainly now, albeit in whispers.

The fiends on the Murder Slopes had vanished as suddenly as they had appeared, but no one doubted that they would soon be back – they or others of their ilk – and that they could strike anywhere at any time they pleased. Everything Lord Malkin had feared three years ago had come to pass.

Tenaxus felt guilty again, for her recent self-absorption, but she still didn't know what to do. The Emperor had given her no answers. She had tried to write a sermon to deliver in the trenches, to make sense of all that had happened, but for the first time in her life the words wouldn't come to her.

Lord Rex's latest plan was taking shape. The Krieg, having failed to climb the Citadel Mountain, would instead force a way in from below. This would entail a two-pronged attack by the 269th Regiment with an Inquisitorial force at their head.

Rex himself would lead a second assault upon the Lower Gate: the most vulnerable of the main three still, and the only one damaged.

His primary target, however, stood at the end of the Citadel Ravine. This huge, sheer-sided chasm was like a slice cleaved out of the mountain, running almost through it north to south, close to its western tip. It led to a blast door twelve storeys high, fifteen feet thick, which protected the citadel's main armoury.

The Krieg were to fight their way along the chasm, up to that great steel edifice, and blow a hole through it. From inside the armoury, they could climb up through the mountain's labyrinthine undercroft, surprising the traitors from below while cutting them off from their weapons stores.

The sky was remarkably subdued on the day Tenaxus visited the 269th Regiment's trenches. The lightning storms that had battered Vraks for weeks had finally relented, which the inquisitor lords considered a propitious sign.

She travelled with Lord Malkin in his personal Land Raider, *Mae Virtus*. He had fought with the 269th before, in the Green Hell, and would do so again. He invited the confessor to fight alongside him, training his unblinking augmetic eye upon her.

She didn't appreciate being made to feel judged, more used to judging. Meeting the inquisitor's glare, unflinching, she answered, 'When the time is right, my lord.'

As soon as she could, she slipped away to tour the trenches. She was looking for a vantage point from which to see the Basilica of St Leonis. She found one, perched atop the parapet of a mortar emplacement. She knew it was dangerous to raise her head like this, though there had been a recent lull in shell-fire, as if the guns of both sides had grown weary. She judged it worth the risk.

She hadn't been so close to the basilica in decades, since her youth. This was her first view of it from the north, unobstructed by the citadel's other structures. Its apse end jutted out over the mountainside, beside the Priory of the Argent Shroud, which teetered on the ravine's western edge. Tenaxus' magnoculars roved over its tarnished façade. She winced at each window broken but was comforted that, despite everything, the building appeared structurally intact.

Her gaze drifting downwards, she saw masked skulls mounted on the citadel's ramparts. They had appeared within hours of Tyborc's regiment's defeat. Zhufor was gloating. The bitter irony of it was that Leonis' hallowed spires would not be destroyed by him and his band of traitors, rather by Imperial firepower.

Tenaxus' right hand probed beneath her red and silver robes to rest on her bolt pistol in its holster. She hadn't yet fired it on Vraks, believing words a more effective weapon. Across the Imperium's shrine worlds, there were legends of confessors who had turned back armies with a few well-chosen words. She had dreamt of marching into the Citadel of Vraks and having its occupiers fall to their knees before her as she made them confront their apostasy.

She knew it wouldn't happen. The sight of Inquisitor Lord Rex might strike the fear of the Emperor into them; Tenaxus had questioned enough prisoners to know they feared their treacherous masters far more than they did her. *Perhaps,* she thought, *had I been here at the start, had I had a chance to pit my words against those of the apostate cardinal...*

Too late now. Words had always been enough for Confessor Tenaxus, but words had failed her now. So, what did she have left?

Four of the 269th Regiment's companies lined up along their forward trenches.

Tenaxus had girded herself to make a speech, but Inquisitor Lord Malkin beat her to it. He stomped along the rows of stiff-backed soldiers in his bulky armour, berating them through a laud hailer. He didn't shy away from the fact that they might be facing daemons – by now, they knew as much – but he reminded them that their regiment had done so before and, unlike some, hadn't broken.

The real daemons, he proclaimed, were the ones that dwelled inside them, whispering heresies directly into their minds, weakening their hearts. The Emperor, he promised, would smile upon the Korpsmen who resisted those seductive voices and simply did their duty.

Tenaxus wondered how many times before they had assembled like this to hear similar words. She wondered if this time felt any different to them. Then it struck her that for most of these young soldiers, this would be their first time and their last. Did they think about those who had stood in their places before them?

Lord Malkin said almost all that Tenaxus could have said. She would have sounded as if she meant it too. Not once, however, did he mention the basilica, nor its holy relics. He spoke of salvation not at all, but of vengeance and destruction.

The confessor watched as thousands of masked figures scaled their ladders in virtual silence and streamed towards the foot of the Citadel Mountain. She thought her presence, at least, might give them inspiration, but rather they inspired her. The Leman Russes of the 19th and 21st Tank Companies led the Death Korpsmen into battle, while super-heavy Macharius tanks ploughed across their trenches, one passing almost over her head.

Once her trench had emptied out around her, Tenaxus turned and trudged back through the mud to the regiment's command dugout. En route, she heard a fresh rumbling of engines and raised her head to look.

Far above her, circling the citadel's spires, were the cruciform silhouettes of Imperial Marauders. Bombers. She felt her stomach tightening. Their target, she reminded herself, was the Lower Gate spur on the south slopes of the mountain, which stood in the way of Lord Rex's infantry force. The holy basilica was safe from them. As safe as it could be. For today.

She thought she might find Malkin in the dugout, alongside Colonel 269, but he had returned to *Mae Virtus*. She made the regiment's command staff aware of her presence but kept out of their way. She sat with her heavy book of catechisms open on her lap and recited its contents fervently under her breath, her restless hand tracing the outline of her staff's aquila.

Once again, she failed to make the Emperor hear her prayers.

Vox-reports revealed an unexpected obstacle in the Death Korps' way. They had been aware that a gully, a natural fault in the earth, crossed their path. It was marked on their tactical maps. What they hadn't realised was how wide and deep it ran at the very point at which they were to cross it.

Traitors had dug into that gully and even secreted tanks in it, their turret weapons level with its edge. They had bided their time until the Krieg were almost upon them, then unleashed a withering hail of fire in their direction.

Third Company's captain died in the opening salvo, along with six of his platoon commanders. As the Krieg's three Macharius tanks searched vainly for a way across the gully, two were blown apart by hurled explosives. The colonel was forced to redraw his plans, quickly pulling his troops back to more defensible positions, sending in reinforcements prematurely.

They were meant to have secured the gully within hours of leaving their trenches. Instead, the battle for it went on into the next day and the next. Krieg Korpsmen made it into the gully and fought an arduous battle to clear it of militiamen and mutants, also facing Traitor legionaries in steel-grey armour. From the black-on-red iron halo symbols on their pauldrons, Inquisitor Lord Malkin, voxing in from his idling Land Raider, identified these as Steel Brethren – which brought the total of Chaos Space Marine warbands identified on Vraks to eleven.

Tenaxus continued to monitor developments. She rested when she could, bedding down in a Korpsman's vacated bunk, just a shelf gouged into a narrow tunnel's wall. Normally she had no trouble sleeping, whatever battle was being fought elsewhere, no matter its stakes. During those days, though, she dozed for barely an hour at a time and, upon waking, couldn't sleep again for wondering what she might have missed.

Towards the third day's end, to her relief, the captain of 16th Company reported that the gully was in Krieg hands. Korpsmen would regroup along it overnight and, on the captain's order, continue their southward march towards the ravine at dawn – considerably behind schedule and having taken more casualties than expected by this point.

Ahead of them still stood a pair of enemy strongpoints at the ravine's mouth and, halfway along it, a gated wall with towers.

The battle for the Lower Gate, in the meantime, was going rather better.

Tenaxus itched to hear more news of it, but didn't want to tie up the 269th's vox-caster. Lord Malkin's Land Raider had a caster of its own, though, and he voxed updates to the trenches, more obviously wrapped in morale-boosting maxims than might once have been the case.

The Lower Gate's towers had been reduced to rubble, and a force of Titans, led by *Praetorian*, was blasting at the gate itself. Lord Rex had personally led a raid on a defence laser silo and disabled it with demolition charges. Predictably, a force of Traitor legionaries and daemon engines had emerged from the St Leonis Gate above them, grinding down the Pilgrim's Road, but Lord Malkin expressed confidence that these too would be vanquished.

For many long hours after that, there came no further news. Lord Malkin spoke only to remind the Krieg infantry: *'You must fight with all your might, for even when the battle here seems hopeless, still it serves to keep the enemy distracted from battles of greater import elsewhere.'*

On the fourth day of fighting, Tenaxus shuffled into the command dugout, bleary-eyed, to hear that the citadel's Lower Gate had been captured and secured. By Malkin's account, a magnificent battle had resulted in the traitors being crushed by the hammer of the Emperor, the survivors scurrying back behind their last remaining walls. He exhorted the Krieg to take heart and redouble their efforts, for if the armoury could be taken too, then the citadel itself would shortly follow.

His words may have galvanised them, for they gained more ground that day than they had on any other and, early on the next, the first Korpsmen finally set foot inside the ravine. The colonel requested, and Lord Rex negotiated, assistance from the Legio Astorum, and Tenaxus gazed upwards in awe as the Reaver Titan *Astor Tyrannis* strode sure-footedly across the trenches.

Another day of frustration ensued, even so.

To the right of the ravine stood the citadel's Northern Bastion. Though it had been shelled heavily, knocking out its defence lasers, still the remains of its walls provided ample cover for traitors with stubbers and mortars. The 16th Company had been poised to swoop upon it when they were redirected to the gully. Depleted in the fighting there, now they lacked the strength to complete their primary mission, and even the Titan's cannons couldn't help them make much headway.

In the meantime, progress along the ravine was measured by the foot and in the number of Krieg lives expended. Minefields and tank traps packed the earth, while weapons fire swept the approach to the wall and towers. Imperial artillery had provided suppressing fire, aimed at the citadel above, but now was running low on ammunition; as a result, emboldened traitors were appearing on the clifftops, firing down at sitting targets who could find no cover from them.

Lord Rex was holding forces in reserve, Thor Malkin among them. He had delayed their deployment once already, and late that evening he did so again. Tenaxus understood his reasons, but felt disappointed all the same. For Rex's plan to stand any chance of success, first the Krieg had to be in position, and they were still far from it. So, for now, they were left to the slaughter.

She noted that, at some point, in their vox-reports, they had ceased referring to the Citadel Ravine by its official designation. They had a new name for it. They were calling it the Death Pit.

Feeling hopeless and useless, Tenaxus hopped aboard an unloaded Trojan, riding it to a newly established supply dump in the west. From there, a free Land Raider conveyed her to the Lower Gate – not that much of it remained.

As she had suspected, the battle here had been harder and closer than Malkin had admitted. The burnt-out shells of Imperial tanks and Chaos war machines still smouldered. The broken shell of another disabled Titan cast a gloomy shadow over the scene, and the Krieg were digging burial pits. It didn't matter.

The 88th Army had won its first substantial victory in what felt to the confessor like an age. Lord Rex was mustering his forces, considering his next move – which would depend upon what happened in the Death Pit – and the general air of purpose made for a welcome contrast to the despondency prevailing in the north.

Tenaxus listened to tales of the battle, wishing her own eyes had seen it. Lord Rex had thrown close to a hundred tanks against the gate, supported by three Reaver and four Warhound Titans – not to mention the lord inquisitor himself and his retinue, who were soon seen in the thick of the melee.

'He wielded the power of the storm itself,' more than one Korpsman told her.

'Lord Rex captured lightning in his sword and smote the traitors with it.'

'He put himself in a lascannon's way to protect a lowly Krieg platoon. He took the full force of the blast upon his shield, and it lit up the heavens.'

Nor was Hector Rex the only Inquisitorial warrior to have impressed even the phlegmatic Krieg. A full day of fighting had seen the Lower Gate captured, but it had changed hands five times more during an ensuing night of carnage. The rising sun had found the gate traitor-held again, whereupon the lord inquisitor had called in his reserves of last resort.

Steel-armoured Space Marines had roared onto the scene in silver Land Raiders, leaping from them with force halberds glowing blue, striking like lightning. Unleashing a storm of weapons fire and psychic powers, they had torn into daemon engines and exorcised them screaming back into the warp. The sudden violence of their appearance had ended the battle in mere minutes, whereupon they had quickly disappeared, having never spoken once.

Tenaxus had heard a name whispered among the Inquisitorial retinues. *Grey Knights*... Before, she had known them only by the gaps they had left in accounts of wars past, never having questioned anyone who admitted to setting eyes upon them. Perhaps, she thought, no one here was expected to live long enough to tell of their existence.

'I ought to have been here,' Tenaxus sighed, forgetting for a moment the Krieg Korpsman with whom she had been speaking.

'For what purpose, ma'am?' he asked her.

She stared at him, surprised.

'The battle was won without you,' the Korpsman stated.

The following day, one last assault was made upon the Death Pit.

Lord Rex finally activated his reserves, and fifteen Deathstorm drop pods plunged out of the cloudy sky. Slamming down behind the ravine's bisecting wall, they sprung open to reveal assault cannons, which strafed their surroundings blindly. Many of the wall's defenders were cut down in mere seconds and, as the traitors reeled, a second wave of pods rained down upon them.

Their impacts shook the ground, setting off small rockslides in the canyon walls. From the pods emerged one hundred and fifty battle-brothers of the Space Marines Red Hunters Chapter, led by four inquisitors in power armour.

They had dropped into a trap, and they knew it.

At the far end of the Death Pit, the huge armoury door rolled open, and through it stomped a black and yellow Reaver Titan of the treacherous Legio Vulcanum. Swarming about its heavy feet was a mob of baying, drooling mutant scum, which flowed towards the new arrivals like a tidal wave of sewage.

A small handful of them reached the Red Hunters, through the purifying bullets of their boltguns, but no sooner had they laid their filthy claws upon their foes than chainswords tore them limb from limb.

The Reaver was a far bigger threat, its volcano cannon and gatling blaster alternately melting and chipping away at ceramite and adamantine. The Space Marines were also prey to plunging fire from the inner keep above them, as well as from the bridge that spanned the canyon, connecting the keep to the rest of the citadel.

All this, however, was no more than delaying tactics, for the traitors had certainly expected the drop pod assault and had prepared to counter it.

Conspicuously absent from the battle at the Lower Gate had been the Chaos lord Zhufor and his united Khornate warbands. They emerged from the armoury now to flood the Citadel Ravine, with Zhufor as always encircled by his Terminator bodyguards. The Red Hunters, caught out in the open with no escape routes available to them, had only one hope, and that was to break through the wall behind them – which had been their plan all along.

As many Red Hunters as dared turned their backs on the Chaos Space Marines. They attacked the wall across the Death Pit, knowing that four companies of the 269th Krieg Siege Regiment would be mounting a simultaneous assault upon its other side. Through their combined efforts, the wall would surely break, but it had to happen quickly. It was their only hope.

The Krieg colonel stiffened and muttered an oath to himself. To Confessor Tenaxus, it sounded like 'Jurten's blood!'

'What is it?' she demanded. 'What's wrong?'

He ignored her, barking into his comm-bead: 'All units, advance! Now!'

The colonel clapped his driver on the shoulder, and the Centaur's engine roared to life. It jolted forwards, and Tenaxus had to brace herself against its soot-smeared sides and against her fellow passengers. This was no way, she thought, for someone of her station to travel – in a dirty, ramshackle, open-topped carrier without any seats.

No, she corrected herself, *this is where I ought to be.*

Tenaxus had finally confessed something to herself. It had taken the lowliest of the Krieg to make her see it. She had convinced herself that the Emperor was deaf to her prayers. The truth was that He had answered her plainly enough, but she was the one who hadn't listened. She knew her duty now, and she accepted it.

She had returned to the north, to Colonel 269's dugout, to tell him she would fight with him. The colonel had accepted her offer without comment, and thus she had found herself here, jammed into the back of the Centaur, elbow to elbow, knee to knee with the six members of his command squad.

Of these, only one, the non-Krieg-born commissar, had spoken to her, updating her on their mission objectives. He had talked of the Red Hunters with hope in his voice; they were blessed, he had said, to be in the presence of Angels. Clearly, he had not been on Vraks for long.

Time had crawled by, hours upon minutes, and Tenaxus had longed to stretch her cramping legs or peel off her stifling gas mask. Now, on the move at last, she felt more relieved than apprehensive.

The colonel listened to more reports through his hidden earpiece. He took a deep breath before announcing to his squad, 'The assault was launched ahead of schedule. It seems a vox-message failed to reach us, or was never sent.'

'But why would–' the commissar began.

'It may have been assumed that we would see the drop pods and take them as our signal to attack, but with cloud cover and the lip of the ravine in our spotters' way…'

'What are our orders, sir?' a veteran watchmaster asked.

'Our orders haven't changed. We attack that damn wall with everything we have – and just pray we aren't too late.'

'That cannot be,' the confessor asserted, in a voice almost too low to be heard over the Centaur's engine and the booming of guns towards which they were speeding. 'The Emperor decrees a path for each of us, whether our eyes see it or not – and thus, we are precisely where He requires us to be.'

They clattered across a temporary bridge, thrown up by Krieg engineers across the gully that had given them so much trouble a few days ago.

The half-demolished strongpoints at the head of the Citadel Ravine loomed in their sights. As they drew closer, they converged with other vehicles, including Lord Malkin's Land Raider, its laud hailers blaring. Two Death Rider companies came galloping to join them from the west, and Tenaxus spotted a Stormblade tank with its massive plasma blastgun – known, with good reason, as a Titan-killer.

Soon, Krieg infantry were streaming about them too. Their road was strewn with rubble, but tanks with dozer blades ahead of them had swept the worst of it aside. The sheer walls of the Death Pit rose around them, hemming them in. The enemy's wall stretched across their path, and fire flashed in the slits of its gate towers.

Tenaxus kept her head down as bullets pinged off the Centaur's armour plating. The colonel tapped his driver's shoulder again. 'That's far enough,' he judged, and the driver stamped on the brakes to bring them to a juddering halt.

Two grenadiers dropped the tailgate, leaping down from it. Tenaxus and the rest of the command squad followed suit, leaving only the driver and gunner aboard. The colonel's standard bearer unfurled the regimental banner as Tenaxus drew her pistol. On the colonel's word, the Centaur lurched forwards again. The colonel, his command squad, and Tenaxus advanced along the Death Pit in its wake, benefiting from its cover. The vehicle's only weapon was a short-range, pintle-mounted heavy stubber, but as it drew closer to the wall it sputtered gamely into action.

Tenaxus saw the incoming shell just a fraction of a second before it struck the Centaur squarely on its glacis. The blast wave caught her as she dived, stealing the breath with which she had tried to yell a warning, and she rode it to the ground, where burning shrapnel rained down on her back. She rolled to smother the flames taking hold in her robes. Her Krieg allies were already picking themselves up around her. The Centaur was immobilised, smoke hissing from its engine compartment, its two crew members slumped bleeding in their seats.

The vehicle's shell still offered shelter. Scrambling back up behind it, Tenaxus levelled her bolt pistol across it. She was looking for a target in the wall, a traitor's head behind a gun barrel, but the distance was too great and the intervening smoke was growing thicker. Needing to get closer, she began to round the Centaur, but a volley of bullets sent her back to where she had begun.

The command squad was likewise pinned down here, their standard badly singed, its bearer nursing shrapnel wounds. 'Incoming!' their watchmaster warned, directing their attention to their rear; Tenaxus heard an engine and whirled to see the Krieg Stormblade barrelling towards her.

She leapt out of its way as it clipped the crippled Centaur, sending it spinning into the canyon's side. The Stormblade had a clear run at its target now, and the wall's blindsided defenders were hastily retraining their heavy guns upon it. Shrugging off their first bout of mortar fire, it lashed out at the gate in the wall once, twice, three times, before its blastgun was finally disabled, its ceramite plating cracked and its crew compelled to abandon their vehicle.

Tenaxus held her breath, waiting for the smoke to clear, but the Krieg on foot were already pushing forwards, using the distraction they'd been granted. The next sound she heard behind her was a thundering of hooves as Death Riders swept along the ravine. Then she heard a watchmaster yelling to their squad, 'They did it!' Still unable to see for herself, she turned to the nearby colonel, who had been listening to his earpiece and gave a satisfied nod. The gate had been vaporised.

The Krieg still had to force a way through it, as traitors now came pouring through the gap to engage them. Tenaxus saw diseased militiamen and ogryns, abhuman beastmen with tails and snouts and horns, and mutants sporting even more hideous deformities. Everywhere she looked were disgusting profane symbols, but what vexed the confessor most was the sheer size of the enemy force, for it told her that behind the wall, things had not been going well.

She prayed she might be wrong. She prayed that, beyond her line of sight, the Red Hunters were still fighting and all these efforts wouldn't come to nothing. The Krieg would fight on either way, that much she knew.

The Death Riders' charge had been stalled by heavy fire from the wall's still-standing towers and by the last few unexploded mines before them. Tenaxus winced as steed after steed was consumed in blossoms of flame, or shredded by bullets and shrapnel, collapsing underneath their riders, in some cases breaking their limbs, pinning them in the dirt. She watched as infantrymen closed with the degenerate hordes to find themselves outnumbered, overwhelmed, torn apart by filthy teeth and claws. She watched as not one of them gave up.

Each Korpsman had a duty and wouldn't shirk from it – now, it seemed, more than ever, as if recent events, rumours of a regiment's disgrace, had only stiffened their resolve. Each one was fighting for the Emperor, for the home world, each driven by the need to make a difference, even if it was only by taking a bullet so the Korpsman behind didn't have to. Tenaxus felt humbled by their faith.

She brought up her pistol again, wanting to make a difference too.

She fired twice into the seething mass of traitors, but through the smoke and confusion she couldn't see the results of her efforts. Her next shot was forestalled as Krieg heads strayed into her sights. She needed to get closer, but she saw no way to do so. Not without risking her life.

Perhaps, she had said to a young Krieg captain many years ago, *it is I who have committed the sin of conceit...*

She thought of Tyborc now and wondered again about his fate. She thought of colonels Adal and Thyran, of Captain Fodor and Lieutenant Marot. She thought of the Hero of Hangman's Hill. She didn't have to ask herself how any of them would have acted in her place.

Confessor Tenaxus turned her head upwards and, at that moment, Vraks' sun, close to its midday zenith, found a gap between the clouds. Its rays streamed through the windows of the Basilica of St Leonis the Blind, on the cliff edge high above her, and were refracted into myriad colours by remaining stained-glass fragments.

My soul cannot rest until I have seen the tomb of the blessed Leonis freed. She had said that too and meant it, so now her soul could never be at rest.

She returned her pistol to its holster.

She gripped her huge, oaken staff two-handed and twisted the golden, double-headed eagle atop it. The staff thrummed in her hands as it was wreathed in golden energy. From somewhere, she wasn't sure where, she heard the augmented voice of Inquisitor Lord Thor Malkin, spurring her on to glory.

She had lost track of Colonel 269 and his command squad. As Tenaxus had wrestled with her daemons, they had moved on, leaving her behind. Abandoning the cover of the Centaur's wreck, she fell into step alongside a squad of grenadiers as they charged gung-ho towards the enemy.

She thought she glimpsed their regimental standard, fluttering ahead above the melee, a symbol of defiance, and she felt pride and fury bursting from her chest and heard herself screaming admonitions that came to her unbidden.

'Prepare yourself to face the Emperor's wrath,' she bellowed, 'for He has seen into your black, shrivelled hearts and He–'

A shell exploded in her path, engulfing her in fire and metal.

Confessor Ignea Tenaxus was dead before her body hit the ground. With time to reflect, she would surely have counted her blessings, for she lay within sight of the holy shrine, the light from its windows playing over her. She may even have confessed her relief, not to have been made to witness its ordained destruction. The Emperor had indeed rewarded her devotion.

XIV

The Krieg Korpsman was a relatively recent arrival to Vraks.

He had been among the last batch of reinforcements brought in from the home world, straight from basic training. The traitors' defence lines had already been broken and the 88th Siege Army was closing in around the all-important citadel. He was led to believe that, as long as the war here had lasted, it was almost won.

He had been assigned to the 150th Krieg Siege Regiment. He had ridden by rail and then by armoured carrier across the grey expanses of the Van Meersland Wastes to a dugout in the west, where he had laid his bedroll.

Just a few hundred fellow new recruits had made the journey with him – the 150th had not been depleted as some regiments had been – and he had lost track of most of them as they were subsumed into the larger force.

His days for the next two years were filled by routine chores, only broken up by stints on an Earthshaker crew, themselves comprising long hours of repetitive activity. All this took place beneath a constant hail of shell-fire, so on many days suddenly there were fires to extinguish and bodies to be buried.

One night, more memorable than most, saw a ragged band of mutants invading the Korpsman's trench. He was pleased to think that a las-beam from his gun had slain one, although he couldn't be entirely sure of it.

His new comrades felt pride that theirs had been the first regiment to engage Vraks' traitors. They hadn't been so honoured since, which was why so many of them survived to remember. When off-duty, they talked more than the new recruit was used to, though they only had one thing to talk about. He listened to their tales of the war, even the ones heard second-hand, some dating back to before his birth, because he thought he might learn something from them.

Several times, his regiment packed up its equipment and rolled its artillery units forwards through already-dug earthworks. Their largest-scale relocation came after First Line Korps was disbanded, and saw them moving clockwise around the citadel. Weeks later, they occupied trenches vacated by the 143rd Regiment after their successful capture of the curtain wall gate.

The Korpsman had been trained to be patient, but he sensed the frustration of some of his older comrades. He wondered if he might come to feel as they did. Some died of diseases in their beds, and he was saddened by the waste of life. When at last the time came for his regiment to go over the top, he welcomed it.

He faced little fire on his dash across no-man's-land, for the traitors had all but abandoned the curtain wall. An engineer company blasted through it with demolition charges and, wading through the rubble, the Korpsman saw the base of the Citadel Mountain, scant miles ahead of him.

* * *

Since then, he had been a great deal busier.

The traitors may have run, but not too far. The Korpsman's sergeant opined that, having failed to hold the wall, they may have been denied the citadel's shelter by their unforgiving masters, so instead had had to go to ground in whatever boltholes they could squirm into.

They had to be rooted out of weapons pits and bunkers, which meant charging headlong into small-arms fire and over mines. It meant fighting blade to blade against desperate militiamen with nowhere left to run to. It meant that, as close as the Krieg were to their goal, every intervening foot had to be hard-won by blood – then fortified and held, which often meant digging through the night.

Our unknown Korpsman felt less restless now, for this was what he had been trained to do. This was just like being back at home.

His sergeant had been wrong, however, in his implication that the traitors outside the citadel gates had been abandoned – for, without warning, vile creatures had appeared as if from nowhere to reinforce them.

The Korpsman heard reports of, and sometimes glimpsed through battlefield smoke, brass daemon engines scuttling on spider-like legs. It was said in the trenches that to gaze upon such horrors for too long was to risk insanity. He felt blessed that the Emperor had provided a bulwark against them, in the form of his Angels of Death and mighty god-machines. Hearing the thunder of their cannons and missile launchers, the rending of metal as Titans clashed around him, never once did he feel insignificant. He knew he had his part to play in this battle, as did they.

He waded into multitudes of gibbering heretics, who spat diabolical names in his face as if expecting their dark gods to lend them strength to best him. He took satisfaction in proving to each of them in turn his God-Emperor's greater strength.

Each night, the Korpsman slept the exhausted, dreamless sleep of the content, regardless of the guns still thundering about him. Each morning, he recited the Krieg Litany of Sacrifice and assumed that his next sleep would be his last. Each evening, returning to his bunk, he acknowledged and accepted the responsibility placed upon his shoulders by another day of life.

On his worst day, flying fiends swooped upon his squad.

He mistook the first for an airborne vehicle because of the way it moved, slicing the air rather than riding its currents. His sergeant yelled a warning, an instant before a stream of yellow-green fire stripped his body to the bone.

Hitting the ground behind a rubble heap, the Korpsman was startled to find a sticky green gobbet eating through his sleeve. Desperately, he scraped it off against a rockcrete hunk, from where it continued to hiss at him balefully.

The flying thing wheeled around and came in for another strafing run.

The Korpsman saw it properly now, saw that although it bristled with metal protuberances, it was also encased in rotting flesh. Its elongated body hung unnaturally from a pair of droning rotor discs. Its only discernible features were a large, unblinking eye and, beneath this, a mouth stuffed with gun barrels.

He rolled onto his back as its shadow passed over him. He switched his lasgun to its rarely used full-auto setting, judging the power consumption to be more than warranted. He loosed off a dozen shots, and thought two struck their target, which let out a nerve-jangling shriek.

His comrades were firing too, and his platoon's other squads also rushed to their assistance – too late to stop the fiend from vomiting another stream of sticky fire, which immolated two more Korpsmen.

Worse, its cry was answered by two more: angry screeches, part animal, part friction of metal upon metal. A junior officer yelled to the Krieg to scatter, as three shapes circled overhead, their incessant drones boring through our Korpsman's ears, into his brain like drills. Yellow-green fire spewed down over and over again, sometimes claiming two or three victims at once, those unable to separate in time, spattering and burning more.

The Krieg responded in the only way they could, taking shots where they could see them, and a bolt from the officer's pistol struck a rotor, turning its drone into a throaty rattle. A fiend came spiralling to earth, but the Korpsman's satisfaction at its downfall was short-lived. To his horror, it alighted upon his dead sergeant's chest. Metal mandibles busied themselves in its mouth, and his horror turned to fury as he realised that it was feeding, replenishing itself, upon the corpse.

Ignoring the imminent threat of the other fiends above him, he loosed off las-beam after las-beam at the one squatting brazenly before him. He burnt dead skin off its body, revealing pulsating, blackened organs in steel cradles. Other nearby comrades joined in the assault, beneath which it began to wither.

Abandoning its feast, it pushed itself up into the air, the machinery in its maw clicking and whirring. It fixed its glassy eye upon our unknown Korpsman, who flattened himself behind his rubble, knowing it wouldn't shield him from a direct hit from those barrels.

He heard several more las-cracks and then a larger blast by far, felt the shockwave of it rolling over him and rippling his greatcoat.

Raising his head, he found the daemon engine gone. A mound

of ashes marked the spot above which it had hovered, his sergeant's resting place, while patches of bubbling, yellow-green bile and what looked like insect larvae were strewn about this in a circle. Burnt and battered comrades picked themselves up from the ground – though some stayed where they had fallen, unmoving.

In its death throes, the fiend had had one final trick to play. Blind fortune alone had spared the unknown Korpsman the force of its spiteful explosion.

He had no time to dwell on his narrow escape. A second explosion, behind him, grabbed his attention, the flaming remains of a second fiend spattering down. The third, badly wounded, made a suicidal dive towards the largest remaining concentration of Death Korpsmen, who worked their triggers frantically, punching las-beams through its eye, but couldn't keep it from bursting in their midst.

The dust settled slowly upon over a dozen Krieg corpses, their platoon reduced almost to half-strength in a frantic, fateful minute.

The unknown Korpsman's hand stung. He peeled off his now-ragged glove and cast it aside. Unhappy at exposing broken skin to Vraks' atmosphere, he quickly applied a salve and a bandage from his backpack.

On Krieg, his instructors had warned him of the horrors that lurked behind the cracks in reality, but they couldn't have prepared him fully for them. As uncompromising as his training exercises had been, they had only pitted him against soldiers like himself. Today, he had proven himself against something far worse.

Perhaps, he thought, it hadn't been a bad day, after all.

Two squadrons of Thunderhawk gunships dropped screaming from the clouds.

They looped around the Citadel Mountain and streaked westward towards the landing site, and even jaded Krieg grenadiers in their trenches glanced upwards to follow their contrails overhead.

Resplendent in charcoal grey and yellow, the gunships belonged to the Adeptus Astartes Red Scorpions Chapter. They had sent a small strike force to Vraks four years before, to make the first breach in the curtain wall. Now, thanks to the diplomatic efforts of Inquisitor Lord Rex, they had returned in greater numbers.

The flypast was a show of strength to friend and foe alike. With the citadel's laser defences mostly disabled, by the time its occupiers could scramble their own few flyers, the Thunderhawks were gone, and so the traitors were left knowing that the agents of the Emperor's vengeance upon them had arrived.

The Red Scorpions' coming had been heralded for weeks by inquisitors, priests and commissars. Though it was broadly welcomed by the Krieg, there were some – chiefly those who had been here the longest – who questioned its necessity. The unknown Korpsman's latest sergeant muttered darkly about how this was a judgement upon them. There had been too many failures, he opined, most notably and recently upon the Murder Slopes.

The Krieg rarely talked about that day. The unknown Korpsman still didn't really know what had happened and knew better than to ask. Before that day, he had often heard the name of Veteran Colonel Tyborc spoken, but not since.

The capture of the Lower Gate, in contrast, was freely discussed in the trenches, with an emphasis on the Krieg's decisive role in it. It was claimed that, while angels and daemons did battle about them, the dogged perseverance of the 269th Regiment had laid the real groundwork for their victory.

The outcome of their battle in the Citadel Ravine received less attention. A hundred and fifty Red Hunters and four inquisitors had been slaughtered in the Death Pit, their bodies left to the mercies of the enemy, but the Krieg held the canyon mouth, so that was something. Like the 263rd Regiment before it, the 269th had been deemed no longer viable, such was the extent of its losses. The difference was that its number had been retired with honour.

The 150th moved around the Citadel Mountain again. The unknown Korpsman settled into new trenches, in the north. Only one regiment was now stationed in front of his own – the 158th, a fellow member of 12th Line Korps – and they were the next required to sacrifice themselves.

At 205830.M41, the 88th Krieg Siege Army launched its final, decisive assault upon the Citadel of Vraks.

On the south slopes of the Citadel Mountain, Red Scorpions in Land Raiders, Razorbacks, and Rhinos struck out from the destroyed Lower Gate, up the Pilgrim's Road. From the north-east, an Inquisition strike force led by Hector Rex himself scaled the mountainside towards the Cardinal Gate.

Joining Rex's team alongside inquisitors, Red Hunters, and two Militarum Tempestus companies were Krieg grenadiers of the 150th and 158th Regiments. A small part of our unknown Korpsman wished he could have joined them, almost wished he might live long enough to be so honoured.

His regiment's rank-and-file members had no part to play in the operation, other than to stand vigilant against a possible attack from the rear. He was led to believe that this was more likely than it seemed. On at least two occasions, Traitor Marines of the Alpha Legion, led by the Chaos Lord Arkos, had appeared behind Imperial lines without warning to wreak bloody carnage.

The sky was overcast that morning, like an omen. By midday, it was black like midnight, but lightning crashed around the

Citadel Mountain, although there was no rain. Standing sentry in a dugout with magnoculars, it was hard to see anything at all. For reasons he couldn't explain, the Korpsman was filled with a sense of foreboding that no amount of prayer could dispel.

His magnoculars roving over the mountainside, he picked out bright red figures and strained to see Krieg greys and blacks among them. The Imperial Thunderhawks were back, screaming in to pound the traitor-held gates with bombs and rockets. Despite this, a darker column was disgorged from the Cardinal Gate, high up on the north face of the mountain, streaming towards the oncoming reds.

Soon, he could see nothing through the smoke of battle.

Further news reached him in slower, less reliable ways. A ragged cheer from a neighbouring trench presaged his sergeant's announcement to his squad that, on the mountain's far side, the St Leonis Gate had fallen.

Accounts were vague and somewhat contradictory, but the Red Scorpions had ploughed a furrow through daemon engines and Traitor Marines of the Black Brethren of Ayreas, and though their standard bearer had been felled and their high commander dragged wounded from the field by one of his Apothecaries, their armoured Dreadnoughts and lightning-clawed Terminators – the latter teleporting into the gate bastion itself – had won the day.

Their salvaged, frayed banner had been raised above the gate by the wounded commander himself, and this had been a signal to his battleship in orbit, which had commenced a bombardment of the citadel.

The storm raged louder and more savagely than ever before – but even as it did so, the Krieg received more sobering news.

The 158th Siege Regiment had also attacked the mountain from the north, but further westward, between the Cardinal Gate and the Citadel Ravine. Like the 263rd, they had perished on the

Murder Slopes. Unlike them, they had fought to the last – and, as importantly, they had achieved their objective, which had been to distract and divert the traitors' forces. It would be said of them that their sacrifice was crucial to the victories won elsewhere today.

The unknown Korpsman's shift had ended. He ought to have rested, so as to be ready for when next he was needed. Instead, he kept his magnoculars pressed to his gas mask's lenses – just for another minute or two, or ten, he told himself. Just to see what happened next.

Thus it was that, when lightning tore open the sky, in a sickening swirl of ugly, brooding colours, shredding clouds and knocking a Thunderhawk into a tailspin, he found himself staring right into the rift.

The Korpsman dropped his magnoculars, covering his eyes – too late, for the images were already burnt into his brain. Hearing stifled gasps around him, he knew his comrades had seen it too: a huge, daemonic figure with blood-red skin and tattered, bat-like wings. It put him in mind of whispered descriptions of the horror encountered by Colonel Tyborc's regiment, though if anything – if possible – this one was larger and more fearsome-looking even than he had heard.

He couldn't bear to look at it again.

He couldn't help but look.

With a casual beat of its mighty black wings, the monster, the daemon, soared towards the mountain. It landed atop the ramparts of the Cardinal Gate, beneath which Inquisitor Lord Rex and his allies were still locked in desperate battle.

It perched there for a minute, bathed in the fire and shrapnel of exploding shells, entirely unaffected by it. Then, throwing back its head, it roared its master's profane name, the name of the Blood God, the sound of which rolled across the sky like thunder to the unknown Korpsman's ears, so far away.

The daemon flexed its wings again, rose into the air, and then plunged into the fray, and the mountainside was engulfed in a violent storm of psychic energy, which caused the Korpsman's brain to ache until he could look at it no longer.

An armoured column of Gorgon assault transports heaved its way up the winding service road towards the Citadel of Vraks.

Each vehicle carried a fifty-strong platoon of the 150th Krieg Regiment. The unknown Korpsman stood wedged between comrades in a musty troop compartment. Some, the longest-serving, declared that they had never thought to see this day. He felt as if it had come with precipitous speed.

His mind kept dragging him back to the horrors he had seen upon this very mountainside. He tried to tell himself that he was honoured, for he had witnessed Lord Rex's defeat of the daemon at the Cardinal Gate – although in truth he had comprehended little and cared to remember even less.

It was said that the daemon's massive axe had torn through power armour as if it were paper. Space Marines of two Chapters – the Red Hunters and one other, whose name was never spoken – had mounted a valiant defence against it, subjecting it to powerful psychic attacks that had made it writhe in agony.

Enduring all this, it had hacked and battered through its foes, seizing battle-brothers one by one, hurling them from the mountain, before planting its cloven feet firmly in front of the gate, barring the path to it, and even some Krieg grenadiers had confessed quietly to quailing in its shadow.

Lord Rex hadn't even broken step. Bellowing invocations against the corruption of Chaos, he had set upon the daemon with Arias, his Nemesis force sword, rumoured to have been blessed by the Emperor in person. His storm shield had deflected axe blows strong enough to cleave the mountain.

It was said that a halo of divine light had shone around the lord inquisitor in battle. With hindsight, the unknown Korpsman was convinced that he had seen it: a bright, golden pinpoint of hope to reassure him that the Emperor had been with His servants that day.

At one point, it had seemed as though all was lost, as though the daemon was too strong, but then Lord Rex had channelled all the strength remaining in his muscles and, more so, the indomitable power of his mind into his holy sword, and thrust its blade into the daemon's chest. He had sent it screaming back into the foul realm that had spawned it and had sagged to his knees then, exhausted, his shield and armour shattered.

That one blow, it was said, had won the war.

The Emperor's forces now held two of the citadel's three main gates. They could bring their artillery up the service roads and pound its structures at close range. Within hours, the last remaining void shields were overloaded, and grand towers began to crumble. Repeated Marauder bombing raids hastened the destruction.

The Korpsman had watched from afar as the main spire of the Basilica of St Leonis the Blind had collapsed in a plume of dust and smoke, and he had joined in the cheers raised from the Krieg trenches. It occurred to him that some of his comrades had waited long years for that symbolic moment, an inconceivable length of time to him. Perhaps he was one of the few to reflect, for a moment, on what the basilica had symbolised before, in a time now long dead and buried.

The Gorgon strained and juddered as it bulled its way through rubble. Holding on to a grab rail, the unknown Korpsman knew he must be passing through the wreckage of the gate. He was one of the very first Krieg to enter the citadel, a thought that humbled him. Had he been assigned a different number, his fate could have been very different, with some other Korpsman now here in his place. He represented all of them, all those who hadn't made it.

The Gorgon's worn brakes brought them to a screeching halt. A sergeant slammed down the assault ramp at the vehicle's rear and, three by three, Death Korpsmen spilled out into the gloomy grey light. Their assignment was to clear the outer ward of the citadel of traitors, and so they streamed towards the bombed-out shells of barrack buildings with their bayonets fixed.

Simultaneously, Space Marine drop pods rained from the sky, disappearing behind what remained of the Cardinal's Palace, while the ground beneath the unknown Korpsman's feet thrummed with the passage of Hades drills through the mountain, conveying engineers into its undercroft. Behind him, Demolishers filed through the Cardinal Gate, and behind them he saw the looming silhouettes of a pair of Titans.

He didn't think he had ever felt so confident before, so assured of victory.

The Korpsman felt invincible.

Three more days of fighting did little to change his disposition.

The remaining traitors had no leaders left to guide them, no plan, no hope, but proved the most fanatical of all. Many bore the marks of heresy in the form of abhorrent mutations, and yet still they couldn't see it. They dug themselves into the deepest positions they could find, fighting to their last breaths with every weapon available to them. More than once, when a building appeared to have been cleared, more traitors would leap out from some cranny, brandishing blades, and try to drag one last foe to the grave with them.

They behaved as the Krieg would have done, in that respect, but the Korpsmen felt only contempt for them, for they were too mad to understand the utter futility of their defiance. When they deprived the Emperor of a Death Korpsman's life, they took less of value from Him than they knew.

The remains of the citadel quaked beneath the force of holy vengeance long delayed. Demolisher cannons and Titan missile launchers summoned more destruction down upon it. The unknown Korpsman had seen Red Hunters marching into the Cardinal's Palace and had heard that yet another Astartes Chapter, the Angels of Absolution, had engaged the Alpha Legion in the basilica's wreckage.

He had seen no Traitor legionaries himself. A commissar had taken to a hailer to crow that Zhufor had fled with his followers. 'Not for the first time, he quails from meeting the Death Korps of Krieg in battle!' A part of him was glad, but another part frustrated because the Butcher of Vraks had escaped being called to account for his many atrocities.

The Korpsman had been slashed across the forearm while deflecting a knife thrust from his neck. He had strained a ligament in his thigh while dodging another. He was weary, but that didn't stop him. He had drained his lasgun power packs but been handed more. For once, there were plenty to spare, as quartermasters could finally strip the Krieg bodies on the Murder Slopes.

His squad had been making its way westwards through the citadel and thus were privileged to enjoy an unrestricted view when Lord Rex unexpectedly mounted the steps of the Cardinal's Palace. He glowed with a pure, holy light, the source of which the Korpsman couldn't see. His voice was amplified through his fluttering cherub. He addressed the traitors rather than his soldiers, as the apostate cardinal, Xaphan, must once have addressed them.

He presented Xaphan's severed head to them.

As a once-human being, it was barely recognisable: a sorry mass of weeping eyes and pustules. The lord inquisitor had found it attached to a writhing Chaos spawn in a squalid cell beneath the Priory of the Argent Shroud – proof of Zhufor's boundless contempt for his supposed ally. Xaphan had been used, Lord Rex had proclaimed, as had his followers. Where once his eloquence had inspired a misguided crusade, what remained of the cardinal had drooled and gibbered idiotically before being forever silenced.

It seemed to the Korpsman that the traitors fought with markedly less fervour after that. Their last illusions stripped from them, they knew now the wages of their sins and most wished only to die, to be put out of their misery.

In a rare quiet moment, he overheard a muttered exchange between his sergeant and a lieutenant, which surprised him. On the steps, Lord Rex had had an entourage behind him, among them a bone-white-armoured Angel to whom his own eyes had been inevitably drawn.

He recalled that there had been a Death Korps colonel with them, but the Korpsman hadn't known him and had thought nothing of it. From the colonel's build and bearing, however, the lieutenant had felt sure he had met him before.

He doubted himself only because he didn't understand how it could possibly have been – that Colonel Tyborc had wound up a hero once again.

With a blinding flash of lightning, daemons appeared amid the ruins.

Some had blood-red hides and hooves and horns, like the one exorcised by Lord Rex, only mercifully smaller. Others were squat grey mounds of undulating, putrid flesh with single eyes and snouts. Cackling, they sprang upon their closest targets, hacking into them with blades that glowed like burning embers and pestilence-dripping plague knives.

The unknown Korpsman and his squad circled each other, looking for any clear shot, wary that another fiend might suddenly materialise behind them. He saw one as it sprang up onto a window ledge, partway up the surviving façade of a demolished office building. He snapped up his gun and squeezed the trigger.

The fiend's head whipped around to face him, its red eyes burning so intently into him that he felt they might ignite his flesh. With a bestial snarl and a flex of corded muscles, it hopped down from its perch and vanished between rubble heaps.

The squad backed away from where the daemon had been seen, sweeping the ground with their lasguns, trying to anticipate where it might re-emerge. The unknown Korpsman blinked and saw its shape atop a mound, from which it leapt upon one of his comrades. He got off two shots at it, both missing, as the daemon's hellblade flashed and sliced its prey's head from his shoulders.

Masonry shifted underfoot and turned his ankle. The daemon, as if sensing his weakness, came bounding towards him. He strafed it with a full-auto burst, as his comrades did the same. It staggered, almost fell but recovered itself.

It was so close now that the Korpsman could feel its presence, like a wave of sickness emanating from it, a wave of unadulterated hate. His every nerve shrieked at him to run, but instead he readied his bayonet, swallowed down his rising gorge, and braced himself to feel the daemon's filthy touch upon him.

He heard a sharp, distinctive hiss, saw a ripple in the air.

The hiss became a roar and he recoiled from a searing heat. The daemon shrieked as its red skin blistered and blackened, and then it was simply gone. The huge, flat, blue and golden foot of a Legio Astorum Titan stamped down to the Korpsman's right, pulverising bricks and sending chips of rockcrete flying.

The Titan had saved his life with its melta cannon, but already it was moving on before he could signal his gratitude to its crew. He doubted they had even seen him, anyway. He was beneath their notice.

Still, the unknown Korpsman had just faced down a daemon, an actual daemon, without giving in to panic and without letting go of his sanity. He had even played a part in its defeat, he fancied, if only by slowing it a little. He withdrew his trapped foot from the rubble, testing his weight on it. It would hold. He knew that pride in himself was inappropriate, but he felt a deep sense of relief that, when he had been challenged, he hadn't let anybody down.

Ahead of him, another red fiend stood surrounded by two Krieg squads. Its glowing blade sliced through one, two, three of them, but the others refused to relent, closing the gaps around it, keeping it penned in. Their bayonets lashed out, drawing thick, dark ichor from the daemon's twisted body. They were making it bleed – for were they not Death Korpsmen, after all? Were they not soldiers of Krieg? They were afraid of nothing, and so no power could possibly defeat them.

The unknown Korpsman glanced over at his sergeant, who nodded and ordered his squad into the fray.

Seeing flashes through the sundered walls and broken windows of the Basilica of St Leonis the Blind, he knew that a monumental battle was being fought therein, between powerful forces almost unknowable to him, but the battle out here, his battle, was equally important.

The deeds of the unknown Korpsman were never officially recorded.

It's more than likely that he died in the Citadel of Vraks, or in the tunnel network underneath it, as almost half the members of his regiment did in the painstaking weeks of mopping up that followed.

Another possibility is that he survived to tell his story, perhaps even earned himself a name before expiring on another battleground, another world.

Whatever his fate, it matters little. He was just a number on a list. A tiny cog in a huge machine, but without him the machine would have sputtered to a halt.

What mattered was that he did his duty and, in so doing, made a difference – and certainly he must have gone to his rest secure in the knowledge that he had.

One of millions of numbers, but every one had counted.

The Krieg would remember them, every single one, in their own ways: in their routines and through their rituals. They would thank the Emperor for the lives they had been given and pray that their deeds had found His favour.

Every single one of them had been a hero.

XV

Veteran Colonel Tyborc's squad fanned out across the dank, dark cellar. Provisions had been stored here, but now there were only empty shelving racks and broken crates and barrels. Crippled, deformed traitors had crawled down here to die, and the stench of rotting flesh seeped through the colonel's mask.

Scraping, snuffling sounds came from the furthest, darkest corner. Tyborc hand-signalled in that direction, but everyone had heard them.

A twitch of movement prompted a fusillade of las-fire. Kicking a crate aside, the colonel looked upon a shrivelled mutant body, which had drawn its last shuddering breath. Slimy entrails spilled from its burst-open stomach, as if something had been feeding on them. The colonel was about to warn his squad when two creatures pounced from the shadows.

He had seen their like before: once guard dogs, keeping Vraks' labour gangs in order, even then so large and fierce that only an ogryn's strength could control them in turn. Like everything else in the citadel, they had devolved into something ineffably worse. Possessed by warp spirits, now they were feral daemon hounds, with matted fur, razor-sharp claws and slavering maws.

One sank fangs into Tyborc's arm, through armoured mesh. It tried to drag him to the floor, but, gritting his teeth against the pain, he battered its head into the rockcrete wall. He broke its neck, but couldn't loosen its tenacious grip.

Two comrades rushed to his assistance. One thrust a bayonet into the hound's crazed eye; the other shattered its jaw with a hellgun butt. Tyborc reeled as the hound let go of him. His greatcoat had been shredded in a whirlwind of scrabbling claws. Blood gushed from his arm.

His comrades were beating the daemon hound into the ground, but it was still a snarling, spitting, clawing ball of fury. Taking careful aim with his newly issued bolt pistol, he ended its defiance with a bullet to its head.

The cellar lit up briefly and a stink of burning hair assailed his nostrils. A flamer had set the second hound ablaze, but still it careened into the wielder like a comet and tore out his throat with its teeth before finally expiring.

Tyborc lit a lumen cube. He had resisted doing so before, relying on Krieg night-vision, but some creatures had them beat in that regard. As he hefted it over his head, its soft light flushed another hound out from beneath a dusty rack. This one looked sickly, with a hind leg gnawed to the bone – by its ravening fellows? It glared, snarling at the intruders in its lair, its dark red pupils shrinking in the unaccustomed light. Then it hurled itself at them but was beaten back by bolts and las-beams, its three claws skittering on rockcrete.

Two more attempts it made, but after the third its black body sagged and its profane animating force drained from it. The Krieg ascertained that the room held no further threats, then set about tending their wounds and stripping the equipment from their fallen comrade, mouthing a quick prayer for him.

The sounds of weapons fire, of bestial howls and growls and tortured screams came to them, echoing along the tunnels of the undercroft. There were chambers and galleries, storerooms and cells still to clear of slithering, snivelling mutant wretches and skulking, twisted warp beasts. There were heretics and traitors still to feel the force of the Emperor's judgement.

He was reminded of another battle fought in a similar environment, many years ago. Fort A-453. In many ways, the defining event of his life.

So much had changed since then and yet, in some ways, nothing had.

He had spent weeks confined to his quarters, a comfortable prisoner. He wasn't sure why he deserved such preferential treatment – because of his rank? Or his name?

His only visitor, apart from the servitors who had brought him food and water, had been Thor Malkin. Expecting fire and thunder, Tyborc had been surprised when the aged inquisitor lord had spoken to him calmly, albeit gruffly.

'I can't fully explain why I ordered my regiment's retreat,' the colonel insisted. 'It can only have been that sheer panic overruled my judgement.'

Lord Malkin shook his head. 'I doubt that. A soldier – a Death Korpsman of Krieg, no less – of your reputation.'

'Perhaps, my lord, my reputation has been overblown.'

'Of your achievements, then.'

'Never have I faced… what I saw on the Murder Slopes before.'

'Few people have, nor could they.'

'As to the rest, I have simply found myself in the right places at the right times to do as any Korpsman would have done.'

'Any Korpsman?' Malkin's augmetic eye had flashed keenly.

'My lord, I am prepared to accept the consequences of my actions.'

'Are you sure of that, Veteran Colonel Tyborc?'

'Whatever they may be,' he had stated.

'I am gratified to hear it.' A ghost of a smile had played about the inquisitor's thin, dry lips. With a faint whir of his armour's servos, he had turned and stomped back towards the door.

'My lord,' Tyborc had called after him. 'If I may... Might it be possible to speak with Confessor Tenaxus? There is much I wish to say to her.'

The inquisitor had paused in the doorway, not turning around. 'Confessor Tenaxus,' he had growled, 'is unavailable at present.'

Another week had passed before a messenger had brought him a sheaf of papers, along with a fresh set of uniform badges.

Confused by the latter, he had broken the seal of the lord inquisitor himself on the former and read with disbelieving eyes. He had checked outside his door to find no sentry stationed there.

Colonel Tyborc had been ready when, an hour later, a coterie of aides had arrived to escort him to Lord Hector Rex's war room. He felt there must have been an administrative error, which everyone would know as soon as they clapped eyes upon him, but he followed the orders given to him.

He joined his fellow officers – other members of the 88th Army's command staff – around the grand table, across which a series of tactical hololiths scrolled. Lord Malkin was present, but he spared the new arrival not a glance. General Durjan met his gaze, but Tyborc couldn't read his thoughts behind his face mask.

At the table's head, Lord Rex was deep in disagreement with

a pair of white-armoured Space Marines. Tyborc would come to know them as Angels of Absolution: a Successor Chapter to the Dark Angels, sent by Supreme Grand Master Azrael to finish the job he had begun nine years before.

He had noted some prominent absentees about the table, and known he must have missed much during his confinement. Later, perusing the rolls of the dead, Tyborc would see such familiar names as Inquisitor Adso and Lord Marshal Arnim Kagori upon them.

For now, he had studied the hololiths laid out before him, familiarising himself with the current situation on the ground. He had listened to Lord Rex's plan to attack the citadel's Cardinal and St Leonis Gates at once, while sending the 158th Krieg Regiment to perish on the mountainside.

It had occurred to Tyborc that this was little different to the plan proposed by Lord Kagori before him, as by Lord Zuehlke longer since.

He had felt Rex's intense glare upon him and, with some trepidation, turned his head to face him. The Lord Inquisitor's curt, approving nod had reassured him.

It was in that same war room, long weeks later, that General Durjan had made the long-awaited declaration: that the Citadel of Vraks had fallen.

Having stood against attacks from within and without – from dissident labourers and would-be looters – for ten thousand years, and in defiance of the Emperor for twenty, the once-thought-impregnable fortress endured no longer.

Tyborc had expected to feel elated; instead he just felt empty.

He had started to feel like a prisoner in that room, so was glad when Lord Rex summoned his command staff to him for the war's concluding battles. Having not seen action since the

Murder Slopes, he was a little apprehensive too. He feared his own reaction, should another daemon challenge him.

He had ridden up the Pilgrim's Road in an ornate Land Raider. He was privileged to accompany the lord inquisitor himself, and the grey-armoured Space Marines of his Chamber Militant, into the Priory of the Argent Shroud. Once a fortress in its own right, the building remained structurally sound despite the pounding it had taken.

They had found it infested by near-formless Chaos spawn, though there had been daemon engines too: brass and iron blood slaughterers and blight drones, whose bloated bodies burst to spread their pestilence. One by one, they were torn apart by sacred lightning cast by Imperial force weapons. Beside Rex and his Astartes, Tyborc felt himself almost surplus to requirements and, not for the first time, had wondered if the intent had been to humble him.

He had witnessed the summary execution of the apostate cardinal, at least of the gibbering wreck into which he had devolved, without ever managing to close with the creature itself, nor see a clear shot at it.

He had been present for the sobering discovery of the Battle Sisters of the Argent Shroud, also confined to the dungeons underneath their former sanctuary. Unheard of since the earliest days of Xaphan's uprising, presumed killed after they had taken arms against him, it was clear that they had suffered unspeakable tortures and been rendered quite insane.

'Their faith armoured them,' Lord Malkin growled, 'else they would have succumbed to possession as other captives did. A credit to their Order – but they have experienced too much for the stench of the daemonic ever to be cleansed from them. They will be cared for by the Ordo Malleus, so they can at last be at peace.'

The Sisters were loaded aboard a Thunderhawk, blankets covering their heads to preserve their reputation, and spirited away. Turning from the sad procession, Tyborc had accompanied Lord Rex to the steps of the Cardinal's Palace, where he had stood beside him as he had presented Xaphan's head to the masses.

Shortly thereafter, the Angels of Absolution had emerged from the basilica's ruins, through its great arch that somehow stood inviolate while the grand spires and towers behind it had collapsed inward and flames guttered in their rubble.

They had brought out their Chapter Master's body.

Another Thunderhawk had set down on the plaza. The Angels had rested their leader's broken helmet on his head, but hadn't managed to conceal the fact that half his face was missing. Four battle-brothers had borne him up the loading ramp as a Chaplain walked alongside him, intoning prayers and sprinkling holy water. Tyborc and Lord Rex had joined others standing by with their heads bowed in reverent silence.

Though Chapter Master Yafrir had spoken little in the war room, his words had struck a chord with the Krieg colonel. Tyborc had come to the realisation that absolution was not what his Chapter offered, rather what it sought. This had made him feel a distant kinship with these Angels, though he knew nothing of their sins. Most assuredly, Yafrir had taken a stride towards absolution today.

Next, the Angels had brought out their prisoners: almost a score of Alpha Legion traitors, stripped of their imposing armour, barely still alive. They had made for a sorry procession of bruised, burnt, broken husks in warded shackles. Tyborc had looked for their leader, but couldn't tell – and would never know for sure – if Lord Arkos had been among them.

He had wondered why the prisoners weren't handed over to the Inquisition. Only later would he learn that this was the price demanded by the Dark Angels' Supreme Master Azrael for his timely intervention on Vraks. Lord Rex had made the deal reluctantly, and the Ordo Malleus would later conclude that Arkos was indeed likely entombed in the Angelicasta – the Tower of Angels – to be subject to Azrael's vengeful ministrations for a virtual eternity.

For now, there was work yet to be done.

'Tear this tainted structure down!' Lord Hector Rex had bellowed. 'Let no stone remain upon another, no desecrated shrine remain intact. Burn out the corruption that spread from this benighted mountain peak across a world, and purge the heretics in whose black hearts that evil found purchase and festered!'

On his voxed cue, the sky had lit up again.

The bridge that spanned the Citadel Ravine had been collapsed, leaving no route to the inner keep, but now this was battered by barrage bombs and melta torpedoes from an Inquisitorial strike cruiser in low orbit.

Thanks to Malkin's research, it was believed that inside the aedificium, a warp portal had been opened: the source of the rifts that had spat so many horrors out across this world in recent years. Testimony tortured out of dying traitors suggested that Zhufor had escaped this way and might return with reinforcements. No Imperial victory could be declared – or mean anything at all – until that portal was destroyed and its threat forever ended.

As the bombardment eased, Lord Rex's Space Marines had charged in single file towards the ravine's edge and, firing the turbines in their jump packs, had been propelled across it. Some hadn't made it all the way, smashing into the mountainside beneath the keep but clawing their way up it.

Tyborc had seen lights flashing in the ruins ahead of them

and known that more battle-brothers were arriving, directly from their ship's teleport chamber. The inquisitor lords had also been prepared for this, with both Rex and Malkin being helped into jump packs by their aides and leaping after their allies.

With no way to follow them and no specific orders, Tyborc had been left to his own devices. He had seen just one way in which he could make himself useful.

Deeper and deeper into the labyrinth.

The chambers here had mostly been converted into makeshift medicae facilities and barracks, as traitors had sought shelter from relentless Imperial shelling.

Tyborc had been fighting in this darkness for almost a week now, since assembling an ad hoc squad from the orphans of three others. He had lost count of the number of cowering militiamen and mutants they had despatched, each more wretched than the one before, still chanting desperate entreaties to daemons that had either been vanquished or left them to their fates.

He had lost Korpsmen too, but replaced them by merging his depleted squad with others. They had absorbed a pair of engineers, who had fought their way up from the mountain's base level by level, so it seemed their job was almost done. He would almost be sorry when it was, for at last he was back in his element.

Vox-links down here were intermittent, but Tyborc had garnered some news from reports, learning more when the tunnels twisted back upon themselves and he ran into friends instead of foes.

He heard that, on the surface, the fighting had come to an end. He heard whispers of another daemon, even larger and more fearsome than the others, if such could be imagined. Lord Rex had engaged it inside the aedificium and, assisted by inquisitors and Space Marines, had overpowered it. No Korpsman had been present to witness this no-doubt titanic struggle, but all had seen the sky itself trembling and flaring with its holy fury.

Tyborc heard that, as soon as it was over, Thunderhawks had swooped upon the landing pad in the inner keep. The Adeptus Astartes had left Vraks, and it soon became apparent that the Legio Astorum had also quietly withdrawn. Tyborc was not sorry to hear it, as it meant their work here was considered done. The last shots of this war would be fired by the Krieg, as were the first.

He was leading the way along a pitch-black tunnel, in a bubble of soft lume-light, when an engineer hissed, 'Sir!' and showed the colonel his handheld multi-scanner, which read body heat ahead of them.

'In the Emperor's name, who goes there?' Tyborc demanded.

The ensuing silence told him that the answer wasn't 'friend'.

Turning back, he cued his comrade with a nod. The engineer plucked something from his belt. He scuttled forwards, dropped to one knee, and bowled a small, cylindrical canister ahead of him. It skipped, rolled, clinked along the tunnel, and the engineer hurried to rejoin his squad as they backed away from it.

The canister was swallowed up by darkness, but Tyborc heard its activating hiss. Seconds later, a thin, yellow-green cloud rolled along the tunnel, over him. He sucked on dry, sterile air from his rebreather's reservoir. Once, chem-weapons would have been a last resort, but now he employed them without a second thought.

He heard the gratifying sound of traitors choking in the dense heart of the gas cloud. He heard dragging footsteps, moving away from him. He waited minutes longer to let the gas disperse along side passageways, before resuming his squad's advance. Slumped against the tunnel wall they found a heavily mutated, slowly liquefying corpse. Insectoid mandibles clicked feebly in its mouth. The gas had caused bubbles to form on a half-grown carapace.

The mutant twitched, and Tyborc shot it twice. He edged his way around its smouldering remains, not wanting its filth on his boots.

The tunnel brought him out onto a metal gantry, which curved away from him to each side. The ringing echoes of his footsteps told him he was in a cavern, with a roof some way above him and a floor some way below. Lume-globes were strung from overhead wires, but none were fully functional. A couple of globes sparked intermittently, revealing the brooding shapes of ancient, rusted tanks below, the sad leavings of Vraks' once-bountiful vaults.

The sounds of fighting were louder in here, drifting in through other openings, reverberating from the cavern walls. Somewhere, water dripped. Hence, Tyborc didn't hear the creature behind him until it was almost too late.

It had been clinging to the rock above the tunnel mouth. It was wounded, and the spatter of a droplet of its blood on the gantry was what alerted him. As Tyborc whirled around, the creature was already leaping at him. It was another insect-featured mutant. Compound eyes erupted from its head like boils. Saliva dribbled from disgusting mouthparts. Its carapace betrayed exposure to the Krieg's corrosive gas, which had likely driven it out of the tunnel ahead of them.

Instinctively, Tyborc leapt backwards, away from his attacker, throwing up his bayonet between them. Bristling black legs slithered over him, slimy claws snapping at his greatcoat. He lurched into a flimsy safety rail and felt it giving way.

His blade sank deep into the mutant's thorax, sticky green fluid spurting over his gas mask lenses, rendering him almost blind.

He needed a second to wrest his pistol back from the mutant's sucking wound, but he had to let it go as he was falling. His flailing left hand struck the gantry's edge and clung to it, fingers stinging, arm screaming as he tore his bite wounds further open. With a desperate effort, Tyborc's right hand also found a hold.

He dangled there, a helpless target, feeling the weight of his armour-threaded greatcoat, rebreather, and backpack more heavily than ever.

He considered letting go.

The drop would kill him as surely as the mutant would, but he wouldn't have to suffer its violation – and after all he been through, at last he could rest, his duty done. Just let go, that was all he had to do.

Tyborc thought about his comrades and held on.

He heard the cracks of lasweapons, saw the soles of muddy boots stamping on the metal mesh above him. He had not revealed his name to his new squad, and of course they had only seen his badges, not his face. He wondered if they knew who he really was. He wondered if they knew his shame.

Almost certainly they did, he thought, but they did their duty by him all the same. He was a colonel, their commander, and nothing else mattered.

The body of the insectoid mutant plummeted past him, buzzing as half-formed membranous wings beat frantically but couldn't hold its once-human weight aloft. Tyborc heard its wet splat on the rock below. His left arm was numb, his fingers losing purchase. Gloved hands struck out, catching him by the wrist even as he lost his grip. Grunting with the effort, a Korpsman hauled him up until his elbows found the gantry and he hugged it.

Then Tyborc heard more buzzing and spluttered out a warning.

Another mutant dived from the dark recesses of the cavern roof, and this one had evidently mastered its insect wings. It hovered beyond the broken rail, beyond bayonet reach. Lasbeams sizzled past it or glanced off its chitin exoskeleton. Tyborc's squad scattered as the mutant spat at them, a thick, noxious yellow-green stream. Most of it struck the wall, but both engineers were spattered and had to shed their tunics as steaming bile ate into them.

Another patch was melting through the gantry's mesh, and Tyborc almost put his hand in it as he pulled himself up and to his feet.

He didn't have a weapon. The last mutant had taken both pistol and attached blade with it in its death dive. He snatched a shotgun from an engineer, who wasn't using it in that moment, still scraping acid from a congealing greatcoat.

'Aim for the wings!' he bellowed.

They seemed to be the mutant's most vulnerable areas, already holed by las-beams. His Korpsmen followed orders, and Tyborc worked his trigger finger. The shotgun felt better in his hands than his bolt pistol had, despite the pain in his arm that made it hard to steady and aim the weapon.

The mutant spat again, into a Korpsman's face – he reeled into the rock wall, screaming, clawing at his mask as it melted into his flesh – but one of its wings was shredded and it spiralled away from them, dropping out of sight.

Tyborc looked around his squad. Its assigned medic was already by the fallen Korpsman, but could likely do no more for him than hasten the end of his pain. His engineers were ready to resume the fight.

'We need a way down to the cavern floor,' he declared. 'Those things, both of them, may be crippled but still alive down there.'

He set off along the gantry, looking for a ladder, knowing his squad would be behind him, knowing that death could be lurking in any of the dark tunnel openings he passed, knowing he was ready for it – ready, that was, to fight it, for one thing had become clear to him while he was hanging over the abyss.

One thought had filled his mind in the moment before he was saved.

Emperor, he had prayed, *don't let me die. Not yet.*

It seemed strange that it was finally all over.

Tyborc stood in the wreckage of the north wall of the citadel, close to the shattered basilica. Centaurs and Gorgons were collecting weary but fulfilled Death Korpsmen, conveying them back down the winding roads of the mountainside.

Though smoke still choked the air, it was clearing just enough to discern the maze of shattered earthworks scarring the grey earth of the Van Meersland Wastes for miles around. There was much activity in the Krieg trenches, as their occupants gathered up weapons and equipment and slowly began to withdraw.

So many had come so far, so close, never to have reached their goal. Troop ships were on their way to Vraks, to take them directly to their next theatre of war. Tyborc didn't know where he would be when those ships left the system. He couldn't picture himself aboard one. That life, the life he had lived before, seemed a very long way away now. It felt like someone else's life, the life of a dead man walking.

A scrape of movement told him he wasn't alone. The imposing form of Hector Rex loomed over him. Tyborc snapped to attention guiltily. How distracted must he have been not to have heard the lord inquisitor's approach?

After all he must have been through, Rex didn't look tired at all. Had another daemon sprung up at that moment, Tyborc didn't doubt he would have pulled his sword from its scabbard and gleefully run it through.

'At ease, veteran colonel,' Rex growled. It was the first time he had addressed Tyborc directly since that briefing in his office months ago. Before the Murder Slopes. 'We may not meet again,' the great man said, extending his right hand to Tyborc. 'I thank you for your stalwart efforts in the Emperor's service.'

'My lord,' Tyborc stammered, his own hand small in Rex's grip, 'it has... It has been an honour... far greater than–'

'Than you feel you deserve?' Rex glared down at Tyborc from on high, and his cybernetic cherub launched itself from his shoulder to hover beside him like a vulture anticipating a fresh carcass.

'Why me, my lord?' He could think of nothing else to say. Nothing but the question that had tortured him for weeks, and which now he had nothing to lose by voicing. 'Why did you ask for me? Why did you spare me? After I...?'

'I had need of your expertise.'

'But surely there were others who–'

'I needed someone on my staff who understood the Krieg, who had lived and fought alongside them, who knew their strengths – and their limits.'

'General Durjan–'

'Someone,' the lord inquisitor continued, talking over Tyborc, 'with the rare and precious ability to think for himself.'

'Not everybody feels that way, my lord.'

'Once I release you from my service, you will again be subject to the discipline of Krieg high command. How do you imagine they will treat you?'

'I will be court-martialled,' Tyborc answered without hesitation, 'then executed for disobeying orders, cowardice and potentially for mutiny.'

'A dreadful waste.'

'In their position, I would do the same, else others might follow the dishonourable example I have set. I see no other option.'

'I do,' said Rex.

The two men stood together for a moment, surveying the devastation all around them. Tyborc's arm ached and it was beginning to rain.

'You have been on Vraks from the start, since before the first shot of the war was fired – is that right, veteran colonel?'

'For eighteen years, my lord.'

'Then you know the 88th Army's mission brief. You know what we set out to achieve those many years ago.'

'To reclaim this world for the Emperor.' Tyborc paused for only a moment. 'Instead, we've made it worthless to Him. We have poisoned Vraks' land, razed its buildings, emptied its storehouses, desecrated its holiest sites.'

'A waste of time. A waste of resources.' Rex's eyes drilled into his soul again. 'A waste of life.'

'By the time you took command, my lord, nothing else could be done.'

'However?'

He explained carefully: 'In my judgement – formed, you understand, with the benefit of hindsight – it may have been better had we never come here.'

'Elaborate.'

'A simple blockade around the system could have contained the problem. The apostate cardinal was one man with an unskilled, untrained labour force behind him. Starvation would surely have turned his traitors against him.'

'Not soon enough,' Rex growled, 'for certain factions within the Departmento Munitorum, more in the Ecclesiarchy.'

Tyborc thought of Confessor Tenaxus.

He hadn't heard from her, or anything of her, in months. He was sure she must be dead. Having no official role in the 88th Siege Army, she would not have been counted in wastage reports. He had not chosen this spot by chance. Had Tenaxus survived, this was surely where she would have been. The Basilica of St Leonis the Blind. She would have been mourning its loss.

He wondered if Leonis' bones, at least, could yet be salvaged. Fragments, perhaps, but it would take a decade of sifting through the ruins, and for what? What purpose would it serve? They would only be memento mori.

'Instead, our spilled blood and rotting flesh drew monsters to this world. Our hubris sowed the seeds of its destruction.'

'When people tell of the Siege of Vraks,' Lord Rex promised, 'they will mark the noble sacrifices of Chapter Master Yafrir and our Chamber Militant's Brother-Captain Arturus, now interred within a Dreadnought. They will count the Imperial Titans and their princeps lost. But they will speak of our victories too.'

'They will certainly speak of you, my lord.'

'They will tell tales of lords and angels, but also of the brave and noble soldiers of your world – their ceaseless, selfless efforts in the Emperor's service, their millions of lives given gladly in compensation for their lords' misjudgements.'

'I am... gratified to hear it.'

'They will speak of the message sent by the Siege of Vraks.' The lord inquisitor drew himself taller, as if preaching to an unseen crowd. 'That the Death Korps of Krieg will stop at nothing to punish those who turn from the Emperor's light, even burn a world to ash before allowing such heresy to take root there.'

The cherub had settled on its master's shoulder again, and Tyborc had the sense that he had passed another test. His final test.

'And perhaps they will speak of Veteran Colonel Tyborc, the Korpsman who broke his conditioning to become so much more than he was.'

'My lord, I only–'

'I'm extending your secondment to the Ordo Malleus indefinitely. The slates will be drawn up before sunset today. Your high command will not refuse my request. They may even be relieved to think that I am watching over you.'

Tyborc didn't quite know what to say, whether thanks or apologies were merited. He thought of Tenaxus again, the twitch of her lips in humour, sweet incense clinging to her robes. He remembered the promise she had extracted from him. *Any chance you are given to make a real difference, you must take it.*

'Your honoured name,' said Rex, 'need not be tarnished by recent events.'

He demurred: 'No. Names are unimportant. I understand that now. Life, on the other hand...'

He was being offered life. A longer life, perhaps, than any Krieg Korpsman before him, when he had already lived so long, but he no longer wondered why. The Emperor, it seemed, thought he needed more time to atone. He had chosen this path for His servant, but in time it would lead him to the same end as any other.

'I was told I could be a hero,' he reflected, 'and my sin was to believe it. I thought I could inspire my people, make them somehow better. If Confessor Tenaxus were here, I would tell her she was wrong.'

Inquisitor Lord Rex raised an eyebrow.

'We of the Krieg cannot be heroes,' said Veteran Colonel Tyborc, 'for heroes live forever, while we are born only to die.'

ABOUT THE AUTHOR

Steve Lyons' work in the Warhammer 40,000 universe includes the novellas *Iron Resolve, Engines of War* and *Angron's Monolith,* the Astra Militarum novels *Death World, Ice Guard, Dead Men Walking, Krieg* and *Siege of Vraks,* and the audio dramas *Waiting Death* and *The Madness Within.* He has also written numerous short stories and is currently working on more tales from the grim darkness of the far future.

YOUR NEXT READ

KRIEG
by Steve Lyons

The Death Korps of Krieg lay siege to a hive city on the outskirts of Warzone Octarius, desperately trying to prevent untold masses of orks and tyranids spilling out into the Imperium. How far will the ruthless Korpsmen go to achieve victory in a seemingly unwinnable war?

YOUR NEXT READ

MINKA LESK: THE LAST WHITESHIELD
by Justin D Hill

Cadia has stood in grim defiance against the enemies of the Imperium for ten thousand years, an indomitable bulwark against the forces of Chaos… but now, the 13th Black Crusade has come, and there will be no victory. Here, Minka Lesk will be tested in the very fires of a world's destruction.

For these stories and more, go to **blacklibrary.com**, **warhammer.com**, Games Workshop and Warhammer stores, all good book stores or visit one of the thousands of independent retailers worldwide, which can be found at **warhammer.com/store-finder**

YOUR NEXT READ

THE LION: SON OF THE FOREST
by Mike Brooks

The Lion. Son of the Emperor, brother of demigods and primarch of the Dark Angels. Awakened. Returned. And yet… lost.
